TIES THAT BIND

PAM RHODES

With love,

Pam Rhodes

Hodder & Stoughton

ISBN 0 340 76537 2

Typeset by Palimpsest Book Production Limited,
Polmont, Stirlingshire
Printed and bound in Great Britain by
Mackays of Chatham plc, Chatham, Kent

Hodder & Stoughton
A division of Hodder Headline
338 Euston Road
London NW1 3BH

Chapter One

'For heaven's sake, Graham, give it to me! You're pointing in completely the wrong direction!'

'How do you know? I'm the one with my eye to the camera!'

'You're making a fool of yourself!' Celia's voice hissed in his ear. 'I knew you would if you had another glass of that punch. Stop wasting everyone's time, and hand the camera to me!'

For a moment Graham thought about arguing, but he'd been married to Celia too long to believe he'd ever get the last word. With a shrug of the shoulders and a wry grin, he handed her the camera without comment, and ambled over to take his position at the edge of the group posed and ready for their photograph.

At the centre of the crowd Gwen caught her husband's eye, a knowing look passing between them. The two brothers had always been close, although Graham was two years younger than Richard. That his sociable, easy-going baby brother should have chosen such a sour, bossy woman for his wife was a complete puzzle to Richard. On countless family gatherings in the past, Celia had been so patronising and critical that Richard had sworn never to invite her again. But today was a special occasion, the celebration of twenty-five happy years of marriage for Richard and Gwen. No one could dampen their happiness on such a heart-warming family occasion – and like it or not, Celia was family.

Graham felt an arm go round his waist, drawing him into the group. 'Never mind, Uncle Graham. At least we can all blame her when the photos don't come out.' He smiled down gratefully into the face of his niece, Susie. At twenty-three, Richard and Gwen's daughter was a stunner. She'd always had great fashion sense even as a teenager, and her new job as part of an account managing team at a leading London advertising agency had given her the confidence to dress with individual style. The two silver studs piercing each ear, and the wild spiky auburn hair would hardly be Graham's choice – but then, as Susie always said, he was a fuddy-duddy. A terrific uncle, of course, but a fashion dinosaur; and somehow he rather liked it that way.

After the heavy downpours of the week before, the warmth of the late spring sunshine was a pleasant bonus for Gwen on what was already a wonderful day. The anniversary party had taken a lot of planning, tracking down bridesmaids who had been children at their wedding a quarter of a century before, but who now had strapping teenagers of their own; arranging a reunion of some of the gang from his university days as a surprise for Richard; organising transport and accommodation for old friends from all corners of the country. It had been exhausting, frustrating, and she'd enjoyed every minute of it. Now, as she surveyed the lawn in front of the golf club which was filled with people she loved, she felt cherished and warmed by the affection around her. A movement at the edge of the crowd caught her eye, and she laughed out loud as she spotted Richard, with his fair hair and tall, wiry frame, being hugged by Aunt Madge who, at nearly eighty and more than seventeen stone, was almost as wide as she was tall. The old lady had razor-sharp eyesight and a mind to match and she relished her undisputed role as matriarch of the Moreton family. Dear Aunt Madge. And dear Richard. Gwen couldn't remember a time when he wasn't central to her life. He was the heart of her, her strength and purpose. Without him, there would be no life at all.

'Everything worked out just as you planned it then!'

Gwen spun round to see her closest friend, Tricia, standing beside her.

'Great, right down to the sunshine! Isn't it good to see them all again?'

'How come they've all gone grey, when we don't look a day older?'

Smiling, Gwen slipped her arm through Tricia's. 'Just lucky, I guess.'

'Does it seem like twenty-five years ago? Do you remember how cold it was the morning of your wedding?'

'I didn't need to borrow something blue. I was covered in goosebumps. I even nipped into the loo before the reception and put my old vest on under that lovely white dress.'

'Whatever did Richard think of that on your wedding night?'

'Nothing. We got to the hotel, ordered a pot of tea, and he was asleep before it brewed.'

'Passionate chap, your Richard.'

'Not particularly, and that's never really mattered. He has other qualities I value more. He's comfortable, reliable, solid . . .'

'Boring?'

'Perhaps. Other people might think so.'

'But you like him just as he is.'

'I love him just as he is. I wouldn't change one single day of the past twenty-five years.' Her face darkened for just a moment. 'I might have changed a thing or two before then . . .'

In complete understanding, Tricia nodded with sympathy.

'. . . but I do love that dear man of mine! Perhaps that makes me the boring one.'

Tricia laughed with her, until the glimpse of a familiar figure in the crowd wiped the smile from her face. Gwen followed her gaze.

'How are things? Has Mike said anything?'

'I've not bothered to ask him. He'd only deny it.'

'Perhaps you've got it wrong.'

'Oh no, he's definitely up to something.'

'Maybe he's feeling his age, and all the exercise and new clothes are just about getting himself a younger image.'

'More likely a younger model. There's a woman in this, I know it. Come on, Gwen, I recognise the signs by now. We've been down this road enough times.'

'Who is she? Any idea?'

'Someone he's met through the garage probably. Maybe a customer.'

'What are you going to do?'

'Wait till he slips up, until I have something concrete to go on.'

'Then you'll give him an ultimatum?'

'Why bother? I'll probably just leave him.'

'You wouldn't! Not after all the time you've been together?'

Tricia's face was drawn as she turned towards her friend. 'I've stood by that man for years, and he's had affair after affair. I've got to be worth more than that, to myself if not to him. I've had enough. This time, I've had it.'

Wordlessly Gwen drew Tricia closer, as they looked over to where Mike was talking to Richard.

'You ought to come down the gym with me. Do you good!'

'Probably – but I reckon the garden gives me all the exercise I need.'

'Ah, but you don't get all the girls in skimpy leotards bouncing about in front of you in the vegetable plot, now do you?'

Richard chuckled. 'Well, you've got a point there, but I

don't think the girls would be interested in an old codger like me.'

'But that's it, Richard. You're old before your time. What age are you? Fifty yet?'

'Forty-nine.'

'And you're already describing yourself as a codger! You'll be thinking about buying a bungalow next.'

'Funnily enough, Gwen and I were only discussing bungalows the other night. Now Susie's settled up in London, we're rattling around in the house these days.'

'For pity's sake, listen to yourself! Barely out of your mid-forties, and you sound like a pensioner.'

'Well, I'll probably be retiring in a year or two ...'

'Then what? The most exciting events in your life will be whether you have a bumper crop of home-grown runner beans, and what's new on telly! Richard, my boy, you're in serious need of help.'

'You forget, Mike, that I know exactly how old you are. Fifty-one later this year. You should be thinking about slowing down too. Sell the garage perhaps? Get more time in at the golf club to work on your handicap? Take Tricia away on a cruise while you're still young enough to enjoy it?'

'I'd rather take one of those leotard lovelies from the health club.'

'You're a dirty old man!'

'Well, at least I've not forgotten how much fun that can be.'

Laughing, Richard looked over towards their wives on the other side of the green. 'Well, you should keep an eye on your Trish. She's always been a smasher. Someone will steal her from under your nose if you don't look after her.'

Mike took a leisurely swig from his beer, emptying the glass as he gazed over towards his wife. 'She's OK. We have our ups and downs, but we understand each other pretty well.'

'She turns a blind eye, you mean.'

Mike grinned. 'She knows what I'm like. I can't change. She knew what she was marrying.'

'That was nearly thirty years ago. Most people have settled down a bit by now.'

'Started to become old codgers, eh? I'm not ready for that, Richard. Never will be.'

'Poor Trish.'

'Why? She's got the house of her dreams, she's never short of money, and I always come home in the end.'

'How would you feel if she went off with someone else?'

'She wouldn't.'

'She might.'

'Never. Not the sort.'

'You'd be too hard an act to follow, is that it?'

'She'd think so.'

'Well, I hope you're right, Mike, for both your sakes.'

'Come on, old man, lighten up. You need a drink – and so do I.'

Sitting at a table near a cluster of rhododendron bushes, Celia cast an eye around the faces she recognised. For the moment she was alone, which infuriated her because she felt it was her husband's duty to stay by her side. Graham, however, was predictably across the green laughing loudly in the midst of a group of men who were plainly having a joke-telling session. They might be amused. Celia clearly wasn't.

'You look as if you've swallowed a sour lemon.'

Aunt Madge was beating a meandering, somewhat unsteady path towards Celia, perhaps because of the state of her legs, more likely because of the number of sherries she'd already tucked away that afternoon. Celia leapt to her feet and began snapping out orders to guide Madge through the docking procedure on to the chair beside her own. Madge brushed her aside as if she were a troublesome mosquito.

'You stick to bossing about that husband of yours. I can

manage to sit down perfectly well by myself, thank you. It's getting up that's the problem.'

'Are you well, Madge? I heard you've been poorly.'

'If you call a bit of a cough "poorly", then I suppose I've been better.'

'Bronchitis, Gwen said it was.'

'They only call it that because they want me to give up my ciggies. I'm seventy-nine, and I've been smoking for more than sixty years. I hardly think it's going to cut me off in my prime, do you? I like smoking and I'm not stopping just because of a bit of a cough, whatever that daft young doctor says!' Madge glared at Celia, willing her to argue. Celia, however, had done battle with Madge for too many years not to know when argument would be futile. Instead she sniffed huffily, and took a tiny sip from the one glass of wine her diet allowed her that afternoon. For several minutes the two women sat in silence, surveying the scene. Eventually, it was Celia who spoke.

'Nice do.'

'Hmm.'

'The weather forecast was bad. It was supposed to be raining by lunchtime, and then where would Gwen have been.'

'Indoors, I expect,' was Madge's curt reply.

'I've often wondered about them choosing this time of year for a wedding.'

'For twenty-five years, that's what you've wondered?'

'Well, that – and why Graham and Richard's mum was so against the marriage from the very start, of course.'

Madge gave her a cool glare, then turned away as if uninterested. 'I have no idea what you mean.'

'Really, Madge, that is a surprise, you being Elsie's sister and all. You know why she didn't want her Richard to marry Gwen. It was quite a mystery at the time, I've heard, although I barely remember it myself, of course, as Graham and I had only just started going out. Still, it's all so long ago now, what can it matter if you let me in on the mystery at last?'

7

'The mystery', began Madge, her voice conspiratorial, 'is how, even after all these years, you still keep going on about that — as if it mattered! Now make yourself useful and get me some of those profiterole things. Plenty of chocolate sauce, mind. I'm not on one of your stupid diets.'

Susie stood a little apart from the crowd. She'd known most of the people there for as long as she could remember. It wasn't a huge gathering, because her parents had never been particularly gregarious people. They lived an orderly life in a neat, pleasant house, keeping mostly to themselves except for the few neighbours they'd come to know over their twenty years of living in Brampton Avenue. Their closest friends had been made through work, Richard in his accountancy business, Gwen as a part-time librarian. To one side of the green Susie recognised the small crowd from the local drama group who were always glad of Richard's help with scenery and props. And there was dear Aunt Madge enthusiastically tucking into a plateful of something definitely fattening, next to a stony-faced Aunt Celia who was constantly glaring in the direction of her husband. After all, not only had he escaped her clutches for a while, but he was obviously enjoying every minute of it.

'Penny for them.'

She turned to greet Richard with a smile.

'I was just thinking what a lovely occasion this is, and how proud I am of you and Mum. And I was thinking too that although I know just about everyone here, I don't belong as I used to. I've not just moved away, I've moved on. Do you know what I mean?'

Her father slipped his arm round her shoulders and drew her close enough to drop a soft kiss on her auburn hair.

'This will always be your home, you know that.'

'Of course, and I'll never stop visiting. But I have another home now in London, and that's where I belong.'

'You're happy there?'

'Yes, Dad, I really am. I'm loving every minute. I love the

work and the people, I even like the dust and noise and the hugeness of the place. It's all so different from what I knew here in Chesham. I get a great buzz out of being a London girl. I always knew I would.'

Richard smiled, hugging her. 'We're too small-town for you now, eh?'

'I don't fit in any more. It's nice to pop back for a while, but I couldn't live here again.'

'Your mum misses you.'

Susie snorted. 'I bet! She couldn't wait to get rid of me.'

'That's not true.'

'We fought like cat and dog, you know we did. It was a relief for both of us when I moved out.'

'Just because you couldn't always see eye to eye doesn't mean that she doesn't miss you. The trouble with the two women in my life is that they're so alike.'

'You're joking! Mum and me? I don't think so.'

'Both as stubborn as each other.'

'We couldn't be more different. She hasn't got an ounce of spontaneity in her. Her life is completely planned and organised, a neat routine for every hour and minute.'

'If you think that, then you don't know her at all. At heart, she's quite a free spirit, your mum.'

'Oh yes? I never saw it.'

'She came from a background where to do the "right" thing was a way of life, and it's suited us to stay that way. But given another chance, and perhaps another husband, I've always thought Gwen could have been quite different.'

His daughter didn't answer, her face a picture of disbelief.

'Where do you think you get all your creative talents for art and design from? Your mum, of course.'

'So why hasn't she followed up anything like that for herself?'

Richard looked fondly over to where Gwen was deep in conversation with Tricia. 'Opportunity perhaps? And I'm

9

probably at fault for that. I've always liked the thought of her being at home whenever I am, and she's come to believe that's where she belongs. It's suited me for her to be a backroom girl, and I think over the years that's drained her confidence to try anything new or different.'

'Exactly. So how can you possibly say we're alike? She'd never have considered the idea of living anywhere but here.'

'Oh, there was a time when she would have liked to.' Richard's pale blue eyes clouded over with memory. 'Her parents were very tough and rigid in their expectations of her. She was desperate to break away from them, and in the end she went to university in Edinburgh. And when it came to looking for a job once she'd got her degree, her own mother was already bedbound with her cancer. Gwen never really had the choice to live anywhere but here.'

'It might have been the making of her if she had.'

'You don't understand how it was then, Susie. It might have been the swinging sixties, when we were all supposed to be smoking pot and hanging from the chandeliers, but in fact we were much more under the thumb of our parents than you could ever understand today. We talked big. We were going to change the world. We were going to put right all the problems the previous generation had created for us. And yet on the whole, when push came to shove, we did what our parents expected of us.'

'All talk and no trousers.'

He smiled. 'That's me!'

'Never. You're just a great dad. You always have been.'

'Well, be a great daughter, and bring your mum back into the golf club building in a few minutes. I want to surprise her.'

In the end, it wasn't just Gwen who was drawn back into the clubhouse a few minutes later. Sensing that something was about to happen, most of the guests wandered in too. As Gwen came through the garden doors, she was greeted by the sight of a beautifully iced cake shining brightly with twenty-five candles. Then her eyes were focused on the pool of light towards one side of the room, where Richard sat at the piano smiling at her as he played. Tears misted her vision as she recognised the tune. 'Sous le Ciel de Paris' had been their special song during their honeymoon. What a romantic time that had been. For Richard with his flair for languages, and Gwen with her love of art and history, their time 'under the Paris sky' had proved magical and perfect.

With slow steps, she moved over to rest her hands on his shoulders as he played, marvelling as always at his ability to be able to pick out any piece on the keyboard without knowing a note of music. By the end of the song the gathered crowd were all swaying and humming along with him, bursting into applause and cheers as he drew to a triumphant conclusion. Then he rose to take Gwen in his arms, hugging her to him before handing over a long white envelope. Her face alight with curiosity, fingers fumbling to slit it open, she pulled out a thick blue travel wallet.

'Paris!' she gasped. 'We're going to Paris!'

'About time, don't you think?' he said, his eyes full of warmth and love. 'In two weeks' time, on Saturday morning, I'm going to whisk you away for a whole week of romance and reminiscing!'

She giggled. 'We're not staying at the same hotel, are we?'

'What? The one with the cockroaches and the decidedly dodgy doorman? No, my darling, this hotel is the equivalent of the Ritz, because I love you even more now than I did twenty-five years ago.' Then he kissed her soundly as a sigh of approval rippled round the delighted crowd, and Gwen thought that no one anywhere in the world could be happier than she was at that moment.

* * *

Susie was thinking about her parents as she drove back down to London later the following evening. Having a mum and dad who lived in a semi-detached in Chesham, and plainly still loved each other after a quarter of a century, would be something of a novelty in the circle in which she now moved. Life in an up-and-coming advertising agency was fast, decisive and cut-throat. Keep up, or keep out! If you didn't come up with inspired ideas faster than all the other bright young things, you'd find your seat taken by someone else in the time it took to refill your cup of decaffeinated coffee.

At first, she'd found the place terrifying – the casually stylish people who spoke to one another in media jargon which excluded anyone who wasn't in the know. For weeks she'd kept her head down and her ears open, absorbing names, faces and facts until she finally found the courage to venture her own opinion once in a while. In the end, it was her uncanny skill for drawing cartoons which gave her the break she needed. Her account team had been locked into a panic-stricken search for a fresh approach to promote a rather tired brand of breakfast cereal. Susie, as the most junior member of the team, was supposed to be taking minutes at their meeting until the account manager, a Mrs Munster lookalike with her long white face edged by a shock of sable-black hair, dramatically snatched Susie's pad out of her hand. The top page was covered with drawings of a cheeky cartoon character with whiskers and thick glasses which made his eyes seem enormous. 'That's it!' declared Mrs Munster (who was called Hilary, and actually quite nice once you got to know her). And Barley Bill was born.

The success of that campaign opened doors for Susie, but not fast enough when her aim was to get right to the top. She was determined that, one day, her opinion and input would be sought after in the same way that Deborah McCann's were now. Deborah was the agency's golden girl, glamorous, sophisticated, popular and right on the ball when it came to new ideas. She even had a boyfriend to match. Paul Armitage was quite the most wonderful man Susie had ever laid eyes on. With his thick dark hair, light hazel eyes fringed by long brown lashes, tall lean frame and pop star's face, Susie had been smitten since her first sighting of him. Not that he'd noticed her, of course. Why should a man who was one of the hottest names in photography, and on top of that, had Deborah McCann as a girlfriend, give a second glance to the new office junior? He did smile at her once, when she'd taken him a beer during a particularly long and hot shoot. He'd even asked her name, although he'd probably forgotten it seconds later. But the image of that smile was imprinted on Susie's mind, and haunted her daydreams. She grinned to herself as her car sped along towards London. Well, there was no harm in dreaming, was there?

She hardly dared think about her conversation with Hilary before she had left the previous Friday evening. Apparently there was the possibility of a photographic shoot in Rome in several weeks' time for a new line of women's office and business wear from Italy which one of their team's clients, a large department store, wanted to promote. The job was likely to come at a particularly busy time for the agency, and they were having difficulty finding someone to oversee the shoot. If things became desperate and they simply had no alternative, would Susie consider going?

Would she?! They had to be joking! Hoping her expression gave nothing away, she casually agreed that she could probably fit in a trip if really necessary. It was only then that Hilary mentioned there was talk of Paul Armitage being the preferred photographer for the session. Susie kept a suitably straight face all the way down to the ladies, where she locked herself into a cubicle and danced up and down with sheer excitement, punching the air with triumph and anticipation.

The thought of those minutes locked in the loo made Susie laugh out loud as she turned off the main road and headed down towards the flat she shared in West Hampstead. Perhaps she'd hear more about the trip this week? And just maybe she'd be able to hide the fact that while the thought of the job was daunting enough in itself, the prospect of spending time in the company of Paul Armitage was simply terrifying.

What did one wear for a romantic trip to Paris? Gwen sighed as she eyed the collection of clothes in her suitcase. No fancy undies. No little off-the-shoulder number. Richard would probably laugh out loud if she turned up in anything like that. No, she was right to pack her sensible warm nightie (well, it would still be cold at this time of year), her favourite twinset and comfy shoes. Anyway, after twenty-five years, the romance of their marriage didn't rely on frivolous trimmings. Their love was firmly based on unspoken understanding, shared goals and compromise on both sides. Perhaps their marriage hadn't had much in the way of passion, but then she of all people knew how painful and destructive passion could be. If only Richard would open his mind to the torment she still felt, the depths to which her thoughts sometimes plummeted. But it wasn't in the nature of the man to dwell on the past. Their lives together were calm and ordered, and passion would now be a poor substitute for the deep love they shared. Wouldn't it?

Gwen glanced at her watch. Five to nine. By this time the following evening they'd be in Paris, probably having dinner on the banks of the Seine. A bubble of excitement clutched at her stomach as she closed the case with a snap.

She was ready at last – and Richard had had his bag packed for days. He'd be home from the drama rehearsal in half an hour or so, and that would be it. Off for a week!

With such an early start in the morning, it was a shame he'd had to go along to the hall for the rehearsal that night, but with the next production coming up in just three weeks' time, work on the lighting and scenery were badly behind. Besides, Gwen knew how much he enjoyed his evenings with the group, as he beavered away preparing the staging for each show.

If she hurried, she'd just have time for a soak in the bath before he got back needing a sandwich and cup of tea. Ten minutes later, she lowered her aching shoulders under the hot bubbly water with a deep sigh. Eventually, thinking she should wash her hair, she allowed her head to slip beneath the water. She had been resting like this for quite a while when she became aware of a strange sound. Thumping? A noise in the street outside? She sat up with a start. No, it was closer than that. Someone was banging on her own front door.

Panicking now, she climbed out of the bath, and hurriedly tied her dressing gown round her. Wrapping a towel over her soaking hair, she ran downstairs to stand behind the front door.

'Who is it?'

'Oh Gwen, thank God! It's me, Mike. I couldn't make you hear the bell. Open up!'

Something was wrong. Through the glazed pane she could see that Mike was not alone. Was that someone in uniform beside him? A policeman! For one breathless second, time stood still as a shiver of cold premonition rippled through Gwen's body. She unlatched the door, and suddenly Mike was beside her, propelling her through to the lounge.

'What's happened?'

'Come and sit down.'

'I don't want to sit down. Tell me! Where's Richard?' She heard her own voice as if from a distance, shrill and unnatural.

Mike glanced towards the policeman who had followed him through. Then he turned back to place his hands on her shoulders. 'I don't know how to tell you this, Gwen, but there's been an accident.'

'Where's Richard? I've got to go to him. Is he hurt? What happened?'

'He was up a ladder working on the lights above the front edge of the stage . . .'

Gwen's hand shot to her mouth to stop the choke of horror that gripped her.

'And he fell? Is that it?'

'The ladder couldn't have been stable. We all saw it moving, but we couldn't get there quickly enough to stop him. He tumbled at such an awkward angle, and when his head hit the corner of the stage . . .'

'Oh God . . . Mike, tell me he's OK. Dear God, let him be OK!'

'He's dead, Gwen. He was dead before the ambulance even arrived. There was nothing anyone could do.'

From somewhere within her came a wail of raw pain like that of a wild animal trapped and sensing its own death. And as she plummeted down the dark pit of despair, she screamed and screamed but no one could hear. Nothing could reach her.

Nearly one hundred miles away, Roger Davis sat in his battered old Land Rover as rain drizzled down the windscreen, making the cold dawn light even bleaker than usual. It was Monday morning, not yet six o'clock, and already he'd had enough.

Perhaps he was getting too old for this game. Perhaps only younger men had the stomach for farming these days. He only knew he was tired, worn out with work and worry, and the constant fear which gripped his stomach and gnawed at his mind. He couldn't make ends meet. He now operated with less help, working harder and longer than he'd ever laboured in all his lifetime of farming, and he still couldn't make the books balance. They'd beaten him, those bureaucrats in Europe. The faceless rulemakers had broken him so successfully that not only could he not do any more, he simply hadn't the energy to try.

He'd been aware of himself climbing into the Land Rover when he should have been heading for the milking shed. The truck would be coming to collect that morning's milk just after eight, and the dairy herd were impatient. But he'd been up twice in the night with calving, and now his limbs wouldn't move, and his mind was blank with weariness. He knew he should get out and get cracking. Instead, he watched emotionless as ceaseless raindrops zigzagged down the windscreen.

He thought of Margaret, remembering her rounded form snuggled warmly in their bed as he climbed out that morning having barely slept at all. In all their years together – coming up for forty in a year or so – he couldn't remember a cross word or a night apart. They were too down-to earth a couple to use fancy words or extravagant gestures. He simply knew that she was his reason for living. Without her, he was nothing. Now, wouldn't that surprise Margaret? To her, he had always been the strong one, the decision-maker for both of them. Her role was to support, his to lead. Even as children, when she'd trailed round behind him as he worked on her dad's farm after school, there had been a comfortable companionship between them. He protected her. She felt cherished by him. They were two halves of a whole, incomplete apart and resiliently steadfast together.

So why, when his lifetime's work was about to crash around his ears, was he pushing her away, avoiding her anxious looks, brushing aside her perfectly reasonable questions? Because he couldn't admit, even to her, that he was out of answers. The shame, the despair, the pain the truth would bring her, were more than he could bear.

When her father had asked him to take over Hall Farm shortly after their marriage, the burden of responsibility for this land which had been nurtured by her family for centuries was a welcome challenge. For years he had risen at dawn, and fallen into bed at nine, exhausted and fulfilled by this farm he loved. And now the calves he would have sold for £60 three years ago wouldn't even fetch him the price of a kingsize Mars bar. As debts mounted, the bank had been as patient as they could be. They knew he was a grafter, but he knew it wasn't humanly possible for him to work any harder. And even then, it simply wasn't enough. It would never be enough.

A light tap on the window broke into his thoughts. Guiltily he opened the door to find Margaret standing there in her dressing gown, rain dripping down on her as she held out a cup of steaming tea.

'You all right, love? Only I didn't hear the milking machines.'

He was out of the car in a flash, ushering her back towards the house. 'I'm fine. Just having a spot of shut-eye. Good job you came! Go inside then, I'll be back for breakfast just after eight.'

And as Margaret found herself propelled back inside the kitchen door, she knew she'd been dismissed. If only he'd share his worries with her. Did he really think she didn't know, didn't realise?

With a sigh, she tipped the cup of tea she'd made earlier for herself down the sink. Somehow she wasn't in the mood for it any more.

Chapter Two

The sun shone. It shouldn't have done. It should have been a dismal day to match the mood of the small crowd of people with dark suits and pale faces who gathered that morning in the crematorium to say their farewells to Richard Moreton. The death of this man they knew and loved at the age of forty-nine had shocked them all. How could this happen? How could the life of a contented, healthy family man be snatched so suddenly and cruelly by one tragic moment, the slip of a ladder?

As the coffin made its slow way down the aisle, all eyes turned in sympathy towards Gwen, who walked stiff-backed and expressionless towards her seat in the front pew. Susie was at her side, cheeks raw from what had probably been days of crying. Her shoulders shook pitifully as the service continued.

'We brought nothing into the world, and we take nothing out ...

'The Lord is my Shepherd ... abide with Me ...

'In the midst of life, we are in death ...

'Blessed are those who mourn ...'

There's nothing blessed about mourning, thought Gwen through the fog of her grief. It's a living death. Without Richard, what have I to live for? And as she watched the coffin slide out of sight behind elegant wooden doors, a vice-like grip of pain tore at her heart. She almost cried. Almost. She would not break down. She would *not* break down.

She turned to Susie, who was sobbing quietly beside her. 'Come on, my love. They're waiting for us.' And mother and daughter supported each other as they made their uncertain way out of the door towards the Garden of Remembrance where the wreaths lay.

Beautiful flowers. Richard had loved flowers. But these had been cut at their best, and would soon be dead – like him. He'd always hated dead things.

'Does everyone know the way?' Celia's stage whisper was loud enough to be heard across the whole crematorium. 'Do any of you need a map? Ask Graham if you do. Or you can just follow us. Now, who's taking Aunt Madge?'

There was nothing like a tragedy to bring out Celia's organising instinct. She'd appeared at Gwen's house immediately she'd heard about the accident, and taken over. She'd fussed and clucked and issued orders. She'd spent hours on the phone passing on the news, her voice dramatically lowered as she related every unfortunate detail. While Graham sat whitefaced at Gwen's side, Celia was in her element.

'She didn't even *like* Dad!' hissed Susie angrily. 'Why doesn't she just leave us alone?'

'She's family, love. And at times like this, you realise how much you need your family.'

'Uncle Graham is family. That woman may be his wife, but I hate her, *hate* her!'

Gwen reached out for Susie's hand as their eyes met in complete understanding. And throughout the following week they clung together, battered by the events of each day, dreading the sleepless nights almost as much as the prospect of yet another morning.

About thirty people came back to the house after the cremation. The subdued mood was soon replaced by the pleasure of old friends meeting again, albeit at the most unexpected and tragic of occasions. As the tea flowed and sandwiches were handed round, bottles of wine and spirits appeared for those who needed something a bit stiffer to get through such a difficult day.

In a daze, Gwen allowed herself to be hugged and sobbed over. Like a distant onlooker, she listened to all the usual reassurances.

'Still, he had a good life – and we've all got to go some time . . .'

'At least he didn't suffer . . .'

Life goes on though, doesn't it, Gwen? Richard would want you to get on with your life . . .'

'I know just how you feel . . .'

No you don't, snapped the voice in her head. You could never know. No one understands how close Richard and I were, how pointless life is without him.

Gradually people began to drift away, leaving with promises that they'd be in touch soon. With relief, Gwen plunged her arms into a sinkful of soapy water to tackle the pile of plates, cups and glasses which were littered all round the kitchen.

'Oh no you don't!' Tricia whispered in her ear, gently taking a cup from her and handing her a towel.

'Trish, I need to be busy.'

'I understand that, but you look all in. I've just put the kettle on again. Go and keep Madge company.'

Reluctantly, because she hadn't the energy for an argument, Gwen sank on to a seat at the kitchen table next to Madge who was cleaning her spectacles on her cardigan. The gnarled old hand reached out to cover Gwen's. No words. None needed.

'Right!' began Celia, bustling in through the kitchen door with a notepad in her hand. 'There's a lot to discuss. Hurry up, Graham, take a seat.'

Following behind them, Susie stood unnoticed at the door, catching her mother's eye across the table.

'Now,' continued Celia, oblivious to the irritation on the faces of those around her, 'has the will been read? Not that we want to know the contents, of course – except that we'd like to be sure you're well provided for. What exactly did it say?'

'Oh, I'm fine,' replied Gwen quietly. 'Richard had his affairs in good order.'

'But this house will be far too big for you now. You should think about selling it, and Graham and I will organise that for you.'

'No, Celia, I'm not ready to make decisions like that just yet.'

'But you are alone now. You need to take stock of your situation, make sensible changes.'

Gwen smiled wryly. 'I'm not capable of thinking anything sensible at the moment.'

'Well, of course you're not – but you don't need to. Just leave everything to us.'

Leaning against the dresser in a corner of the room, Graham squirmed uncomfortably.

'Mum doesn't want to sell the house, Celia.' Susie's voice was cold and hard. 'She's just made that quite clear.'

'And she also said that she's not able to make sensible decisions for herself at present. As her family, we must rally round and make those decisions for her. That's the only way she'll move forward.'

'She's not ready to move forward. She lost Dad less than a week ago. Just lay off, will you?'

As if nothing had been said, Celia turned once more towards Gwen.

'And what about a job? You only work part-time at the library, don't you? Will that be enough to make ends meet? Would they take you on full-time if we asked them?'

'Aunt Celia . . .'

'Susie, you're just a child. You don't know about these things. Your mum mustn't be allowed to go into decline over this. She has to pick herself up and rebuild her life. Richard would want that. Isn't that right, Graham?'

Madge pushed her seat back noisily as she staggered to her feet.

'Time for us to go. Come on, Graham, take me home. And you'd better take that insensitive oaf of a wife with you, unless you can think of anything better to do with her. Drowning perhaps?'

'How dare you?'

'Oh, age helps! You're always saying I'm senile. Now get your coat, Celia, and let these good people go into decline in peace.'

And with a wink over her shoulder, Madge ushered Celia and Graham out of the house.

'That woman!' exploded Susie the moment the door was closed. 'She's like a vulture! I bet she was going round with that notebook putting a price tag on everything, working out how much she could sell it for.'

It was then that Tricia started to chuckle. She couldn't help herself — and it was infectious, because in spite of all the sadness of the previous few days, Susie and Gwen found themselves joining her in a mixture of laughter and tears. For minutes they giggled and cried together, hugging each other because it felt so good, like a gushing tap relieving the pressure of the shocking, emotion-filled days they'd all been through. At last, spent and tearstained, they kicked off their shoes while Tricia filled the only three clean glasses they could find with generous tots of gin and a splash of tonic.

'She's right though,' said Gwen at last, 'I do need to get my act together. I'm not used to being on my own. I don't even know what it costs to run this house. Richard always took care of the bills.'

'You'll learn. You'll be fine.'

'And you're not alone. There are two of us left in this family.'

Susie leaned across to put an arm round her mother's shoulders, drawing her close.

'But you don't like me!' grinned Gwen. 'We haven't got on for years.'

'Losing Dad changed all that. It's us against the world now, isn't it? And we Moretons have got to stick together against the wicked Celia. Right?'

'Right!' And as Gwen leaned forward until their heads were touching, she thought how proud Richard would be of Susie, and how lucky she was to have the most wonderful daughter in the world.

Susie made a point of visiting almost every weekend after that. Together the two women discovered a new and comfortable closeness in which they could cry, laugh and reminisce about Richard with complete freedom. To Gwen's delight, Susie even opened up about her job, an area of her life which she had previously shared often with her dad, but rarely with her mother.

One weekend about five weeks after Richard's death, Gwen could tell Susie was excited about something the moment she stepped out of the car.

'I'm going to Rome! That job's come up. I leave on Friday.'

'Susie, that's wonderful. How long will you be away?'

'Not long. I'll be back on Tuesday.'

'And how many of you are going?'

'Oh, there'll be a few of us. The models are being recruited in Italy, as well as the make-up and hairdressing team, and the department store will be sending their own people to look after the clothes. I suppose the photographer will have an assistant or two with him as well, but I'll be the only representative from our agency.'

'Wow, they must think highly of you then.'

Susie giggled. 'I don't know. I hope so.'

They opted for fish and chips that night, which they ate sprawled out on the settee, with Susie barely stopping for breath as she gushed with enthusiasm about her coming trip. Gwen watched her affectionately, thinking how pleased Richard would have been to hear her news. It was strange how unlike her father she was. He had been a handsome man, tall and lean, with thick blond hair and pale blue eyes. His daughter was short and dark, with thick unruly dark red curls which spilled over her shoulders, and generous curves which Susie hated at a time when hips and busts were definitely out of fashion. She's like me, of course, thought Gwen with a smile. Better not tell her that.

The following morning, as Susie packed to head back down to London, Gwen pushed an envelope into her hand.

'What's this?'

'A cheque. Buy yourself some nice clothes for Rome.'

'There's nothing wrong with the way I dress, Mum.'

'Nothing at all. But I bet you could find something special to add to your wardrobe.'

'You need your money. You shouldn't do this.'

'Yes, I should, and your dad would want me to. He'd be so proud of you.'

'Thanks, Mum,' was Susie's muffled reply as she hugged Gwen before driving away with mist in her eyes.

Three counties away at Hall Farm, Margaret pulled the joint of lamb out of the oven for a final basting, glancing up at the kitchen clock as she closed the Aga door. Twenty-five to one. Kate and Martin would be here soon. Untying her apron, she made her way upstairs to the bedroom to splash cold water over her face and pull a comb through her hair before her daughter and son-in-law arrived.

A movement outside the window caught her eye, and she looked out to see Roger walking away from the milking shed towards the greenhouse where he grew his beloved geraniums. Over the years, they had become a passion for him, a glow of pleasure in a life that had become increasingly hard. He looked tired now, and it was only lunchtime. Margaret sighed. These days that was nothing new.

She sat down heavily on the bed, her heart going out to this dear, hardworking husband she'd been married to for nearly four decades. He'd always been an ox of a man, broad and strong, yet the last few years had taken their toll on him. He seemed smaller and more frail, his shoulders hunched, face lined, his mind constantly preoccupied. But it was the distance between them which worried her most. From the very beginning, when they'd been childhood sweethearts, they had always been friends first and foremost, sharing secrets and troubles. Now, for the first time in their long years together, he was excluding her. He wouldn't discuss the farm finances. He refused to be drawn on the long hours he was putting in, or his obvious exhaustion. He remained tightlipped and aloof, getting up at the crack of dawn each day and falling into a sleep like death at night.

The sound of a car coming into the yard broke into her thoughts. Kate was here. Smiling broadly, Margaret hurried downstairs to greet the visitors.

Lunch was an informal affair, with the four of them seated around the large scrubbed kitchen table. Margaret glanced across at Kate and thought how lovely she looked, her long blonde hair tucked neatly behind her ears, pale blue eyes bright and alive in her often rather serious face as she laughingly told her parents about a comical incident at school that week. That a daughter of theirs should not only take herself off to university to become fluent in French, but go on to be Head of Languages at the biggest private school in Colchester was a source of immense pride to her parents. Margaret watched how Kate's slim elegant hands and expressive face brought the story to life, and her heart lurched with love and thankfulness that this beautiful young woman should be part of their family. And it was good to see the way Martin glanced at Kate, his interesting, friendly face beaming behind his glasses, eyes full of shared affection.

'Actually, Mum and Dad,' continued Kate as she leaned across to clasp Martin's hand, 'we've got a bit of news for you.'

'We've been waiting until we were completely sure,' Martin went on, 'but it looks as if we're all in for a rather special delivery later this year. We're expecting a baby.'

In an instant, tears filled Margaret's eyes as both she and Roger got up to hug and congratulate them.

Kate held her mum tightly. 'You know how difficult it's been. We'd almost given up hope.'

'But everything's OK?' asked Margaret anxiously. 'No complications after all that treatment?'

'No,' smiled Martin, 'it seems fine. They say they'll keep a special eye on Kate after all her problems, but hopefully the pregnancy should go normally.'

'Just one baby, is it?' asked Roger. 'Only if my ewes have special fertility treatment, they end up with triplets!'

'That was my first question,' laughed Kate, 'and yes, they're sure. Just one baby – and that's all we need, just one perfectly healthy, much-loved baby.'

'What about work? You'll have to give up, I suppose?'

'Probably. It's April now, and the baby is due at the end of October. I may well just leave at the end of the summer term, and decide later if I feel I want to return to full-time teaching.'

'After this long wait, you'll need to stay at home for a few years at least, won't you?'

'Maybe. Maybe not. I'm not sure yet how I'll feel. The whole thing is still so new to me. Perhaps I could do some private language tuition to keep my hand in. Perhaps, if Martin's company is taken over and there's any doubt about whether his contract will be renewed, we'll be needing my income.'

'Well, you know I'll enjoy babysitting any time. Try stopping me.'

'You've always been a wonderful mum. You'll make the best grandmother ever.'

'The proudest.'

'And the busiest! I hope you're in the mood for knitting. I picked up a pattern for a beautiful shawl yesterday.'

For a moment, Margaret thought of how this big old farmhouse came to life with the sound of a child's laughter. It was so long since Kate had been a little girl here, and in the fifteen years since she'd left home for good to go to university, and then on to work in Colchester, Hall Farm had missed the noise and bustle of family life. A new baby would bring life and purpose for them all. Margaret glanced across to Roger, who was smiling for the first time in days as he chatted to Martin.

Yes, a baby would be just wonderful. And perhaps, just perhaps, it would be what Roger needed to draw him back from the problems of the farm to the family who loved him so dearly.

It was the sight of his writing that did it. Sitting at her office desk late on Thursday evening, Susie had been sorting out last-minute details for the trip to Rome the following morning. She had checked and re-checked everything. It was so important that this job went well. After the sadness of the previous few weeks, things had to start getting better.

And then she saw it – her father's writing on a page in her Filofax. He had written an address out for her, and signed it underneath with the silly smiley face he always put at the bottom of letters to her. It had been a secret joke between them, a symbol of the closeness and love which had always been so strong a link with her dad, particularly after she'd left home and begun working in London. Dressed in her smart office clothes, here in their hi-tech, untidily organised West End office, the sight of his familiar writing caught her by surprise, chipping away at the fragile veneer of toughness she'd hidden behind in her struggle to cope with the shock of her father's sudden death. She could do nothing to stop the wave of grief overwhelming her yet again. Would she ever get over this? Would she be able to think of Dad without wanting to bawl her eyes out at the unfairness and waste of losing him? And because she knew she was on her own in the deserted office, her shoulders slumped as she buried her face in her hands and let the tears come.

It was several minutes before she realised she wasn't alone. She became aware of a shadow behind her shoulder, the shape of a person perching themselves intrusively on the edge of her desk. Appalled at being seen in such a state, she groped for a hankie to wipe her eyes, before turning her reddened, tearstained face to see who was there. To her horror, it was Paul Armitage.

'I hope it's not the thought that we're going to be working together tomorrow that's made you cry.'

'No. I'm sorry, it isn't what you think . . .'

She didn't dare look directly at him, fearful of the pity she might see there.

'It isn't that you've heard how difficult I am to work with then?'

In spite of herself, she grinned. 'Are you?'

'Dreadful. It's the artist in me. That and the fact that the sight of a lovely girl in tears makes me want to stop work immediately and cheer her up.'

'I don't usually cry.'

'Then an unusual sadness must have brought this on. Want to talk about it?'

She didn't answer. She couldn't.

'Someone you love?'

She nodded dumbly.

'A man friend?'

'The man who was my very best friend. My dad.'

'Was?'

'He died about six weeks ago.'

'Oh.' In the seconds of silence that followed, Susie could feel him looking at her closely. 'Had he been ill?'

'No, it was very sudden, an accident.'

'Susie, I'm so sorry.' She felt him gently pull her towards him so that her head rested against the rough leather of his jacket. There he held her, not speaking but simply rocking her to and fro as if she were a small child. The tenderness of the gesture surprised her until she felt herself relax against him, sighing as the tension dropped from her shoulders.

'Were you very close?' he asked at last.

'I adored him. You know what they say about dads and daughters.'

'Were you like him?'

'We had the same sense of humour. We laughed a lot together. And I could talk to him, *really* talk to him about anything and everything.'

'I wish I had a dad like that.'

'Why? What's yours like?'

'No idea. He didn't stay around long enough for me to find out. In fact, I'm not even sure he knew I was on the way.'

'So did your mum bring you up on her own?'

'For the first few years. The best years, I suppose, because when she finally did marry, it didn't do me any favours.'

'You didn't get on with your stepfather?'

Paul's tightlipped smile was humourless and bitter. 'You could say that.'

'And your mum? Do you still see her?'

'Whenever I can. She's up in Lancashire, so I pop in if I'm up that way. And I ring her often.'

Suddenly embarrassed by the fact that she was still snuggled up against his chest, Susie moved back into her seat, watching in fascination as he reached out to take her hand.

'I guess you could have done without this Rome trip so soon after losing your dad?'

'It's probably just what I need, something to occupy my concentration and time. It will be all right, honestly.'

He smiled down at her. 'I know it will. And Susie, if you feel down and need a shoulder, I'm here. OK?'

Then, leaning forward to tuck a stray wisp of hair behind her ear, his lips touched her forehead with the lightest of kisses before he turned to walk away.

Bereavement is exhausting. Gwen felt that she was tired all the time, worn out by the shafts of grief which stabbed at her. Richard's shirts still hanging in the wardrobe smelling faintly of his favourite aftershave, the photo of them from last year's holiday, his vegetable garden now abandoned and overgrown: each caught her unawares, knocking her back just as she thought perhaps she was finally coming to terms with the loss of him.

Nights were the worst. She found herself falling asleep at nine o'clock, only to be wide awake again shortly after midnight, her mind teeming with memories of the past and fears for the future. Gradually, the pattern became the same. She'd toss and turn for the first hour, then admit defeat and go down to the kitchen to make herself a milky drink. When that, and an hour or so of tedious night-time television, didn't do the trick, she'd try to think of something exhausting to do. For three nights now, she had ended up scouring every sink in the house until the porcelain gleamed and her hands were red-raw.

I need to keep busy. I must be busy. I have to do something, anything. Sitting in the lounge in the early hours of the morning, Gwen looked around desperately for a way to occupy her hands, fill her mind, soothe her aching heart.

The dawn that crept round the closed lounge curtains that morning found her sitting at the table surrounded by the sketchpads, crayons and pastels she had buried at the back of the cupboard many years before. The pleasure she had once found in drawing and painting had been forgotten for so long, and yet as the hours wore on and sleep still evaded her, she felt the familiar comfort that pouring her feelings out on paper had brought her years before.

She sat back in her chair, looking critically at the array of sheets scattered over the table. There was so much she'd forgotten about the skills and secrets of producing satisfying pictures, much more she'd like to express through brush and pencil. Then, for the very first time since Richard's death, she realised she was coming to a decision. She would go to lessons. That's what she'd do!

She thought of the library where she worked part-time, and Brian, the gentle, bearded man who came a couple of times each week to teach art. His class was always full of students who spoke enthusiastically of his ability to analyse and inspire their work. On several occasions in the past, when she'd been working late, she'd stood on tiptoe outside the door, peering through the glass panel to watch the casual way in which he moved from one easel to the next, admiring here, suggesting there.

She'd like to join that class. And the very next opportunity she had, she would seek Brian out and set the wheels in motion.

The trip to Rome was a whirl from beginning to end, from the moment that the three-strong team from the department store met up with Paul, his assistant Mark, and Susie at Heathrow for their early morning flight. What followed were three days of rushing from one well-known location to another, taking photos of the four precocious young models who had been supplied by the Italian agency. But what they lacked in social skills they more than made up for in their ability to flirt with the camera — or perhaps it was with Paul, as he cajoled and flattered them into the poses he needed. Susie watched in admiration as he chose backdrops, designed lighting and changed film and cameras to create the stylish shots they required. He wasn't just good, he was brilliant.

Susie made sure that she too was totally professional. She arranged the timetable for the whole shoot, organising everything from meal breaks, payments, transport, hotels and insurance to rushing out at the last minute to find the *only* shade of lipstick that one model was prepared to wear. And throughout it all, the intimacy of her time in the office with Paul stayed with her; and perhaps with him too, if his smiles in her direction, or the occasional squeeze of her shoulder as he passed, were anything to go by. He seemed to seek her company, turning down the opportunity to eat out in the city with the crowd in the evening, opting instead to stay in the hotel with Susie to 'talk over plans for tomorrow'. Together they'd sit for hours over a plate of pasta and a bottle of red wine, chatting about almost anything except the work they were there to do. She discovered that he was not as flash and offhand as she had imagined him to be. The sadness of his expression when he spoke of what had plainly not been a happy childhood, his vulnerability when he asked her what she thought of his photos, as if her answer really mattered to him, the compassion in his eyes when he listened without any sense of impatience to her memories of her father, all combined to give her an insight into a man who cared deeply, both for others, and about the hurts in his past.

And then, on the last night, he walked her as usual up to her room, except that this time he didn't leave immediately as he had before, but instead gently drew her to him, looking down into her eyes with exquisite, heart-stopping tenderness before he kissed her. Susie sank into his embrace knowing that this was what she had wanted from the first moment she'd seen him.

And when he took the key from her to open her door, she reached up to kiss him again before taking his hand to draw him inside.

Chapter Three

The moment she walked through the café door, Gwen spotted Tricia in the corner at a table already set with a pot of tea and two gooey chocolate cakes.

'Well?' demanded Tricia once Gwen had got her coat off and settled herself down. 'How did it go?'

'Brilliant! Brian's such a good teacher, really encouraging. He had some interesting points to make about the pieces I brought with me.'

'So he liked them?'

'Seemed to. In fact, he was very complimentary even though he had plenty of suggestions to make about ways to improve my technique and style. I enjoyed it.'

'Good.' Tricia looked approvingly at the sparkle in Gwen's eyes which had been clouded with sadness too often recently. 'When do you go again?'

'His art classes are twice a week at the library, and he was telling me that he runs private workshops in his studio at the weekends too.'

'And you're thinking of going?'

'Should I? What do you think?'

'I think it's great to see you taking up something for yourself again, and I don't mean just since Richard's death. I've felt for years that you've buried your own interests in favour of what he enjoyed doing. All those teas you made for cricket, and the hours you spent at the golf club.'

Gwen chuckled. 'Especially when I hated the game!'

'And we both know that Richard wasn't exactly sensitive to your need to express your true feelings.'

'He thought it for the best. He probably didn't understand how much it still hurt.'

'Well, he should have listened. I've watched how the heartache of all that has eaten into you over the years. Now, at last, you have the chance to do something of your own that you really love.'

'You don't think it's too soon, do you? What will people think?'

'The people who matter, the ones who really care about you, will recognise that this art class is just what you need right now. Don't feel guilty about it. Go ahead and enjoy it!'

A shadow crossed Gwen's face as she dropped a lump of sugar into her cup and took a sip before sitting back in her chair.

'And you? How are things with Mike?'

'Well, I now know who she is.'

'You do?'

'I took a look at his mobile phone bill. One number in particular kept coming up, sometimes four or five times a day. I rang it myself and got an answerphone reply where she gives her name. Barbara Morgan. The only thing is that the message gives her husband's name too. Barbara and Robert Morgan, she says. No wonder Mike always rings her during the day. That must be when her poor fool of a husband is at work.'

'Oh Trish, what are you going to do?'

'I've already done it. I left a message of my own on their machine – and if it happens to be Mr rather than Mrs Morgan who gets it first, that's fine by me. I told her that I knew all about her affair with my husband, and that I don't give a damn. She's welcome to him, and as soon as she likes she can help him collect his stuff which is piled up in our garage waiting for him.'

'You didn't!'

'Oh, I did. I've even moved out his precious golf clubs, and that huge great cactus which he loves and I hate. Getting it all out to the garage took me hours this morning, but it's done now. And I got the locks changed, so dear Mike is in for a bit of a shock this evening.'

'He has no idea that you know?'

'He probably thinks I have a suspicion, but of course I'm not supposed to mind. He always says that I knew what he was like when I married him, and I shouldn't expect him to change now. That man has been my husband for nearly thirty years. We've brought up two children together. Yes, I do expect him to change. Most men grow up. Mine didn't.'

'But Trish, how will you manage? What will you do about money?'

'The same as I always have. Mike will pay for me to stay in my home. I just don't want him to live there with me any more. I'm worth more than this, Gwen. If he doesn't think so, I don't want him around me. He's knocked the confidence out of me over the years, and I've had enough.'

'But you love him. I know you do.'

'Do you? I'm not so sure any more.'

'What do you feel?'

'For him? Not a lot. For myself? Angry, humiliated, relieved that I've finally made the decision to crawl out from under his shadow.'

'Good for you!'

'And now I've made a few changes in his life, I'm planning to make a few in my own. I'm going into London tomorrow for a *really* expensive haircut. Then I'm going to hit the shops for some brand-new outfits. After all, I've got a newly empty wardrobe to fill! I refuse to be good old Trish any more – Mike's wife, the kids' mum, a handy person to have around when tea needs to be made or a raffle organised. Mike apparently needs a new woman. Well, his old cast-off is ready to become a new woman too! And who knows, perhaps I'll even find a new man.'

'Trish, you wouldn't.'

'Wouldn't I? Just watch me!'

After the euphoria of the Rome trip, Paul Armitage disappeared. For weeks, Susie hoped for a glimpse of him, or the sound of his voice on one of the rare occasions when he came into the office. Then, just when she'd almost given up hope, she overheard Deborah McCann saying that he was away on a shoot in Scotland for another agency, but they would be spending the weekend together on his return. Susie's mouth went dry, her hands hot and clammy. Well, what did she expect? Deborah was his girlfriend. She was glamorous, successful and beautiful. What chance would someone like Susie have with competition like that? Did she honestly believe that a chance dalliance in a romantic Italian city had meant anything to a sophisticated good-looking man like him? Of course not.

But that night, Susie cried. Tears soaked her pillow as she cried because she loved her dad, cried because she probably loved Paul, and cried because of a nagging new worry which increasingly filled her thoughts.

Pregnancy was wearing. Kate had been told that the first few weeks were sometimes the worst, but the constant feeling of nausea combined with overwhelming tiredness to make her days of teaching at school seem endless. Because she'd always found tremendous pleasure in teaching the languages which came so easily to her, her current lethargy was a real disappointment. She loved being able to enthuse about words and sounds in a way which brought French to life for her young pupils; but there were times now when she feared she might nod off in the middle of a sentence. This wasn't made easier by the fact that the pupils had not been told about her condition.

'Better to wait a while, until we have decided how to fill your position during your maternity leave,' was the headmistress's sensible suggestion.

But she was too thrilled about the thought of at last becoming a mother to keep the news from her fellow teachers. The years of wanting and waiting were almost behind her, and she longed for the moment when she would finally hold her own child in her arms. And Martin would make such a wonderful dad. The kind, patient, intelligent man she had married more than eight years ago had proved to be not just a dear partner but a real soulmate. A child would be the blessing to complete their lives and marriage.

Complete? She thought about that word as she looked out of her classroom window at going-home time one evening. The girls were filing out of the school building towards the cluster of parents and cars gathered around the gate. She watched as one pupil scooped her small toddler sister up in her arms before turning to hug her mother.

Unexpectedly, Kate caught her breath as she watched the trio set off down the road, overwhelmed by the familiar sense of emptiness which washed over her.

In the light, airy room at the back of the library building, Brian watched as his pupils went to work on the task he'd set them for that lesson. It was a still-life arrangement of garden pots, bare branches and tools. The shapes and colours intertwined with one another in an intricate pattern, and he was interested to see what his students would make of it. Well, one in particular. Gwen Moreton was the most talented student he had come across in years. Not that she knew it. She seemed completely unaware of her ability, and so absorbed in learning new techniques she felt she was lacking

that she seemed to have no conception of the natural talent she
possessed.

As an artist, she fascinated him. As a pupil, she challenged
him. But it was as a woman that she intrigued him most,
self-contained and serious, as though keeping a tight rein on
her true feelings and personality. She was sad, he could see that.
She wore an air of deep hurt about her like a glass shell which
kept others at arm's length. And yet her paintings were free and
expressive, revealing a passion and complexity which drew his
curiosity.

Gwen had been coming to classes for several weeks before
he finally found the chance to talk to her properly. She had
needed a few extra minutes to finish the sketch of the elderly
gentleman who had been their model that afternoon, and by the
time the piece was completed to her satisfaction, the room had
emptied.

'That's good,' he said softly over her shoulder. 'You've
captured his colouring and the contour of his face very well. It's
interesting, though, that you saw such emotion in his expression.
Do you think that sadness was in the subject, or the artist?'

She eyed the drawing critically for a moment, before
slumping back in the chair with a sigh.

'I saw what wasn't really there, didn't I? I seem to see sadness
in everything these days.'

He didn't reply immediately, noting the forlorn defeat in
her slight shoulders. 'I could murder a cup of tea. Do you have
to rush off, or could you join me? I'd like to chat a bit more
about your work.'

From the look of panic on her face, he thought she was
going to refuse. Then unexpectedly she smiled. 'A cup of tea
would be wonderful.' She gathered up her bag and coat and
followed him down the corridor to the canteen.

It was more than an hour later before Gwen finally climbed
into her car to drive home. She glanced in the rear-view mirror
as she switched on the engine, surprised to see an animation

and excitement in her face which she'd not felt for a long time. Painting and drawing had brought that kind of fulfilment and pleasure to her years ago. She'd forgotten. She'd buried the memory of her own satisfaction from painting when the demands of her home, marriage and family took over. Now she'd found that pleasure again, and it was more vibrant and compulsive than ever. These art lessons had turned out to be a brilliant idea. She was loving every minute of them.

She smiled as she put the car into gear, glancing over her shoulder to pull away. Oh yes, and Brian was quite nice too.

Martin knew Kate well enough to understand her preoccupation. They had discussed it often in the past, the sense of emptiness within her, the longing to be complete. In the end, it was he who first made the suggestion that now was the right time to do something about it. She only had to take the first step. If, as a result, there was the real possibility of going further, then she could make a decision. And if there was nothing to find, well, that would be the end of it.

Kate looked up at him, her eyes shining with gratitude. Why, when she had such love around her, from her parents and this dear man to whom she was so happily married, did she feel the need for more?

'Hi!'

Susie stopped in her tracks at the sound of Paul's familiar voice. Holding her breath, she rounded the corner towards the desk where he was comfortably settled in her chair, tanned and unspeakably gorgeous.

'I thought I'd missed you again. You always seem to be away from your desk when I call in.'

'Was I? I didn't know you'd been around.' Words tumbled

out in the wrong order as she struggled to control her thumping heart and shaking hands.

'You look great. How are you?'

'I'm fine.'

'I'm sorry it's been so long. I meant to call you, but you know how frantic I always am.'

Susie's smile was almost convincing. 'Oh, that's all right. I didn't expect you to.'

'I didn't want you to think – well, you know ...'

'Really, I understand. Deborah was saying how busy you've been.'

He nodded, as if not sure what to say next. Eventually Susie filled the awkward silence.

'The photos were wonderful. The clients were delighted. Thank you for that.'

'I really enjoyed that shoot. Rome is always terrific. And this time the company was particularly good.'

She held his gaze for a moment, her voice soft as she replied. 'I enjoyed it too.'

'How are you, Susie? About your dad and everything? Feeling any better?'

'Oh, you know, good days and bad days.'

'I'm always here, if you ever need a shoulder ...'

But you're not, she thought. She dropped her head, unable to bear the kindness in his expression when she knew without a shadow of doubt that she could only ever be a diversion for him. He need never know how thoughts of him had filled her mind and heart since their trip was over. What would be the point? He belonged to Deborah, two golden people together.

Her eyes were tightly closed as she sensed him stand and move towards her. She felt his hand under her chin, tilting her face towards him as his lips gently brushed against hers.

'Take care of yourself, lovely Susie.' With that he was gone, leaving her rooted to the spot. And there she stayed, cheeks flushed, pulse pounding.

Why hadn't she told him? She'd had the perfect chance. So why hadn't she told him she was pregnant?

They agreed to meet on mutual ground in the bar of a large, impersonal hotel just outside town. Mike arrived first. In fact, he was there more than twenty minutes before Tricia was due, with time for two visits to the bar and one to the loo before he saw his wife park her car and walk towards the hotel entrance. She looked different. Something about her hair. Shorter perhaps? Blonder? And he'd not seen that outfit before. Tricia looked good, confident and happy with herself. Not like his wife at all.

She spotted him immediately, then made her way over to the corner table where he sat. He stood to greet her, but they didn't touch. Thirty years of marriage behind them, yet there was an awkwardness between them now.

'Drink?'

'Please.'

'Gin and tonic?'

'I'd rather have a cup of coffee.'

As he went towards the bar to order she watched him coolly, wondering at the detachment she felt in the company of this man she had loved without question, and who'd hurt her so badly. He looked thinner, his face drawn, dark circles around his eyes. His suit needs cleaning, she thought with some satisfaction, and that shirt could do with an iron. Strange, he'd always been such an immaculately dressed man – but then behind every smart man, there's an even smarter woman. Or, in his case, there used to be.

'They'll bring your coffee in a minute,' he said as he placed his own double whisky on the table. He seemed unsure where to sit, beside or opposite her.

Getting no clue from her expression, he finally pulled out the chair across the table from her, and sat down. He took a gulp from his drink, uncertain how to start.

'You look nice,' he said finally.

'Thank you.'

'New hairstyle?'

'Yes.'

'It looks lovely. You look lovely.'

She sighed with impatience, as if the conversation were boring her.

'Mike, you said you needed to talk. I'm here, but as I'm going out this evening, I haven't much time. Can you get to the point?'

The abruptness of her reply took him by surprise. He reached again for his glass.

'I want us to stop this nonsense. I'll come home, and we can just forget about all this.'

'All what? *This* affair, or all of your affairs?'

'They've never meant anything to me. You know that.'

'Do I? Didn't they?'

'You're the only woman I've ever really loved. You're my wife, for heaven's sake.'

'You remembered! Pity you forgot that small detail when it meant something to me.'

'Look, you've made your point. I made a mistake, and I've paid for it. I'm coming home now. It's over. Finished.'

'It certainly is, Mike. Thirty years is a long time, but I've still got a lot of life left ahead of me. I'm sick of being your doormat, and as we agreed our marriage is finished, we simply have to talk terms. I thought that's what we were here to do.'

She watched in fascination as the blood drained from his face. 'Oh come on, Trish. Enough's enough. I've eaten humble pie. I'll make it up to you. I love you.'

She looked directly at him, her voice hard and cold. 'No, Mike, it was me who loved you. What you felt for me was need. You needed your house kept, your schedule organised and your washing done. I did all that for thirty years because of my love for you, and because I needed your love too. It's taken me a very long time to work out I was getting the raw end of the deal. So the deal is off. I no longer wish to remain married to you. We will divorce on the grounds of your adultery. You can decide which particular woman you'd like me to cite by name.'

He stared at her dumbly, as she looked at her watch.

'And if there's nothing else, I have to go.'

'You haven't had your coffee.'

'You have it. You look as if you need it.'

'Trish, please! You can't leave before we've even had time to talk properly.'

'We had thirty years, Mike. Surely that was long enough?'

'I don't want a divorce. I never meant anything like this to happen.'

'Then what did you expect?' She stood up, staring down at him as she spat out the words. 'That I would just carry on being humiliated and hurt, while you were free to continue with whatever you felt like doing?'

'I can make it up to you, I know I can. Just give me the chance and I'll prove how much you mean to me.'

'Oh, I think you've already done that. That's why our marriage is over. My solicitor will be in touch. Goodbye, Mike.' And without a backward glance she left the bar with every eye in the place staring after her.

'Lovely day!'

Roger was just closing the bottom meadow gate when Gillian Bawdon pulled her Range Rover to a stop in the lane. She and her husband, Simon, had been their neighbours for about six years, when they'd bought the old manor house surrounded by six acres of paddock and garden just outside the village. Roger barely knew her husband, which wasn't really surprising as Simon was something big in the City, one of the immaculately pinstriped commuters who caught the fast train from Colchester to Liverpool Street around eight each weekday morning, returning on a regular train in the evening, a copy of the *Financial Times* tucked neatly into the side of his briefcase. Roger couldn't think of a worse way to spend the working day, except that Simon plainly had plenty of money, judging from the small fortune the family had spent on renovating their manor house to give it brand-new old-fashioned features. Odd really. Simon's work in the City enabled him to buy all the pleasures of country living. Roger worked, slept and breathed the country life, yet he wasn't sure he could afford to buy a new tax disc for his old Land Rover at the end of the month.

He smiled as Gillian came to join him and lean over the gate to take a leisurely look at the dairy herd. Roger had decided some time ago that, for a townie, Gillian was all right. But then she had come from a country background, a landowning family up North, so she'd told him. It was there that she first learned to ride, and riding had remained a passion for her, passed on to her two teenage daughters who both owned horses on which they regularly competed in the local gymkhanas. It was that family love of horses which had brought them to the manor house where the paddocks suited their needs perfectly. And, as it turned out, it suited the needs of others too, because over a period of about three years Gillian had steadily built up a business providing lessons, mostly for youngsters, plus livery for six other horses and ponies whose owners hadn't their own facilities to keep them.

Gillian had never been a woman to beat around the bush. 'I'm glad I found you, Roger. I've got a proposition for you.'

'My, I don't get many of those these days!'

'How are things? Any better?'

He shrugged his shoulders. 'I'm not alone. We're all in the same boat. There won't be many small family farms like this left in ten years' time.'

She nodded, gazing out across the tranquil scene of cows grazing on the meadow in front of them. 'Pity. I feel most sorry for young men wanting to come into the business. If, instead of your Kate, you'd had a son who planned to take over the farm in due course, what prospects would he have now?'

'I've been thinking that myself. I wondered what I would do if I were just starting out in farming. This isn't just a job for me. There's no other way that I could live. I work the land. That's what I do, what I've always done.'

She almost reached over to touch his arm in a gesture of comfort and support, but this was a proud, self-contained man who would probably be embarrassed by any show of emotion. Instead, she turned to face him.

'Well, I need something I think you may be able to provide, on a proper business footing of course.'

His eyebrows rose almost imperceptibly. She'd got his attention.

'Well, two things have happened more or less at the same time. I've been approached about providing livery for another couple of horses, and as that's something I enjoy doing, I'd like to be able to say yes. Quite apart from that, Mary Smith over near Fairstead – do you know her? She's taught riding for years, although only in a small way. Well, she's decided to retire, and she wants to find good homes for her seven horses and ponies. None of them are bad, and they're well used to youngsters – and I'd like to have them so that I can expand the teaching side of the business. I've thought about this long and hard. I'd need to take on another teacher, of course, but I'd enjoy the challenge, I know I would.'

'And it's a nice little earner.'

She laughed. 'And it's a nice little earner! I've got more time on my hands now with the girls practically finished at school. They'll be off to university before I know it.'

'So how can I help?'

'I could do with the use of one of your fields, preferably the one that backs on to us. How about if we come to some arrangement for me to rent it from you? And I'll need extra stabling. You've got all those old barns and farm buildings at the side of that field. Is there anything there I could convert into about six stables to begin with?'

'To begin with?'

'I'm not sure just how much demand there will be. I think I can make a go of this, but until I try, who knows if it will work?'

He grinned. 'I reckon if anyone can do it, you can.'

'So the answer is yes?'

'The answer is that I need to think about it, and talk it over with Margaret,'

'Oh, of course.'

'But providing we can agree on fair terms, I don't see why not.'

She threw her arms around his neck and hugged him. She couldn't stop herself.

'No promises, mind!' he gasped. 'Fingers crossed though, for both our sakes.'

When Susie arrived home in Chesham that weekend, Gwen was out. Susie knew she would be. Her mother had been full of anticipation at the prospect of joining the workshop organised by her art teacher at his own studio on Saturday mornings. Susie had been pleased to hear the note of pleasure in her mother's voice, replacing just for a while the sadness which had overshadowed everything for the past couple of months.

In fact, of the four students at Brian's studio that morning, Gwen was the last to leave. Her pencil line study had proved absorbing and time-consuming, so that hours passed by before she looked up to realise that everyone except Brian had gone. Seeing her lay down her pencil and stretch her stiff arms towards the ceiling, he made his way over to inspect her work, pulling up a chair alongside her.

'It's good.'

For a few minutes they discussed the picture, Brian's head close to Gwen's as he pointed out detail, and made suggestions for improvements.

'Time for a coffee?' he asked at last.

'Better not,' she replied, glancing at her watch. 'Susie's home.'

'Your daughter?'

Gwen's face lit up with pride. 'That's right. She works in a big advertising agency in London. She's always had a flair for anything artistic.'

'Gets it from her mum, eh?'

'Oh no, I've not done much art over the years. That's probably why I'm enjoying it so much now.'

'You have great talent, Gwen. In time I think you could have real success as an artist.'

A red flush crept up her neck and cheeks as she fumbled to put her materials away.

'Nonsense. I'm just an enthusiastic amateur.'

'Perhaps that's what you are now, but talent like yours should be encouraged.'

'Brian, this is just a hobby for me, a diversion to keep me from ...' She stopped mid-sentence.

'From what? Thinking? Feeling? Remembering?'

With a sigh, Gwen stopped packing up pencils, and sat back in the seat looking down at her hands.

'All of that, and more. There's nothing to prepare you for the pain of bereavement. Richard died so suddenly. It was such a shock. Perhaps that's what makes it worse for me. I can't believe he's gone. I still expect him to walk through the door, that I'll wake up to find this has all been a dreadful dream, a nightmare.'

A bleak shadow settled across her face as Brian reached out to cover her hand. For minutes they sat together, she unable to speak, he unsure what to say. Finally, it was his quiet voice that broke the silence.

'I lost my wife too.'

'You did? When?'

'Oh, it was way back now, nearly ten years ago.'

'But it still hurts?'

'Not in the same way. The sadness remains, but the pain fades as you make new memories to add to those you shared together.'

'Was it an accident?'

'No, she'd been ill for months. Cancer.'

'Brian, I'm so sorry. Had you been married long?'

'Fifteen years.'

'Children?'

'Two boys, both working away now.'

'They must have been very young when their mother died.'

'John was a teenager, Neil nearly eleven. Oddly enough, when I look back on that whole experience, I realise how much Jean's illness brought us together. In many ways, I got to know my sons better because we shared the pain of losing her. Sometimes it felt like us against the world.'

'I bet you were a great dad.'

'I did my best, but kids need a mum. They missed her. I did too. It must have been very hard for them having a father who was in too much of a state to know what he was doing half the time.'

'You loved them, Brian. That's the most important thing.'

'We planned such a different upbringing for them. We were thrilled when they were born. Jean had always wanted a family, and it was a cruel blow that she didn't live long enough to see them mature into young men.'

'Did you ever think of marrying again?'

He smiled. 'Not really. I've had my moments. One or two ladies have perhaps had more on their minds than friendship. I've enjoyed their company, but I've never been tempted to make any relationship permanent.'

Gwen nodded with understanding. 'How long will it be

before I can mention his name without feeling I want to bawl my eyes out? And do you ever get used to doing everything by yourself? Sleeping alone is dreadful. Waking on my own is even worse. I keep thinking I hear Richard's voice, even catch myself talking to him. Sometimes I think I must be losing my mind.'

'No, I remember feeling just the same – and because of that, I know you mustn't expect too much of yourself. Don't worry what other people think or say. Draw comfort in any way that helps you, and if that means talking to Richard as if he's right there beside you, then that's what you must do. Everyone grieves in their own way, just as they start to pick up the pieces in their own time. One day you will be happy again, Gwen. You may not feel that at the moment, but I promise you it's true.'

She looked down at his hand, which was still covering her own. 'No wonder you are such a good artist. You look at the face and see the soul.'

'No, I'm nothing special. I just recognise what you're going through, and my heart goes out to you. And if you need anything – from your lawn mown to someone to scream at – I'm here.'

'Thank you, dear friend,' she said, turning to face him. 'That's very good to know.'

The kitchen in Hall Farm had always been the place for family discussions. When Kate went over that afternoon to talk to her mother about the decision she'd reached, Margaret sat quietly beside her at the huge pine table where so many memorable conversations had taken place in the past. It was here that Kate had come to sit on her mum's lap when the first day at school hadn't gone quite as well as planned. Every birthday had been celebrated round this table. Margaret remembered all the faces of friends and neighbours who had joined them for meals from beans on toast to Sunday roast. It was in this kitchen that mother and daughter had mixed up and boiled Christmas puddings year after year, and here too that

Margaret had put the final touches to the icing on Kate's wedding cake.

Margaret felt the first fearful stirring of premonition as she listened to her daughter's intense and concerned explanation of her need to take this step. Of course this had to come. Margaret had always known one day it would. So this was the start. Here it began. But where would it lead?

'I just need you to know,' Kate was saying as she reached out to take her mother's hand, 'that I love you very much indeed. Nothing will ever change that.'

Margaret looked down at the clasped hands. 'Yes. I do understand, really I do. Don't mind me, and don't worry about your dad either. I'll deal with him.'

'I may not get anywhere. I just know I have to try, especially now.'

Margaret looked at her for a second, as if making a decision. Then she rose to her feet.

'In that case, I have something which may help.'

It was several minutes before Margaret returned from upstairs carrying a yellowing envelope which she handed to Kate without comment. Full of curiosity, Kate carefully pulled out a handwritten letter and what looked like a very old and brittle photograph. With shaking hands, she began to read.

Gwen pulled up behind Susie's small car which was already parked in the drive. Fired with enthusiasm from her time at Brian's studio, she quickly put the key in the front door, anxious to share it all with her daughter. No sooner had she closed the door behind her than the phone started ringing.

'She's after your cordless drill!' It was the unmistakable voice of Aunt Madge. 'In fact, she'd like the whole toolkit!'

'Madge, whatever are you talking about?'

'Celia of course. She's got a list of jobs lined up for Graham to do at their house, and she's decided that Richard's toolkit is probably a lot better than theirs. She's on her way round to borrow it indefinitely right now.'

'Oh, for heaven's sake, I've got things that need mending here too. I'll just have to learn to use the toolkit myself. I'll happily lend her anything she wants, but I can't give away something I need.'

Madge snorted agreement. 'She's a grabbing little minx, that one. She mentioned Richard's computer too. Says you probably won't need it now, and it would be really useful for her to keep her Women's Institute bits and pieces on.'

Gwen sighed. 'OK, thanks for warning me.'

'Tell her to push off!'

'I might just do that.'

'How are you?'

'Oh, you know . . .'

'Come and see me soon. Bring a bottle of sherry.'

'You're on!' agreed Gwen with a chuckle. 'Take care, Madge. 'Bye.'

Replacing the receiver, she realised with surprise that the house was silent. A blaring hi-fi system was usually a sure sign that Susie was home. Perhaps she'd gone out again? Making her way upstairs to take off her shoes, she peered curiously into Susie's room as she passed the door.

At first she didn't see her. The curtains were drawn, and in the late afternoon semi-darkness she didn't immediately spot the huddled form under the duvet. Asleep? Gwen smiled with affection. No wonder Susie was exhausted when her job in London was always so frantically busy.

'Mum?'

'I'm sorry, I didn't mean to disturb you. Go back to sleep. You must need it.'

'I can't sleep.'

'Well, the rest is still good for you.'

'I don't think I'm resting much either. I can't seem to stop my mind spinning.'

Gwen moved over to sit on the side of the bed. 'Dad?'

'Yes, among other things.'

'Has it been a bad week?'

'More of a bad month really.'

'It's going to take time, love. Losing Dad was bad enough, but because it was such a shock, it's even harder to come to terms with.'

'I seem to be in for more than my share of shocks at the moment.'

Gwen looked at her daughter carefully. Something was wrong, dreadfully wrong.

'Susie?'

'Look, Mum, you and I haven't ever seen eye to eye. We've never been close until this business with Dad brought us together, but then you've always expected too much of me.'

'That's not fair. I only wanted what's best for you.'

'I understand that. It's just that I need you to be my friend right now.'

'Susie, of course I'm your friend.'

'You may not feel that way when you know what's happened.'

'What?'

'I don't need you to judge me. I have no use for recriminations and lectures. I just need help.'

'Of course, I'll do whatever I can. Tell me.'

Susie pulled herself up so that she was sitting with her back propped against the pillows. 'I'm pregnant.'

Gwen felt her head swim, as her own nightmares crowded in on her. She clutched the side of the bed to steady herself, hoping that in the darkness Susie wouldn't see the devastating effect this news had on her.

It was at that precise moment the doorbell rang.

'Leave it.'

Gwen nodded dumbly in agreement with Susie.

But whoever was at the door was not to be put off. There

were two more rings of the bell and a smart rap on the knocker
before Celia's voice floated up the stairs as she shouted through
the letterbox.

'Gwen, dear, whatever are you doing? I know you're in there
because your car's here. Gwen! Can you hear me?'

Susie was out of bed before her mother could stop her.
Thumping barefoot down the stairs, she flung open the front
door to reveal Celia with her face still at letterbox level. She
stood up abruptly, adjusting her expression from guilty shock
to ingratiating sweetness.

'Susie, my dear, how *are* you?'

'I'm ill. So's Mum. We just want to be left alone, so do us
a favour, Aunt Celia? Clear off and pester someone else!'

And with that, the door was slammed shut in Celia's
astonished face.

Chapter Four

That night they talked until the small hours of the morning, finally demolishing a full packet of chocolate biscuits as they sat curled up together on the settee sipping cups of hot cocoa.

'Tell me about this Paul. What does he think?

'I haven't told him.'

'Why not?'

Susie shrugged. 'It's difficult to see him. He's not around much.'

'You could ring him, arrange a get-together to talk things over.'

'I don't want to do that.'

'He should know, Sue. It's his baby too.'

'Look, he's busy. And he's got a girlfriend.'

'I see.'

'You probably don't. You think I was just gullible and stupid, which I probably am – but I don't want to burden him with this.'

'Let me get this straight. You don't want to tell him because he'll think you're stupid. Doesn't he know it takes two?'

'Mum, I have to work with him. And his girlfriend. She's my boss.'

'He can't think that much of her if he slept with you. Have you any reason to think he cares for you?'

Susie thought of Paul, the kindness in his eyes, the warmth of his arms around her. Then she remembered the glamour of the man, his job as a top photographer, the lingering looks he drew from every female member of the agency. And of course, there was Deborah.

'No. I shouldn't think he's given me a second thought.'

'And you? How do you feel about him?'

When Susie said nothing, Gwen looked at her closely.

'You love him.'

Still no reply.

'Well, let's leave Paul out of this for a moment. How do you feel about the prospect of having a baby? You're a perfectly healthy young woman. I've got the time now to help you bring up a youngster. You could get a job locally, if that's what you'd like. There are options.'

'But I love working in London. I've worked so hard for it. I'm just beginning to get somewhere.'

'Then you have a decision to make.'

Susie nodded her head, looking down into her almost cold cup of cocoa.

'And what if I decide to have an abortion? You'd never approve of that.'

'What I think doesn't really matter.'

'Oh come on, Mum, if you were in my position, you'd never consider getting rid of a baby, or giving it away. I know you. You'd keep it – and if I don't, you'll disapprove of my decision, even though you might never be honest enough to say so.'

'Then perhaps you don't know me very well at all,' replied Gwen, staring hard at her daughter. 'But be sure of this. Whatever you decide, I'll support you all the way.'

The old farm building which stood to one side of the paddock had not been used for years. There was a time when Margaret's father had kept hay in it, but when a new barn was built nearer the farmhouse some thirty years before, the building had been left to crumble gently.

As Roger and Simon walked round the old barn together, discussing the work needed to renovate and change the building into a stable block, the two women found themselves trailing behind until at last they decided to lean up against the fence and let their respective spouses get on with it.

Gillian chuckled to see the men deep in conversation. 'They've completely forgotten we're here, and yet we both know that whatever agreement they come to, it will be me who actually plans and organises the work. And whatever price they decide on, it will be the two of us who make it all happen. How on earth can Simon involve himself when he's never here in daylight hours during the week?'

'And Roger is much too busy and preoccupied with the farm to have time to oversee this.'

'Margaret, is he all right? I hope you don't mind me asking, but some days he's looked really dreadful. He's not ill, is he?'

Margaret gazed over towards her husband. 'Physically, he's in good shape for a man who'll be sixty-three in a month's time but what's ailing him isn't physical. He's losing the battle. All his life he's worked this farm. It's his first love, his every thought.'

'Is business that bad?'

'Could hardly get worse. Not that I really know because he won't talk to me about finances these days. He used to. Now he locks up the bills and letters because he thinks I shouldn't worry about such things.'

'And not knowing only makes you worry more?'

'Of course it does, but he's the old-fashioned type with traditional views about being the provider in the family. He thinks the worth of the business is the worth of the man.'

'Isn't there an old-fashioned and very true saying about a trouble aired being a trouble shared?'

'He's too proud to share this, because that would mean

admitting he can't make it pay any more. It's not his fault. He's working harder than ever, but the prices still keep falling. And he's not getting any younger. We both know he can't keep up this pace much longer, but he'd never admit it.'

'What could help? Is there anything?'

'New farm buildings, modern machinery. Successful farms nowadays are almost like factories with all the hi-tech equipment they have.'

'Any chance of you installing what you need?'

'None at all. Roger isn't a factory worker. He's a farmer in the old mould, hands on, working by experience and instinct. That's low priority in farming today. A business mind and computer technology, that's what you need.'

'Perhaps he should retire? Let someone else take the reins?'

'Who? Kate is our only child, and she'll never come back to the farm.'

'Sell it then?'

Margaret sighed. 'I suppose that's what must happen in the end. It's just that all my life, this has been my home. We belong here. That house is the heart of us, always has been.'

The sound of the men's voices coming nearer drew their attention.

'This helps, you know,' said Margaret, nodding in their direction.

'Does it? It's not too much trouble, me taking over this barn, something else for you both to worry about?'

Margaret smiled. 'No, we'll charge you a fair rent, and it will all be a bit extra in the pot. Believe me, every little helps, and that building is hardly earning its keep at the moment.'

'Well, that's true. It's good to know this arrangement works for both of us. And Margaret, if you ever need to let off steam, remember where I am, won't you?'

The older woman looked back at Gillian, thinking how odd it was that having spent her whole life in this village, she'd opened her heart so easily to a relative newcomer. She had older, closer friends here; but when troubles were deeply personal and somehow shaming, it was rather comforting to talk to a comparative stranger who obviously cared.

In spite of the fact that the letter was more than thirty years old, the writing was clear and easily legible. The words were neatly and flowingly written, as if by a hand which was usually confident and artistic.

There was little confidence, though, in the content of the letter, with its emotion-filled message. Kate stared hard at the photo, trying to get inside the mind of the person who filled the frame, the girl who had written this heartbreaking note. Where was she now? What was she like? Did she find happiness in the end? Did she ever think about those events of so long ago?

Apart from the name of a town, there was no address on the sheet, and no signature either.

One name had been included in the body of the letter though. That might be worth investigating. Looking in her own local telephone directory, there was only one family listed with that surname, so it obviously wasn't all that common. Perhaps that would also be the case in the town mentioned at the top of the page? Even though there was no proper address, at least the town name gave her something to go on.

It wouldn't be that easy. A search like this never could be. Nevertheless, even if she drew nothing but blanks, she just had to give it a try.

When Gwen first mentioned the possibility of a part-time job which might interest Tricia, her old friend had jumped at the chance to hear more. So far, Mike had done nothing to alter the housekeeping arrangements for their home even though he no longer lived there. Nevertheless, Tricia knew that if she pressed ahead with the divorce, she could be left with much less to live on. Since the birth of the first of their two sons twenty-eight years earlier, she had never worked. Of course when Mike first took on the garage she'd helped out with paperwork, accounts and phone calls, but as the business expanded, so did Mike's belief that what a really successful businessman needed to be taken seriously was an efficient but extremely decorative secretary. At that time Tricia hadn't minded taking a back seat in the business, as their two boys were a mischievous handful from the moment they were able to walk and talk.

'Tell me again,' she begged Gwen when she called in for a cup of tea the following afternoon. 'What exactly does the job involve?'

'I don't know the details, but Wendy Abbott – you know, she's the chartered accountant Richard often worked with? Her husband, David, has his own business running a rather upmarket agency for medical supplies. He's got an office somewhere in Amersham, and apparently he's doing so well that he would like to take on a part-time assistant to deal with orders and bookings when he's out on the road.'

'Does he know I haven't any proper qualifications, and it's been a long time since I've tackled anything like this?'

'He says he'd like to find someone mature enough to deal intelligently with telephone enquiries. And you can use the computer as well as any secretary.'

Tricia's expression was a mixture of doubt and excitement. 'So what happens now?'

'I've got his number, and he's asked if you could ring. Why don't you call from here?'

Five minutes later, Tricia returned to the kitchen grinning broadly from ear to ear. 'He sounds really nice, and very keen to meet up as quickly as possible. In fact, he's going to call in at the house this evening for a chat.'

'That's wonderful. He must be keen.'

'Or desperate!'

'Trish, you'd be terrific at something like this. What are you going to wear?'

'How about that new blue blouse with the long black jacket? That's smart, but kind of casual too.'

'Perfect.'

'Thanks, Gwen, you're a darling. Must rush! I've got to wash my hair, do my nails, not to mention clean the house from top to bottom. And the front lawn could do with a mow too!'

'Just be yourself. You'll be great.'

'I'll let you know how it goes. 'Bye!'

The slam of the door behind Tricia left the house feeling silent and empty. Listlessly, Gwen collected up their teacups, and automatically began to wash them under the tap.

It was a pity that Tricia had left so abruptly, when Gwen would have welcomed the chance for a good chat with her oldest and dearest friend. So much had changed for the two women in the past few months. Both had lost their husbands. Tricia's husband had gone and love had died. For Gwen, her husband was dead, but the love not only lived on, it filled her every thought with the all-consuming torment of bereavement.

She sat down heavily on a stool next to the breakfast bar, staring absent-mindedly out of the window. Most of all, she would have liked to confide in Tricia about Susie's dilemma. Now Richard was gone, there was no one other than Trish who could possibly understand the tangle of emotions within her.

Susie had asked for her advice. Well, sometimes, with the best will in the world, mothers got it wrong. And Gwen knew without a doubt that if she followed her true instincts and feelings in the advice she gave, Susie would neither understand nor agree.

Best to keep her thoughts to herself. No one can learn from another's experience. Let Susie decide – and then love her through it.

*　　*　　*

Kate called into the main city post office on her way home that evening. Searching until she found the telephone directory covering the right geographical area, she opened the huge tome with a knot of anticipation gripping her stomach. J . . . K . . . L . . . M . . . here it was!

There were just three entries under the surname she was looking for. With trembling hand, she copied out the three initials, addresses and phone numbers.

She'd ring them that night. Yes, that's what she'd do. Ring them later when Martin was with her. Perhaps if he were at her side, she'd be able to find the courage.

David Abbott arrived promptly, as he said he would, at six thirty. Tricia had barely put the vacuum away and finished spraying the lounge with her favourite perfume when the doorbell went. Half an hour and a cup of tea later, it was plain that Tricia was exactly the kind of person he was looking for. He wanted someone who was able to deal with queries in a friendly confident way, and who could be relied upon to place orders and make arrangements in his absence. What Tricia couldn't possibly know was that he had been quite nervous himself about the practicalities of employing an assistant. Suppose he chose someone who turned out to be a clockwatcher, po-faced and humourless?

The warmth of Tricia's personality, combined with her attractive looks and obvious common sense, appealed to him immediately. He didn't want an empty headed bimbo, and this smart, sensible older woman would fit the bill perfectly.

'Look, I know it's short notice, but I'm on the road for two days starting at the crack of dawn tomorrow. Would you consider coming over to Amersham with me right now, to take a look at the office and see what you think? And then, if we can agree terms, you can start as soon as you like.'

Minutes later, the two of them left the house and walked down to where David had left his BMW. He used the remote control to unlock the car, then helped Tricia into the passenger seat. As they drove off, neither of them noticed the car which had just pulled up on the other side of the road, nor the expression of disbelief and despair on Mike's face as he watched his wife being driven away by another man who was obviously not only younger than him, but considerably more wealthy.

With Martin smiling encouragingly beside her, Kate rang the first number. The initials were G.J. She wondered what they stood for as she listened to the ringing tone. There was no reply, until suddenly an answerphone clicked in. Something about the precise coldness in the voice of the woman who asked callers to leave their message after the beep made Kate slam the phone back down on the cradle.

Martin squeezed her hand. 'Like me to try?'

'No, it's all right. I have to do this myself.'

'Do you want to stop? Perhaps have another go tomorrow?'

'No. Who's next on the list?'

'There are only two left. Mr R. and Miss M. Which do you fancy first?'

'Let's keep it alphabetical. Miss M. it is!'

The number rang for so long that she was just about to give up when an elderly-sounding voice answered the phone.

'Yes?'

Kate's throat went dry. She swallowed, trying to decide how to start.

'Who is this?'

'Oh, good evening,' Kate blurted out at last.

'If you're selling something, I'm not interested.'

'No! No, please, I'm sorry. I just have a rather strange question to ask you.'

'Hmm?' The old lady was plainly suspicious.

'I'm trying to trace a man with the same surname as you who lived in your area more than thirty years ago at the end of the sixties. I just wondered if by any chance you could help me. His name was Moreton, Richard Moreton.'

It was a pleasant surprise when Brian rang. Gwen's air of melancholy had remained with her all evening, and his quiet, friendly voice was somehow soothing.

'I'm organising an outing to a rather picturesque spot beside a lake about ten miles from here. We haven't had much chance to work on landscapes, and it should be good practice. There's a nice pub near by, so we can make a day of it.'

'How many are going?'

'I'm not sure yet.'

'When have you in mind?'

'In about a fortnight's time, on the Saturday?'

Gwen smiled. 'I'm sure I could fit that into my busy schedule. The ironing can wait! It sounds great. I'd love to come.'

He sounded genuinely delighted at that news. 'How are you? Coping?'

'Oh, you know, some days are better than others.'

'And today?'

'Not a good one.'

'Can I help?'

'I think you already have.'

'Listen, I've got a book at home I've been meaning to give you. It's about portrait painting, and I've always found it useful. Would you like to borrow it?'

'I'd love to.'

'Are you working at the library tomorrow?'

'Until one o'clock.'

'Perfect. Shall we talk about it over a plate of something in the pub? My guess is you're not eating much at the moment, and I can never be bothered to cook at home when it's just for me.'

She was hesitating. He could tell from the silence at the end of the phone.

'I'm told they do a mean lasagne. Come on, it will do us both good!'

I shouldn't, thought Gwen. I'm in mourning. I'm not supposed to be sharing meals with a man I've only just met. Isn't it disloyal to Richard, when I loved him so much, and always will? And supposing Celia heard about it?

That rebellious thought made up her mind.

'That's very kind of you, although I'm not sure I'll be much company.'

'Then we'll sit in companionable silence. It's still better than both of us eating alone.'

She laughed. 'You're right, and I accept. One o'clock then, when I finish?'

'I'll be waiting in the foyer. Keep your chin up till then.'

And warmed by the friendliness of the unexpected invitation, she said goodbye and replaced the receiver. The phone rang again almost immediately.

'Mum?'

'Susie, are you all right?'

'I've got an appointment. They've just rung me.'

'For counselling? Are you seriously thinking about having an abortion then?'

'Not just considering. I've spent most of yesterday there talking it through, and they say they can fit me in for a termination tomorrow.'

Gwen gripped the kitchen work surface to stop her knees from buckling.

'Mum?'

'I'm here.'

'Will you come? Please?'

'Are you sure, Susie? Are you quite sure this is what you want?'

'There's no alternative. I've thought about nothing else, and

I can't see any other way. I don't want a baby now. It's too early, with the wrong person and in the wrong circumstances.'

'Have you spoken to Paul yet?'

'No.'

'Don't you think you should?'

'Mum, I have to handle this my own way. You said you'd support me. Did you mean only if I do what you want me to do? In that case, just forget it. I'll be fine on my own.'

'No! No, don't worry. Of course, I'll be there. What time tomorrow?'

'They want me in at nine.'

'Heavens, I'd better come tonight then.'

'Oh, Mum, would you?' The relief in Susie's voice was unmistakable.

'I'll just throw a few overnight things into a bag, and be with you in a couple of hours.'

When Susie didn't answer, Gwen knew she was crying.

'Hold on, love. I'll be with you before you know it. You're not on your own. I'll be right there with you.'

For almost half an hour after her strange telephone conversation, Madge's hand hovered over the receiver. Should she ring? Should she let Gwen know about the young woman who had just called?

Her eyes ached, so did her head. And her hips were bad that night. It was hell living longer than you should.

She thought about Gwen as she filled up her hot water bottle from the warm tap. Poor Gwen. Such a devoted wife, now a bereaved widow. Life wasn't fair, taking her husband like that. Richard had been a dear man. A little dull, perhaps, but his heart was in the right place. It had been a terrible blow for them all.

And now this.

That young woman had said she wanted to come and visit.

Madge could tell from her voice that she was very emotional, with so many questions she wanted to ask. In the end, the caller left her number for Madge to ring back and tell her when she could come. Should Madge ring? If she accidentally lost the number and didn't call back, would the girl get the message and leave well alone?

Probably not.

With a sigh, Madge reached out to switch off the kitchen light. Then gathering up her crochet, the *Radio Times* and a bottle of sherry from the hallstand, she shuffled painfully upstairs to her bedroom.

She'd have to think this through carefully. Sleep on it, turn it over in her mind. She must tell Gwen, of course – but in the right way. And heaven alone knew if there was a right way to tell a grief-stricken woman news like this – that a stranger had just rung up out of the blue to say she believed she was Richard's daughter.

Chapter Five

From the outside it looked like a family home, a genteel Edwardian town house, Gwen thought as she followed Susie up the stairs to the main entrance. It wasn't until you were inside the discreet glass doors that you would guess it was a clinic, a place where young women arrived carrying babies, and left no longer pregnant. For just a moment, Gwen's eyes swam with the image of another door, another young woman, her emotions a tangle of fear, love and overwhelming loneliness. Did Susie feel like that now? Gwen reached out to clutch her daughter's hand as the two of them stood at the reception desk where a smiling uniformed nurse pointed them in the direction of the room she had been allocated for the day.

For about ten minutes, they were alone. After they'd made every remark possible about the room decoration, the TV with satellite stations, and the well-appointed bathroom, they both fell silent. Too many thoughts, too much to say, no words enough to express their feelings.

Susie recognised the white-coated doctor who finally came to join them. The doctor was kindly but businesslike. A short discussion with Susie to make sure she was still absolutely certain about the action she was about to take, a signature here, a signature there, and it was done. With the promise that a nurse would be along soon to give her a pre-med, Susie was left to get undressed and into bed. When she was ready, she pulled back the starched bed linen, her face almost matching the colour of the crisp white sheets. Susie, who was usually so confident, a spiky, self-opinionated girl-about-town, looked small, frightened, and incredibly young. Without a word Gwen sat on the bed and drew her daughter to her, holding her slight trembling shoulders, both too overwrought to hide the shine of tears in their eyes.

They sprang apart with embarrassment as the nurse entered. Gwen clasped Susie's hand as the injection was given, watching for minutes as her daughter became more sleepy and relaxed. All too soon, the porter came to take her down to the theatre. Gwen watched helplessly as the trolley was wheeled away, barely noticing the nurse who propelled her to a seat, handed her a cup of tea and switched on the television before leaving the room.

She saw only flickering pictures, heard no more than senseless words. The images in her mind filled her vision as long-buried emotions gripped her throat with pain and fear for Susie – and for herself.

Mike didn't recognise the franked address at the top of the long white envelope. It wasn't until he'd read the letter twice that he realised it came from the firm of solicitors who had a large practice in the centre of the town. Of course, he knew the senior partner, Basil Harthill. They belonged to the same Rotary Club. So Basil would now know that Tricia had started the process of divorcing him. And if Basil knew, everyone at the club soon would.

It had begun. Mike had never thought it would get this far. He had been so sure that Tricia was only sabre-rattling, that she never meant to go through with divorcing him. And now here it was, in black and white. This was the start of the end of their marriage.

A surge of anger coursed through him. How dare she! He

had provided and cared for her all these years, given her two beautiful children. She'd wanted for nothing. Had she?

He glanced again at the text of the letter. Words like 'irreconcilable', 'mental cruelty' and 'adultery' jumped out at him. Suddenly, the anger and fight fell away as he leaned forward to rest his head on his arms, and sobbed like a baby.

'Why doesn't she call? She said she would.'

Martin squeezed Kate's shoulders as he answered. 'Early days yet, sweetheart. Your call must have come as quite a shock. That family has moved on, healed the wounds, forgotten the upset and pain they went through all those years ago. There have probably been other marriages, more children. Then along you come, out of the blue, wanting to rake it all up again.'

'Do you think she will ring back?'

He shrugged, brushing a stray hair away from her forehead. 'I hope so. Let's give it till the end of the weekend, then perhaps, if we've heard nothing, you should write to her, put it all down on paper. Let her know you don't want to cause trouble for anyone, but you just need to know about your past. It's not that you're unhappy ...'

'Oh no, I've had wonderful adoptive parents in Roger and Margaret. They couldn't have been a better mum and dad. It's just that especially now ...' She paused to stroke her expanding waistline. 'I just want to know about my real mother and father. I need to know why they gave me away.'

'Of course, you do.'

'I think it's all happening a bit fast for me. It's been a shock to get this far so quickly. I thought it would take months, and even then perhaps I'd draw a blank.'

'I didn't think that in those days mothers were allowed to give details like names and towns in letters they wrote to babies they were giving away.'

'That surprises me too, but from what Mum told me, that

envelope was sewn into the layers of my clothes so cleverly it simply wasn't discovered until we got home.'

'Who was it addressed to?'

'There was nothing written on the front of the envelope at all, so Mum opened it. That was how she discovered I was called Elizabeth for those few days before I was adopted, so Mum and Dad chose it as my middle name when they had me baptised.'

'Lovely people, your parents.'

'Yes, and I'm so scared I might hurt them.'

'Nothing will ever change your love for them. I know that.'

'I just hope they do too.'

He pulled her to him then and planted a soft kiss on her hair so that, with a sigh, she relaxed into the familiar comfort of him.

'How are you feeling, love?'

Susie turned her head gingerly to look in her mother's direction, taking her time before she spoke.

'Not sure yet. Muggy. As if I've been kicked in the stomach.'

'I'll call the nurse. She wanted to know when you were properly awake.'

The nurse arrived, followed not long after by the doctor, by which time Susie was sitting up in bed with a cup of tea. A matter of hours later, the colour was returning to her cheeks, and her legs stayed beneath her without too much wobbling as she carefully climbed out of bed and, with her mother's help, began to get dressed. By four o'clock, she was sitting in the passenger seat of the car as Gwen lowered herself behind the wheel.

'That's that then.' Susie's voice was barely more than a whisper. 'It's over.'

'So now you have to build up your strength again, and get on with the rest of your life.'

Susie nodded, dropping her head as tears threatened again. 'Nothing to it, huh?'

'This was never going to be easy. You knew that. But you have so much ahead of you, Susie. Put this behind you now. Look to the future.'

'Did I do the right thing, Mum?'

Gwen held her breath for a moment before she replied. 'It was right for you.'

Susie didn't reply, a forlorn picture with her shoulders slumped, head bowed.

'Come on, love, let's go home.'

And Gwen drove away, without a backward glance at the elegant building which looked so ordinary outside, but in which scenes of extraordinary drama were acted out almost every hour of every working day.

There were two messages on Gwen's answering machine when they got back. The moment she heard Brian's hesitant voice on the first, she realised that she'd completely forgotten their arrangement to have lunch that day.

'Stood me up, eh? Don't blame you. They told me at the library that you'd had to rush off to deal with some family emergency. I hope everything's OK now. You will let me know, won't you, if there's anything I can do to help? In fact, give me a ring anyway. No, forget that. Only give me a ring if you feel like it. I'd just like to know you're all right.' There were several moments of indecision as he plainly wondered how he should finish the message. At last the machine cut in, and he was gone. Gwen smiled. Brian was such a confident and inspiring teacher. Funny how answering machines could make mice of men. She must ring him as soon as she had a moment to apologise for not letting him know in advance about her change of plan.

The second message was brief and cryptic.

'Gwen?' It was Madge. 'Where the devil are you? I've got

news. Not necessarily good, but I've decided you should know all the same. Call me. Better still, visit.' And the receiver was noisily replaced.

Gwen sighed. Not more bad news. Hadn't there been enough of that? Whatever it was that Madge had to say could wait for a while. Kicking off her shoes and leaving them where they fell in the middle of the hall, she picked up the cups of tea she'd just made, and wearily climbed the stairs to Susie's room.

Mike was waiting on the doorstep when Tricia got home that evening. It was a shock to see him, not just because she hadn't expected to find him there, but because of the way he looked. Gone was the arrogant air, the immaculate neatness of the successful businessman. He'd lost weight so that his clothes hung on him, and the skin seemed to sag on his much thinner face. This man was grey and tired, nothing like the larger-than-life Mike she had been married to for so many years.

'Can I come in?'

She hesitated, torn between distress at seeing him like this, and the knowledge gained from experience that nothing about Mike was ever quite what it seemed.

'I don't think that's a good idea.'

'Please, Trish. We need to talk.'

'There's nothing to say.'

'I need to talk then. Just listen to me for a few minutes. Please, Trish, please.'

She didn't answer.

'Trish, it can't end like this. Please, for the sake of everything we've shared, our home, our children, our lives. I can't write off thirty years without even talking about it. Can you?'

She looked at him closely then, taking in his shaking hands, the button missing from his jacket, defeat in his expression which she'd never seen before in three decades of marriage. Without a word, she unlocked the door, ushering him in ahead of her. He stood awkwardly in the hall, unsure about how he should behave in this house which had been his home, although some weeks had passed since he'd set foot inside it. It was dear and familiar, his pictures on the wall, his choice of carpet on the floor, his silver letter-opener on the hall table – yet he felt like a stranger.

She didn't invite him into the kitchen, where family conversations usually took place. She didn't offer him a cup of tea, or even something stronger. Instead, she led the way through to the spotlessly neat lounge, where they perched at opposite ends of the plush red velvet settee. Mike realised with a jolt that she intended to keep their conversation formal, her face giving nothing away, not the slightest suggestion of emotion. This was a Tricia he didn't recognise, didn't know, and couldn't talk round. She looked amazing, with her smart new haircut, and a petrol blue suit he didn't recognise. She was poised, calm and beautiful. If Tricia was feeling the strain of the break-up of their marriage, it certainly didn't show. She had said she didn't care, and from the look of her now that was true.

'Well? You need to make this quick. I'm due out in half an hour.'

'Who with?'

'That's none of your business.'

'I've seen him, you know. I know you've got a fancy man already. You didn't hang around, did you? Was he on the scene before you threw me out? Is he the cause of all this?'

'You're talking rubbish.'

'Am I? All this holier-than-thou business wears a bit thin now I know what you've been up to. I'll fight you all the way. You won't get a penny out of me, if I can help it.'

She sighed sadly. 'Let's let the lawyers decide that, shall we? Now, if that's all you wanted to say, I think you should leave.'

'No! No, Trish, that's not what I meant to say at all.' He moved towards her on the settee, distress written over every line of his face. 'I don't want this. I don't want a divorce. I want us to try again. I know I've probably been the worst husband in the world, but I just didn't know how you felt about everything.'

'Didn't you? I told you often enough.'

'And I didn't listen. I didn't understand. But I'll change! I'll be whatever you want me to be. Darling, listen to me, whatever you want, that's what I'll do. Just give me another chance, Trish, please?'

'Until the next time? Until another glamorous customer who's bored with her husband slips you the wink? There've been so many, Mike. I don't want to sit by and watch any more. I can't. I won't.'

'Of course not, my darling, and you'll never have to. I've learned my lesson, and it will never happen again. I love you, Trish. I didn't know just how much until I nearly lost you.'

She looked at him for a while before she replied.

'But you have lost me, Mike. I don't want to be married to you any more. I'm sorry, but I won't change my mind – just as, over all those years, I've never been able to change yours. I'm happier without you. And perhaps, when the dust has settled, you'll be happier too.'

'Never! We've been together for as long as I can remember. We're family. You're my wife. We belong together.'

'I was your wife, and I was worth nothing to you. We only live once, Mike, and I'm not going to waste any more precious time with a man who doesn't value me.'

'But I do! Darling Trish, I do. Just let me prove to you how much.'

She rose to her feet, plainly moved but keeping her expression under rigid control. When he looked up at her and spoke again, it was with desperation in his voice.

'Don't you feel anything for me? You can wipe out everything we've meant to each other, and feel nothing?'

For a moment, her expression softened. 'I have loved you and only you for years. It was never my love that was in question. I've been lonely in my marriage for so long that it's nearly broken me. I long to be with someone I matter to, someone who wants my company, values my love.'

'I need your love. I can't live without you. I know that now.'

'I'm sorry, Mike, it's all too late. I need some space to rebuild my life, and seeing you makes that difficult. I wish you well. I hope you find happiness. I hope we both do. But please, don't come back again. You don't belong here any more.'

It was a beaten man who got up from the settee and left the room without a word. Trish heard the front door close behind him before she sank down on to the seat and buried her head in her hands.

Roger turned the delicate cutting over in his hand, tipping it out of its first-size pot before planting it on into a bigger container. This was a new hybrid of border geranium which he'd not managed to grow before, with its deep magenta petals tinged with gold at the edges. He studied the plants with warm pride. It was impossible to get any shade of yellow into the petals of a perennial geranium, that's what they said. Yet just look at this! The local garden centre should be quite interested in this little beauty. He'd already thought of a name for it: 'Marvellous Maggie.' After all, when it came to little beauties, there was no one to rival his own dear Maggie, his wife Margaret.

He had never been able to pinpoint what it was about these old-fashioned perennials he loved so much. Perhaps it was their resilience, the way they could survive even if they were practically ignored? Or perhaps it was the glorious show they gave in reward for the propagating, feeding and ample amounts of tender loving care he always found time to give them?

His interest had started in his battered, modest old greenhouse. For twenty years, he had experimented with root cuttings he'd grown himself, or swopped through the local plant group. Sometimes he sent away for seeds of unusual varieties from flower societies, growing them on first in the greenhouse, then later in his flower garden which had started as a patch, and now stretched to almost an acre. Best of all, in spite of this being nothing more than a hobby, he made money with his plants, which were in constant demand at every local flower and craft show, Christmas fair and summer fête. He didn't sell them for much. He didn't feel the need to, when his only wish was to share his beautiful protégées with anyone willing to give them garden room. Nevertheless, the feeling of coming home from a show with his old truck empty and his pockets heavy with notes and coins was a pleasure beyond compare. Pity the effort he put into the farm didn't bring such rich rewards.

'There you are, my lovelies,' he said out loud, as the last cutting was tenderly placed in its new pot. He turned slowly to look around his greenhouse with its organised jumble of plants, some in flower, others not yet in bud. With a deep sigh of satisfaction, he reluctantly left the greenhouse to take a last turn round the flower garden before the watery sun sank behind the old farmhouse.

He made his way along the rows of plants, stopping here, tidying there. Tonight though, the brightly coloured blooms didn't hold his complete attention, as other concerns crowded his thoughts. For once, it wasn't the farm that troubled him most. This business with Kate trying to trace her birth parents had shocked him deeply. Hadn't she been happy with him and Margaret? Hadn't they tried to provide her with everything she could possibly need? So why search for the woman who had abandoned her, who had cared so little that she had given her baby daughter away? She didn't deserve any part of their Kate. She had no right to involvement in her life, especially now that Kate was pregnant. This would be *their* grandchild, Margaret's and his. No one else was needed or wanted.

He had watched quietly as Margaret reacted with her usual fairness when Kate told them about the phone call she'd made to the elderly woman who seemed to have news of her natural father. Father! Huh! How could a man who turned his back on his own child ever be called a father! He had heard Margaret reassure their daughter that whatever she decided to do about this new information, they would understand and support her. And he had glimpsed the despair and fear in his wife's expression when Kate was no longer there to see. This could rip them apart, break Margaret's heart — and his. The sense of foreboding rested heavily on him.

'Roger!' Margaret's voice drifted across from the house. 'Dinner's ready!'

And it was his favourite shepherd's pie tonight, that he knew. With a deep sigh and one last look over the garden, he rubbed his hands on his trousers and headed for the house.

By the next day, Saturday, Susie was much better. She even managed to pin a smile on her face as she went off to the bathroom for a long soak in her favourite bubbly concoction. While she was upstairs, Gwen rang Madge. There was no reply, but then Madge rarely surfaced before eleven o'clock in the morning. Still, as her message had sounded so intriguing, Gwen felt it was worth a try.

Brian was out too when she got through to his number. He wasn't the only one to find words failed him when faced with an answer machine, thought Gwen wryly as she struggled to word an appropriate message for him. In the end, she simply said, 'It's Gwen. Sorry I missed you,' and replaced the receiver as if it was burning a hole in her hand.

When Susie finally emerged from the steaming bathroom her eyes were red and swollen, but as she said nothing about the events of the day before, neither did her mother. They had a late breakfast together, splitting the morning paper into halves to avoid the need for much conversation. Finally it was Susie who broke the silence.

'I need to go back tomorrow. I can't miss another day. Must get back for Monday morning.'

Gwen nodded. 'How do you feel?'

Susie shrugged. 'Washed out. As if I've been punched hard in the stomach. I'm all right though.'

'You have to be careful after a general anaesthetic. Don't overdo things. Look, I've got to pop out to do a bit of shopping this morning. Why don't you take yourself back to bed, and see how you are later? And if you like, I'll drive you back tomorrow.'

Susie's smile was thin and grateful. 'Thanks Mum.' She stretched out to cover Gwen's hand. 'For everything.'

Gwen didn't reply. The experience they'd shared the day before was best left with no more discussion. It had brought them closer than they had ever been. For a while, they needed each other. In what had always been a prickly relationship between mother and daughter, that was enough for now.

In fact, when Gwen rang, Madge wasn't still in bed but in Celia's lounge, sitting like a queen in the largest, most cushioned chair sipping from a bone china cup which she wished had contained a little less coffee and a lot more sugar. A dash of brandy might have been nice too; not that Celia would ever think to offer it, when she already kept marks on the brandy bottle to make sure Graham didn't help himself without permission.

'The cheek of the girl! Susie just shut the door in my face – and I was only there to see if I could help her mother. It was indescribably rude. I simply couldn't believe my ears!' Celia's voice was shrill with indignation as she proffered the biscuit barrel. Madge helped herself to two Bourbons which she promptly dunked into her coffee, hoping they might improve the flavour. Celia's long fingers reached down into the barrel to draw out a Jammy Dodger. Nibbling around the edge with infinite care until just the jam centre was left, she then swallowed it in one gulp.

'Going down to London has ruined her, that's what I say. Look at the way she dresses. Her skirts are either ridiculously long, or disgustingly short. And that hair! Why on earth doesn't she get it cut in a nice neat style to suit working in an office? No sense of responsibility, none at all!'

'I like it. It suits her.'

If Madge had bothered to glance up from her biscuit, she'd have seen pure disbelief in Celia's pitying look.

'The one I worry for is Gwen. Hasn't she got enough on her plate without Susie making life even harder for her? Gwen's really not come to grips with Richard's death, you know. She needs to face facts, get her house in order.'

'Oh, for heaven's sake, Celia, leave the poor woman alone!'

'Richard did everything for her. She's simply not used to coping on her own. Graham could help her. So could I. We could organise everything so she has nothing to worry about. But will she let us help? Does she know what's good for her? No! And I blame Susie, really I do.'

'Don't underestimate Gwen. She's tougher than she looks.'

'She can't possibly manage that house on her own. Graham and I have been talking, and we think the best idea would be for her to sell it, and we'll sell ours, then we can buy a much larger place together. Then we can keep an eye on her, make sure she's all right.'

'No doubt you have a new address conveniently in mind?'

'Now you come to mention it, there is that rather nice Victorian place at the corner of Wykeham Road. Graham has always liked that. Says he'd love the garden. And of course, it would be so convenient for the bridge club.'

'Got it all worked out, I see.'

'And do you know,' continued Celia as if Madge had said nothing, 'Gwen's started art lessons? Can you believe it? Her husband's hardly gone, and she's out gallivanting at art classes! Well, that's Susie, isn't it? Gwen hasn't shown an interest in drawing and stuff like that for years, so why on earth should she start now?'

'Seems like a good idea to me. She's got the time, probably more than she knows what to do with. What harm can it do?'

'What harm! What about her reputation? My friend Barbara saw her coming out of the library with that art teacher chap the other day, and they were laughing. Laughing! Can you imagine? And Richard barely in his grave. They'll be calling her the merry widow next.'

Madge spluttered into her coffee cup, her eyes screwed up with laughter. 'Well, good for her. She needs to get some laughter back into her life. She didn't have much of that with Richard around.'

Celia sniffed. 'I don't know how you can say that. He was a dear man, good and steady.'

'Oh, I'm not saying he wasn't. I was very fond of him, as you know. Always have been since he was a small boy. But he did rule the roost at home. Gwen had to toe the line, have his tea on the table when he walked in the door, go where she should go, say what she should say. Couldn't have been much fun for her.'

'I never heard her complain.'

'But she wouldn't, would she? She's not the sort. And she loved him, there's no question about that.'

'Are you saying that things weren't all they seemed in that apparently idyllic marriage?' Celia's question was casual, although her face burned with interest.

'I'm saying nothing at all.'

'What then? What did he stop her doing?'

'Painting, perhaps? She was very good at drawing when he

first knew her, as I recall. I remember her drawing a picture of me once. She must still have been at school then. I kept it for ages.'

'School? They didn't know each other at school. Graham always said they met when they were at university. That's right, isn't it?'

Celia's eagle eyes instantly spied Madge's discomfort.

'Probably. Old age. I forget.'

'Not you. You don't forget a thing unless it suits you.'

The old lady fell silent as she leaned forward to delve into the voluminous shopping bag at her feet.

'Come on, Madge, spit it out. What is all the mystery about how they met? I know there was something. I remember how Richard and Graham's mum always got very tight-lipped when the subject came up. Didn't she approve of Gwen then?'

'No idea.'

'She was your sister. Of course you have an idea!'

'Nothing I can remember. I told you, my memory isn't what it was.'

Celia's eyes narrowed as she watched Madge draw something out of the bag. 'You might just as well tell me. I'll find out in the end. And don't you dare light up that cigarette in here, do you hear me?'

The old lady sighed dramatically. 'You'll just have to take me home then, because I can't stand another moment of your constant chatter without a puff or two.'

Celia stood up abruptly, and flounced towards the door so quickly that she missed what Madge mumbled almost in a whisper as she hauled herself up from the chair. 'Anyway, you may know soon enough. I have a feeling the past is just about to come up and hit us – hard.'

Chapter Six

When Susie returned to work on Monday morning the first person she saw was Deborah McCann, her lovely face framed by long golden hair which flowed over the shoulders of her pale leather jacket. She looks more stunning than usual, thought Susie wearily; or was it just that her own confidence was at such a low ebb that even the lived-in face of cuddly old Bob, the security man at front reception, seemed more attractive than she felt right now?

Deborah didn't usually make a point of speaking to juniors in the agency. The fact that she had found her way to this end of the office at all was surprising. When she turned up at the side of Susie's desk, it became downright worrying.

'You were off on Friday.' A statement, not a question.

'Yes, flu.'

Deborah eyed her closely. 'A lot of it about.'

'Hmm.'

'Busy?'

'Quite. I'm working on another proposal for that big department store account.'

'Of course, you went to Rome, didn't you?'

Dangerous ground. Where was this leading?

'The photos were good.' Deborah's voice was deceptively offhand.

Susie nodded, not sure how to answer.

'But then, they would be,' continued Deborah smoothly, 'if Paul took them.'

'Oh yes, he's excellent.'

'He told me all about the shoot. Amusing. That's the word he used.'

Really! Is that what he thought? 'I'm glad you're pleased with the results.' Susie's face revealed nothing, although she could cheerfully have slapped the other woman hard across the face at that moment.

'You did well – workwise, I mean.' Deborah's eyes seemed to be boring into her.

'Thank you.'

'Keep it up. Concentrate on your own job. And not too many days off. That never goes down well if you want to get on.'

'No, of course not.'

Deborah fell silent as she cast a long, apparently casual glance across Susie's desk. Finally, the long fingers with their immaculately painted nails stretched out to pick out one particular envelope from the pile of post awaiting attention.

'From Rome?'

'Is it?' Susie frowned, taking the envelope from her clasp to study the postmark. It was small and white, with her name and the agency address written in distinctively stylish handwriting.

'Were you expecting something?'

'No. I think all the bills are paid up now. I don't know who it's from.'

There was ice in Deborah's stare.

'Perhaps it's from one of the models?' suggested Susie. 'We became quite good friends.'

'I understand from Paul that none of them spoke English.'

'Oh, we got along.'

'Aren't you going to open it?'

Something about Deborah's arrogance finally goaded Susie enough to look directly at her.

'Not just yet. I'll get round to dealing with the post a bit later.'

'It may be important.'

'So is the proposal I'm working on, and having had Friday off, I've a lot of catching up to do. Concentrate, that's what you said. Nice of you to call by, but I must get on.' And twisting her chair towards her computer, she doggedly ignored Deborah until she finally moved away. Minutes later, when the coast was clear, she picked up the envelope with curiosity, sliding her finger across the seal to pull out a white postcard with an artist's impression of the Trevi Fountain on one side.

They say if you throw a coin into the Trevi, you will come back to Rome. True enough, here I am again. Another shoot. Different models. No Susie. Wish you were here. P.

Susie's eyes misted over. Why did he do that? Why?

Amusing himself, I suppose. And while he was amused, I went through last Friday. Would he have found that amusing too?

She took the card in her hand to tear it into little bits. Then she stopped, changed her mind, and bent down instead to lay it carefully in the darkest corner of her bottom drawer.

Kate's letter was on the doormat next morning when Madge made her painful way downstairs. She didn't open it immediately. Handwritten letters that looked intriguing were rare nowadays, so she put it to one side while she made a cup of tea, savouring the thought of its possible contents. From the Essex postmark, she could guess who had sent it. This was it then. Now she had to make a decision about what exactly she should say to Gwen, if indeed she should say anything at all.

Half an hour later, she was still sitting in her favourite seat with the letter open on her lap. She had pored over it four, perhaps five times, each reading proving more worrying than the one before. Finally she sat back with a heavy sigh, deciding at last on her course of action.

Digging down the side of her comfy chair, she pulled out a pad of notepaper and started, in fine spidery scrawl, to fill the page. Some time later she sat back to survey her handwork – an invitation to Kate and her husband to pay a visit the following Sunday. Four o'clock would be fine. A reply was only necessary if she couldn't come; otherwise, she would be expected.

The job done, Madge folded the note into an envelope, addressing and stamping it immediately before she could change her mind. Then she picked up the phone. Gwen was out. Of course, it was Tuesday. She'd be at the library. Plucking up courage to speak into the darned answering machine, Madge's message was simple and rushed.

'Ring me,' she said. 'Madge.' Then she slammed down the receiver before she realised she hadn't even said hello or goodbye.

The following evening, just as Kate was returning from work in Colchester to find the invitation for that coming Sunday waiting for her, Gwen was in Chesham sitting on the edge of the settee in Madge's lounge. Her face was pale, hands shaking as she read, then re-read Kate's letter. Madge, for once silent, eyed the younger woman with concern, especially when the glass of sherry she offered was totally ignored. Perhaps she'd made a mistake? Perhaps she should just have kept her mouth shut in the hope that this whole unpleasant episode would stay where it belonged, in the past.

Gwen was dimly aware that the trembling which had begun in her fingers was slowly spreading like pins and needles throughout her body. She felt herself collapse back against the settee, her vision blurred, unable to command her limbs or mind. No more, she could bear no more. First Richard, then Susie. Now this.

She had always known that one day it might happen. But why now when she was drowning in loss and grief? Now, when her emotions were in tatters, and her strength gone? It had all been buried for so long – the pain, the fear, the anger . . .

'. . . probably not a good idea.'

Madge's voice broke through the jumble of her thoughts.

'Look at you. I've made a mistake. I should never have told you, with Richard just gone. Ignore it, forget I mentioned it.'

'No!' Gwen's voice was so shrill and loud she hardly recognised herself. 'Don't worry, Madge. It's just such a shock. I'll be all right.'

'I didn't know what to do,' moaned Madge forlornly. 'She sounded nice, well-spoken and everything, but desperate too.'

'And you've invited her to come and see you?'

'Sunday afternoon. Four o'clock. You don't have to come. Perhaps better not.'

Gwen clutched Kate's note to her as if her life depended on it. 'Of course I'll come. Not a day has gone by without me wondering, thinking of what happened. After a lifetime of waiting, I've got to face this.'

That night, Gwen didn't sleep at all. Her eyes were closed but her mind teemed with faces, words and thoughts which demanded her attention and robbed her of rest. At last, hot, tousled and distressed, she thumped her pillow and buried her face into its softness.

'Richard,' she sobbed. 'Tell me what to do. Help me. Don't leave me to cope with this on my own. Can you hear me, Richard? How I wish you were here.'

At their home in Colchester, Kate snuggled up to Martin who was breathing evenly in the darkness. Her husband's body felt warm, reassuring and familiar. Since their marriage, the greatest pleasure for Kate was to feel his body following the line of her own, his arm draped over her as she dropped off to sleep.

Sleep eluded her now. An ache of excitement mixed with trepidation and foreboding jarred in the pit of her stomach. She thought of the conversation she'd had with her mother on the phone that evening. Margaret was her usual, understanding self, although Kate suspected she was keeping her own feelings firmly in check, partly through natural generosity and love for her daughter, and partly because she too was frightened of what this meeting of present and past could bring. Not that Kate was really anywhere nearer finding the mother who had given birth to her more than thirty years ago, then offered her up for adoption when she was barely three weeks old. All she had even now was an invitation to meet a woman who might somehow be related to her father; and for all Kate knew, he might never even have been aware of her existence. As for her mother, perhaps through Madge Moreton she might find a more positive clue – a recent address, a married name? And however loving that young mother might have felt when she wrote the letter which she had then sewn into the back of the cardigan worn by her baby daughter as she handed her away, who knows what life had brought her since? More children? A happy home? A new life where whispers of the past had no place?

Kate turned over restlessly, trying to get comfortable. This was all happening too quickly for her to keep up with her feelings, or be sure what she hoped to find any more. A lifetime of longing to know, the yearning to fill the emptiness which incessantly gnawed away at her, hadn't prepared her for the fear she felt now, when finding her birth parents might actually become a reality.

At that moment, Kate felt their baby shift position within her, and the familiar sense of fierce, overpowering love and protection swept through her.

How could any mother part with her own baby? How could she walk away not knowing what sort of future she was leaving her child to face alone? What kind of mother could do that?

Someone who wasn't fit to be a mother at all.

Wrapping her arms tightly across her stomach, Kate curled up in a ball against Martin, longing for sleep, hoping her seesawing thoughts would allow her peace at last.

In London, Susie too was wide awake. As she heard the clock strike two, she slipped out of bed and padded along to the kitchen where she put a cup of milk into the microwave.

After his card, should she ring him? Should she drop both a note and a bombshell? Tell Paul he was almost a father? Should she have told him before?

She had no doubt that 'no' was the answer to all those questions. Why, then, did she long to hear his voice again? Watch his eyes light up as he talked about the photography that fascinated him, or the family he loved and loathed in equal proportions? There was so much he cared about. Was it possible that he did actually care for her too? Was that why he sent the card? And if he did care, what would he think of her now, if he found out that she'd aborted his baby without even telling him?

The ping of the microwave interrupted her thoughts.

She'd probably never hear from him again. And if she didn't see him, then it was a waste of time and energy to worry. Anyway, he'd plainly had such a bad time with fathers in his own family, he'd hardly volunteer to become one himself, would he?

Unbidden, an image of her father's face slipped into her mind. How she missed talking to him. She'd never stopped being his darling little girl, and there'd been real comfort in the proud, protective way in which he watched over her. She remembered her frustration and embarrassment when she'd first become a teenager, and he'd turned up at parties to take her home at only ten o'clock. She smiled at the memory of their arguments about his dismissive opinion of her first boyfriend, and his fury on her behalf when it turned out that his assessment had been right all along. If only he were here now to wrap his arms around her and make the world go away.

With a sniff which was probably, she told herself, the start of a cold, she grabbed the cup of hot milk and padded slowly back to her room.

Her covers heaving in time with her breathing, Madge was sprawled across the mattress in the upstairs room of her house. The bed was surrounded by mounds of magazines and papers, a stack of photograph albums, an old Decca record player and a pile of Mario Lanza LP's, three large biscuit tins, two jars of Vick, an economy pack of Mars bars, a nearly empty packet of cigarettes, an overflowing ashtray, two half-full bottles of sherry, at least six empties and a canary, asleep on his perch in the cage to one side of the bay window.

Too old to remember, too tired to care, too contentedly drunk to worry about either, Madge snored noisily in dreamless sleep, the television remote control in her hand, with the TV still flickering across the room.

Kate was up early that Sunday morning, and had dressed and re-dressed several times before Martin gently sat her down while he made them both breakfast.

'I've had a thought,' said Kate, the toast going cold on the plate in front of her. 'Could we pop in and see Mum and Dad before we set off for Chesham this afternoon?'

Martin nodded. 'If you like. That's a nice idea.'

'Only I'd like to see them, before I . . .'

'Before you see Miss Moreton.'

'Just in case, you know . . .'

'. . . nothing is quite the same again.'

'Only I couldn't bear to hurt them. I need them to know how much they mean to me, how grateful I am.'

'Darling, they've always known that. But I think you're right. It would be good for you to see them today.'

'Give them a hug.'

'A big hug. They'd like that.'

Kate picked nervously at a crumb on the breakfast bar

surface. 'Perhaps I shouldn't go. I could be opening a can of worms.'

'But could you ever be truly happy if you don't follow up this lead? As long as I've known you, the thought that you don't know who gave birth to you, or why they gave you away, has haunted you. You have a chance today to find out what happened and why. Perhaps you'll choose to leave it there.'

Kate nodded without answering.

'Or perhaps this will be the start of a voyage of discovery which will alter your life forever.'

'That's what frightens me.'

'Change your mind, if you like. Whatever you decide, I'll be right beside you.'

She turned then to smile at him. 'What a very special man you are, the dearest possible person . . .'

'Husband.'

'Friend.'

'Lover.' He leaned across to plant a lingering kiss on her open lips.

'We haven't got time.'

'Really?'

'I'm all dressed up.'

'I think you should change. I'll help you.'

'But I'm pregnant, all fat and lumpy. How can you fancy me like this?'

The response in his slow smile was unmistakable. 'Take it from me. I do.'

Her arms slipped around his neck. 'You're insatiable.'

'Aren't you?'

She didn't bother to reply, when a kiss said it all.

The phone rang just as Gwen got out of the bath. Wrapping a towel around her head, she tiptoed over to the bedside table to pick up the receiver.

'Oh good, you're in.'

She smiled at the sound of Brian's voice. 'I'm sorry, we seem to have missed each other all this week.'

'You've not been to class. Are you OK?'

Gwen thought back over the rollercoaster of events through-out the past few days, and was still considering her answer when he spoke again.

'That bad, eh? Can I help?'

'You already have. I'm glad you're still speaking to me.'

'You haven't forgotten our art outing next weekend?'

'Saturday, wasn't it? Wouldn't miss it for the world.'

'How's Susie?' If he noticed the slight hesitation before she replied, he made no comment.

'In London. Fine, I think.'

'And you? Missed any good lunches lately?'

'Yes, and I'm so sorry about that.'

'Something came up.'

'That's right. Very unexpected.'

'Quite all right. I polished off both our lasagnes, and haven't eaten a thing since.'

In spite of herself, she laughed.

'And because I'm now fainting with hunger,' he continued with a chuckle in his voice, 'I think we should go out for a debauched cream tea this afternoon. Chocolate cake, scones and jam, cucumber sandwiches with the crusts cut off, the works. What do you say?'

'Brian, I can't — not today.'

'Oh. Oh well, another time then.' He sounded hurt, perhaps a little embarrassed.

'Yes, that would be nice, really nice.'

'Right. Well, I must go. See you on Tuesday at the class?'

'Of course. I'll be there. And Brian?'

'Hmm?'

'Thank you. I really do appreciate your friendship.'

'Same here. Take care of yourself, Gwen. 'Bye.'

She replaced the phone slowly, sinking down on to the bed to unwind the towel from her hair. He was nice. Kind, thoughtful, intuitive and still there, even though she'd forgotten their lunch dates and turned him down yet again. Eventually he'd give up, of course. He'd realise she wasn't worth the bother, and let the friendship fade. Why should a lovely man like that stick around to be overlooked and pushed aside?

She sat back against the pillows and closed her eyes for a moment, thinking with dread about what she would be doing that afternoon. Her mind had been filled with nothing else since she'd first heard the news from Madge. And she had told no one. It would have been nice to talk it all over with Tricia, but she was so preoccupied with the break-up of her marriage and her new job that it seemed unfair to burden her. If only there was someone with whom she could share the events of that week. Susie's abortion. The news of the young woman who had appeared out of the blue to stir up nightmares of the past. Difficult experiences to face alone.

Funnily enough, it occurred to her that Brian would understand. He was a good listener, perhaps because of all the challenges he'd been through himself. She recognised instinctively that nothing would shock or surprise him. He wouldn't forbid discussion or dismiss emotion, as Richard always had. It would be so good to be truthful about her fears for that afternoon's meeting with someone in whom she glimpsed genuine empathy. What a relief it would be to share her memories, face her ghosts, and know that the secrets she revealed were in safe and caring hands.

She almost reached out to ring him back but then she thought better of it. Instead, she dialled Susie's number. The phone only rang once before her daughter picked it up.

'It's Mum. How are you feeling?'

'Better, thanks.'

'Good week at work?'

'I had a lot of catching up to do. I wasn't really concentrating much before ... well, before I had Friday off.'

'So you're putting your feet up this weekend?'

'I still feel a bit bushed. They said I might.'

'I love you, Susie.'

There was a moment of silence before Susie replied. 'That doesn't sound like you. We don't say things like that. We never have.'

'Well, we should. So much has happened. I need you to know that I love you without question, no matter what.'

'Something's wrong.'

'Nothing. There's nothing wrong. I just had to tell you how much you mean to me, that's all.'

There was a catch in Susie's voice as she spoke again. 'And I love you, Mum, very very much.'

Roger was in the milking shed when Martin's car drove up the lane towards the farm. Margaret hadn't said they were expecting Kate, especially not today of all days. Wiping the dirt from his hands, he straightened up painfully, and started to make his way back to the house.

He walked into the kitchen to find Kate hugging her mother as if she'd never let her go. Margaret's eyes were glistening with tears. Neither woman spoke.

Then Kate turned towards him. Holding out her arms, she walked over to clasp him tightly to her.

'I'll ring you later.' Her voice was muffled against the coarse wool of his old gardening jersey.

'You do that.' He could bear no more, and without a backward glance pulled away, and disappeared through the door towards his beloved geraniums.

At exactly four o'clock that afternoon, Martin's finger hovered above Madge's bell. In fact, they had arrived in the area almost half an hour earlier, but had driven round the block endlessly rather than arrive before invited. Kate's face was drawn and pale with anxiety, until Martin lent down to plant both a kiss and a smile on her lips. Then he rang the bell.

They heard movement from within. Someone was making their slow, breathless way down the corridor to the front door. And suddenly there was Madge, her hair nearly, but not quite, drawn back into a bun, dressed in her Sunday-best suit, her lips almost covered in vibrant pink lipstick, and patches of face powder standing in blotches on her cheeks.

'My, my!' was all she managed to say as she stared hard at Kate. 'Just look at you! Aren't you a turn-up for the books?'

It was five past four when Margaret glanced at the clock, just two minutes later than the last time she'd looked. She'd been unable to settle all afternoon: bored with the television, too distracted to read, not in the mood for cross-stitch, without the heart for baking. She prowled around the house, adjusting this, tweaking that, until she finally found herself in Kate's old bedroom. To her surprise, Roger was already there.

He turned away guiltily as she came in, but she'd already seen his cheeks wet with tears.

'Oh my dear!' she cried, reaching over to hold him tightly. And there they stood, the hardened old farmer and the childhood sweetheart he'd married, clinging together.

'We're losing her, aren't we? We're losing our girl.'

'Hush, my love,' she soothed, 'hush. I only know we have to let her go – then pray with all our might that she'll choose to come back again.'

They'd had tea. They'd dipped into the biscuit barrel out of politeness. They'd admired the room and the garden. And now there was nothing for it. They had to get down to talking about what was on all their minds.

'Did you know my father?' asked Kate at last.

'Yes. My nephew, Richard.'

'Did he know about me?'

'Yes.'

'And you? Did you know of my existence?'

'I heard from my sister, Richard's mother, that a baby was expected. I knew that the other parents were furious and embarrassed about the whole thing. It was the end of the sixties – all that business of free love and flower power. That might have been all right in Carnaby Street, but in Chesham things moved a little slower. The girl was sixteen, still at school, exams coming up. A baby just wouldn't suit, not at all.'

'So what did she do?'

'I never knew the details at the time. She went away, I suppose, and came back without you. I didn't know her then.'

'And my father? Did he try and keep in touch?'

'Richard was just a schoolboy with his whole career ahead of him. My sister, Elsie, was pretty angry about the mess he'd got into. Blamed it all on the girl, of course. She must have beguiled him, got herself into trouble.'

'And he accepted that?'

'He had no choice. He was studying for exams. He had neither the money nor the courage to break away from his parents. It sounds pathetic when you say it now, doesn't it, but times were different then.'

'What happened to him?'

'He became an accountant, a very good one here in Chesham. Later he married. They had a daughter.'

'I have a sister?'

Madge smiled at the thought. 'I suppose so, yes, though heaven knows what Susie will make of all this.'

'Where is she? More important, where is he? Do you think he'd want to see me?'

The old lady suddenly looked weary, slumping back in her chair as a shadow crossed her face.

'Not possible, I'm afraid.'

'It would cause trouble for him, I suppose, with his wife and family?'

'I'm sorry to have to tell you this, after you've come so far – but he died, Kate, just a matter of weeks ago. He had a dreadful accident a few days after we all celebrated their twenty-fifth wedding anniversary. It was a dreadful shock for everyone, but most of all for his wife. I'm sure you can understand. They were a very close family.'

Kate felt Martin's arm support her as she leaned back against him. Too late! After over thirty years, she was just too late.

Suddenly, there was a ring on the doorbell.

'That's for you,' said Madge, looking steadily at Kate.

'For me?'

'It's Richard's wife, widow now.'

Kate's hand shot to her mouth. 'Does she know about me? Will she be hurt or angry that I'm here?' There was panic in her eyes.

'She knows you're here, and she wants to meet you. You see, Kate, both sets of parents may have tried to keep those two unfortunate lovers apart, but they didn't succeed. They met again, back here in Chesham, after they'd both been to university. He'd always loved her, and even though his parents never approved, he married her – and they stayed together for twenty-five very happy years.'

'You mean ...?'

'I mean that Gwen is your mother, and she's standing outside the door right now.'

The blood had drained from Kate's already pale face. With an unspoken question, Martin sought permission to go and open the door. Kate heard the clock tick, the door open, the sound of muffled voices, and the ticking of the clock again. Then suddenly she was there, the woman Kate had both dreaded and longed to see for as far back as she could remember.

Neither woman spoke, but as Gwen walked through the door to stare at the young woman before her she felt her head swim and her knees buckle beneath her. For in front of her stood a ghost: a girl with the height, colouring, eyes, smile and look of her own dear husband. There was no doubt at all that this was Richard's daughter. And if that wasn't miracle enough, there was more! This lovely young woman was pregnant. Gwen had not only discovered her daughter, but her grandchild too. Hardly knowing she was moving, Gwen stepped forward with her arms outstretched.

'Elizabeth,' she whispered, gathering Kate tightly to her as if she were still the small baby she had once been.

Chapter Seven

It was Madge who conveyed with a nod to Martin that their company was no longer needed. He smiled as the old lady went back to her seat twice before she left the room, first to collect her cigarettes and lighter, then her weekly woman's magazine, obviously thinking they were in for a long wait.

Not that Gwen and Kate noticed anything going on around them. They only had eyes for each other, bound together by an invisible tie which transcended all the pain and uncertainty of the intervening years. For long minutes they stared, overwhelmed, too full of questions to know where to start.

At last Gwen pulled back to gaze closely at her daughter. 'You're lovely. I always thought you would be. Beautiful – and so like your father.'

'Am I?'

'I've brought photos. There's such a lot to show you.'

'But you went on to marry him. You married my father. You were together for twenty-five years, and you never let me know!'

The smile dropped from Gwen's face, her whole body slumped.

'Sit down,' she said at last, 'and let me start at the beginning.'

And as the clock ticked and the shadows lengthened, the two sat side by side on Madge's battered old settee, hands tightly clasped, as if to let go would break the bond between them.

'I was just sixteen when I first noticed Richard, your father. There were separate schools for boys and girls here then, so we didn't meet up much. Anyway, as an only child, I was never very used to the company of boys. My parents were quite strict. Dad was a solicitor and a local councillor, always busy at meetings and social gatherings, which my mum loved. She didn't work, mostly because it wasn't so usual for women to work in those days, but then I'm not sure she would have wanted to do anything as common as work in an office anyway. She enjoyed being at Dad's side when he was at official functions. She was a queen bee in several charity organisations in the town, and very involved at the church. I never remember being allowed to miss a Sunday morning service, even if I was dead on my feet. Appearances and duty mattered to her. That was the way she was.'

'Were they happy together, your parents?'

'In their own way, I suppose they were. She was the boss. She ruled our house with absolute authority. Everything in its place and rules for everything – what time we ate, what we wore, who we spoke to, who was beneath our interest – or at least hers.'

'And your dad allowed that?'

'He put up with it, probably because he was too preoccupied with council affairs and his own work to bother arguing. She kept what he called "a good house", and he liked order around him. It allowed him to get on with the life he really enjoyed.'

'And there were no other children? Just you?'

'She didn't think much of pregnancy first time round. She certainly wasn't about to do it again.'

'Even for your father? How did he feel about that?'

'He probably wasn't allowed to voice an opinion. They had separate bedrooms for as long as I can remember, so I imagine his opinion was of no importance at all.'

'Poor man.'

'A dear man.' Gwen smiled at the memory. 'I was always very close to him. And as I grew older, I got the distinct impression that he didn't mind being excluded from Mum's bedroom. He made other arrangements, I'm pretty sure of that.'

'A mistress?'

Gwen nodded. 'I almost met her once. She worked in his office, and had a flat on the outskirts of town near to the house of a school friend of mine. I was visiting one day when I saw them coming out of her flat together. He had his arm around her shoulders, and she was laughing up at him. I remember feeling a flash of anger, until it suddenly struck me how rarely I heard Mum laugh. He deserved a bit of fun in his life. Somehow, from that moment, I was glad for him.'

'Did he know you saw him?'

'I must have stopped in my tracks so suddenly that I caught his attention. He looked straight across at me with real fear and dread in his eyes. So I just smiled and we stared at each other for a moment before I carried on as if nothing had happened.'

'You never spoke of it?'

'No. It hung in the air between us, but it wasn't mentioned. No need. He knew his secret was safe with me.'

'So what about your own boyfriends? How did your parents feel about them?'

'There weren't any until Richard.'

'Did they approve of him?'

'I never let them meet him. I wasn't sure how they'd react, so I didn't risk it. Besides, as he became more special to me, I didn't want to share him. Mum thought of me only as a child, with no thoughts or feelings of my own except those she allowed me to have. If my parents didn't take to him, and honestly I don't think my mother would have approved of anyone, then it seemed safer to say nothing at all.'

'Tell me about him. What was he like?'

'Tall, fair, very blue eyes with blond lashes just like you. A long wiry frame which suited him well for the cross-country running he always enjoyed as a boy. In fact, that was how we met. My friend Tricia's brother was running in the same race, and she dragged me along to watch.' Gwen's expression softened as she remembered. 'It was really cold, I know that. Standing in a freezing field was the last thing I felt like doing, even though we did end up with quite a nice crowd, including a chap called Mike whom Trish was very keen on. It was at the end of the race that Mike introduced us to his best friend – and that, of course, was Richard.'

'Did you like him straight away?'

'I remember looking at him and thinking he was rather good-looking, but I was probably too shy to make an impact one way or another. What I didn't realise until much later was that he was quite shy too. It was an accident that we ever got talking at all. They were passing hot soup around, and somehow I dropped half of mine over him . . .'

'Accidentally, I'm sure,' laughed Kate.

Gwen's eyes sparkled with humour as she replied. 'Oh, completely by accident. In fact, I was mortified with embarrassment, especially as I'd dropped the other half over myself. There's was nothing for it. We just had to go off to the park pavilion together to clean ourselves up.'

'Of course you did! And did that break the ice?'

'Once we started talking, we never stopped. We never went back to join the crowd either, but ended up sitting on the steps of the pavilion until it was really quite dark. Then, of course, I had to go home.'

'And did you arrange to meet up again?'

'Not in so many words, but we both knew he'd be at the cross-country race the following week, and wild horses couldn't have stopped me being there.'

'So that was the start of it. Difficult, though, if you didn't feel you could be honest with your parents about where you were going?'

'You've no idea! I caught a gleam in my dad's eye once which made me think he had a good notion of what I was up to, but I had no wish to let my mother suspect anything.'

'Did your relationship progress quickly?'

'Do you mean, did we jump into bed with each other straight away? You know, it may have been the swinging sixties, when there was supposed to be all that free love but there was a real streak of Victorianism too, at least in our community. Young people did sleep together ...' she broke off to smile at her daughter '... otherwise, we'd hardly be having this conversation, would we? − but in our group, that only happened after you'd spent months together as boyfriend and girlfriend. A girl who behaved in any other way would be looked down upon as too easy and not respectable to know. In my case, coming from a very sheltered, over-protected family background, it just didn't occur to me. It was out of the question. That was it.'

'Until?'

'Until we'd been together for about six months, meeting secretly most of the time. I'd tell my mum that I was going out with Tricia, and sometimes I was, but it was always in a foursome with Richard too.'

'How did he feel about not meeting your folks? If you went out for so long, presumably he wanted the two of you to be recognised as a couple?'

'Yes, he did, but he knew I was frightened of Mum's reaction, and he didn't want to cause problems for me, especially as I'd just gone into the sixth form.'

'And his parents? Did you meet them?'

'I did, but only a couple of times. They were very keen for Richard to stick to his studies. His father was an accountant, and it was always clearly understood that as the elder of their two sons, Richard would take over the business.'

'Did he?'

'Eventually, yes, although I was never convinced that

accountancy was his own choice. Richard always had a flair for languages, and I often wondered if he should have followed that as a career.'

Kate gasped, thinking of her own post as a language teacher.

'Our friendship grew very gradually, probably because we weren't able to see each other all that often, what with homework, Richard's sport, my interest in art, and family commitments. I liked him, though, because in his shyness I recognised my own. We drew one another out. I remember how we laughed a lot, and went for long walks down back lanes, when we came back blue with the cold, but warmed by the cuddles and kisses we'd snatched on the way. Then we'd walk down to the chip van which often used to be parked at the end of our road, and buy steaming burgers piled high with ketchup and onions. And I'd always keep a roll of peppermints in my pocket so that Mum wouldn't smell the onions on my breath when I got home.'

Gwen paused, looking down to stroke her thumb across Kate's fingers as she went on.

'I'll never forget the first time he told me he loved me. It had been such a wonderful day. For the first time ever, he'd won a county race, and he was so excited, on top of the world. I remember him swinging me round and round, until I was giddy and lightheaded as he hugged me to him. Then he just said it. "I love you." Just like that! It was so unexpected, and yet felt right, really right. So I told him I loved him too, and we stood grinning at each other like Cheshire Cats. In fact, it was that night ...'

Kate squeezed her hand, encouraging her to continue.

'It was on that night that you were conceived.'

'That was the first time?'

'The first and only time. We were here.'

'Here?' Kate glanced around to take in her surroundings. 'In this house?'

'In this very room. This used to be Richard's parents' house. Madge only moved here about fifteen years ago to be with her sister Elsie — that was Richard's mother — when his father died.

Of course, when Elsie passed away some time later, Madge carried on living here.'

Kate tried to picture how it might have looked more than thirty years before. 'That night, his parents were out?'

'It was a few weeks before Christmas, and they were away for the weekend with relatives in Birmingham. They had wanted Richard to go as well, because his brother, Graham, was too young to leave behind and had to tag along. But Richard was seventeen by then with A levels only a few months away. He persuaded them that he had too much homework to do, and . . .'

'. . . instead of eating your burgers in a cold back lane . . .'

'. . . we brought them here. It felt almost like playing house, as if it was our very own home where we could light the fire, put records on, and cuddle up together on the settee.'

'Only this time, you didn't stop at cuddling?'

'It all seemed so natural and comfortable. We were committed to each other. And we were curious. We longed to know what it would be like, how we'd feel together, whether it would change our relationship for ever.'

'And did it?'

'More than either of us knew at the time. We were really close after that, full of love for each other, but we never had the opportunity to do it again. There was nowhere to go, and we were too scared to take risks.'

'But you'd already done that. You were pregnant.'

'Yes, although that didn't occur to me until much later. Looking back, we were so naïve. I suppose we both thought I couldn't get pregnant the very first time. Do you know, we didn't even talk about the possibility? We just couldn't imagine it would happen to us.'

'How long did it take for you to realise what had happened?'

'Months. My period stopped, of course, but I thought that was just stress. I found the sixth form quite hard work, and there was a lot of pressure on us to get to grips with our A-level studies. It wasn't until I found I was regularly wearing my skirt unbuttoned under my cardigan that the truth occurred to me.'

'What was Richard's reaction?'

'Disbelief. Fear. We had no idea what to do. We had no money, and no one to turn to except our parents, and the thought of talking to them filled us with dread. Richard was as much out of his depth as I was.'

'This is a hard thing for me to ask, but did you think about having an abortion?'

'No, not really, because for months I just ignored the possibility that I really was pregnant. I do remember very clearly, though, the first time I felt movement inside me. First of all I panicked – but then there was a sense of awe too. Suddenly, there was someone else involved apart from just me. The responsibility was terrifying, but wonderful at the same time. In some ways, I grew up in that moment, although in reality I was still a very immature schoolgirl from a sheltered, over-indulged background, and simply couldn't cope with what had happened.'

'So what did you do?'

'In the end, I plucked up courage to speak to my dad. That was in May, and I hadn't even seen a doctor, although I must have been five months pregnant by then. I didn't really mean to tell him, but he came up to my room one evening and asked if I was all right. I couldn't reply. Just burst into tears, and it all came pouring out.'

'How did he react?'

'He was very shocked. After all, this was his darling little girl we were talking about. He was most furious with Richard. It had to be his fault, of course. He must have led me astray, talked me into something I couldn't have wanted to do. He didn't want to know about the fact that Richard and I loved each other. He swept that aside as juvenile and unimportant. I felt belittled, outraged and terrified all at the same time.'

'Did he calm down eventually?'

'It took a day or two, and I was incredibly relieved that he didn't say a word to Mum until he'd really thought things through. All I knew was that I was summoned into the lounge one evening where they were sitting at the table together, Mum in floods of hysterical tears, and Dad trying desperately to calm her down. I shall never forget or forgive her reaction. She turned on me with such fury and vitriol, as if I had done all this deliberately to spite her. Hadn't I thought of our family reputation at all? Or how it would affect my studies, because I'd obviously have to leave school, and everyone would know why? What would people at the church think not just of me, but of her for having such an inconsiderate tramp of a daughter? And I wasn't to think there was any possibility I was going to keep a baby here! She practically had me thrown out in the streets with my bags packed before Dad managed to talk her round. The most terrifying part of the evening was when Dad made a phone call to Richard's parents, and the two of them locked me in my room so that they could go round to accuse their daughter's seducer. I think I could happily have ended my life at that moment. Not once did my mother ask if I was all right, or what I wanted to happen. My opinion was irrelevant. This was just an embarrassing inconvenient mess they had to sort out. I was expected to go along with whatever they decided. The sense of being powerless and manipulated was overwhelming. I had no choice, and I didn't know how I could change things to give myself any.'

'And Richard's parents? Were they furious too?'

'The most humiliating thing in my mother's mind was that Richard's father was an accountant, a professional. In fact, being a solicitor himself, my father knew him slightly through business, and the men were quite practical about it all. The mothers, though, were beside themselves, throwing accusations and blame in every direction except their own. Poor Richard. I think if my mother could have organised a lynch party that night, he would have been strung up then and there.'

'What happened in the end?'

'I never went back to school that term. My mother went in to see the head teacher, and told her I'd had a nervous breakdown, and needed complete rest. She said I'd be back in September for the new term, and that was that. Everyone must have thought I'd gone away, although in fact I became a complete recluse for the next few weeks, not allowed out at all, or even near the windows. If anyone came to the house, I had to hide. Worst of all was the fact that I was completely cut off from Richard. My mum watched me like a hawk. She even had a lock put on the phone. I was alone, totally alone.

'I was aware of arrangements being made. No one discussed them with me, and it wasn't until six weeks before you were due to be born that Mum told me I was leaving the next day for London. Through some church organisation, she'd managed to arrange for me to go to a home for "wayward" girls there. The plan was that I would disappear to the city, have the baby, give you up for adoption, and come home as if nothing had happened. It was that simple to them. I disappear, and so does the problem.

'Dad took me up in the car. Mum couldn't bring herself to go there, probably in case somebody saw her. I shall never forgot my first view of that house. It was a huge Victorian mausoleum of a place, freezing cold and gloomy, with high ceilings, peeling paint, brown lino, cold water, metal banisters and bedsteads. The receptionist woman judged me as no better than I should be with her first glance in my direction. After that, there was only formality, a regimented, efficient system which took no account of the homesickness and desperate unhappiness of the young women in their care. They expected us to be contrite, ashamed and sensible enough to take their advice.'

'Did you meet the other girls? What were they like?'

'There must have been about two dozen girls in when I was

there. We slept in dormitories which had six beds each. We were just thrown together, and that was the most comforting part of it all. One of the girls – Brenda was her name – was only fourteen, a baby herself really. We just clung to each other. Each of us had our own story, but the feeling of guilt and failure was instilled in us all. There was so much distress and fear. All of us dreaded having our babies, mostly because we had no idea at all about the actual process of giving birth. No one explained, and somehow none of us dared to ask. It was as if the staff assumed that if we'd managed to get ourselves pregnant, we must know what happened next. In fact, I didn't have a clue.'

Kate reached out to quieten Gwen's fingers, which were picking nervously at the material of her skirt as she spoke, eyes glassy and dark in her pale face.

'And me?' asked Kate quietly. 'Did you think about the baby you were carrying? What I'd be like, whether I'd be healthy?'

Gwen turned towards Kate, although her eyes were distant with memory. 'I remember being given a bag of baby things: nappies, powder, a little nightie and cardigan. There were some knitted booties too, and a crocheted shawl that had obviously been used several times before. But the moment I saw that tiny cardigan, and buried my nose in it so that I could smell the baby who had worn it before, the reality of you came over me. I knew nothing about babies. I was an only child, there were no little ones close to me in the family. I couldn't imagine someone tiny enough to fit that little cardigan, and the need to protect this small, fragile being inside me awakened a fierce sense of belonging and love. That was the first moment I recognised what my feelings were towards you. I loved you. No one would ever love you as I could. I couldn't entrust your care to anyone but me.'

'Wasn't there some way you could have kept me?'

'I knew that's what I wanted. I sat down and wrote to Mum and Dad telling them how I felt, begging them to help me keep my child, their grandchild.'

'And? Did they reply?'

'Not a word. I was allowed one phone call home a week, and I was never allowed to speak to my father, only Mum. When I tried to mention the letter, she put the phone down on me.'

'No discussion.'

'None at all.'

'What about Richard? Were you in touch with him?'

'When I was at home I wasn't allowed to contact him, but while I was in London I had the freedom to write to him again. I decided it wasn't a good idea for me to write to his home, so I dropped a line to my friend Tricia instead. Her boyfriend, Mike, was Richard's best friend. It was those two who helped us to stay in touch, and for that I will be eternally grateful. To this day, they are still dear friends of mine.'

'Had Richard's feelings changed while you weren't in touch?'

'Yes. He still said he loved me, but he obviously felt as powerless as I did. He seemed beaten down by his parents saying that I'd trapped him. It was all my fault, as far as they were concerned, and he was forbidden from having anything more to do with me. As my parents were saying much the same thing to me, I understood exactly what he was facing, but honestly, that was nothing to the pressure I was under. He was the only one I could pour out my heart to about that awful place, and how frightened and depressed I was. I even told him that I was trying to work out how I could keep you, but he was very adamant that I couldn't come back with a baby. It was out of the question, even to him. My letters were long and rambling and smeared with tears as I wrote. His were distant. His world hadn't changed at all. He had no real idea of the hell I was going through. Nobody did. It was a nightmare time of misery, fear and loneliness.'

'Did you have anyone with you when I was born? Your mother perhaps?'

'Not then, no, and I wanted her there so much. She may

have been a difficult woman in many ways, but I felt small and young and unable to cope. At times like that, you need your mum. There's no one else quite like her.'

Kate nodded grimly in agreement, although Gwen didn't notice, so lost was she in the hurts of her past.

'I remember my waters breaking, and not knowing what that was, whether something was wrong. There was a nurse who was older and more senior than any of the others I met, who told me very sternly to be sensible and pull myself together. To this day, I don't know what she meant, but I've never forgotten the feeling that I was somehow being childish and naughty. After that, through all the contractions, I tried hard not to cry out so that I wouldn't be a nuisance to anyone.'

'Was it an easy birth?'

'No, but most of it was just a fog to me. Afterwards, I gathered that my body wasn't really built for giving birth to babies, and you were lying awkwardly, having a great deal of difficulty coming out. The labour seemed to go on endlessly, but no one thought to tell me what was happening, and I didn't know if the immense pain I was feeling was usual or not. Now I know that it wasn't, and that you were in great distress. Suddenly, there was a panic. A doctor appeared, I heard urgent voices, and before I knew it I was being wheeled down a long corridor. When I came to several hours later, I was alone in a side room somewhere.'

'With me?'

'No. I looked for you. No sign of a baby, and no one else in sight either. I felt incredibly weak and sore, I do remember that, and it took a while for my mind to clear enough to work out where I was. I shouted and shouted and it seemed like ages before anyone appeared. Thank God *that* nurse had been taught something about bedside manners, because she was really concerned and kind to me. She told me there had been complications, and that you had grown so weak during the long labour that your heart actually stopped beating. More than that, apparently I'd haemorrhaged severely as you were born, and needed an immediate emergency operation. She gave me something to drink, and told me I should rest, and I found it hard to make her understand that I needed to know about you. Were you all right? Were you a boy or a girl? She kept saying that the doctor would have to explain everything to me, and scuttled off as if she were afraid to tell me. I thought I screamed at her to come back, but I couldn't hear my own voice. It felt as if I ran out of energy and simply couldn't keep my eyes open, although I'll never forget the terrible feeling of foreboding as I drifted off again.

'It was light when I woke. I became aware of a doctor at the side of the bed as I opened my eyes, and I called out for my baby. He explained then that my daughter was being cared for in a special baby unit because the birth had been traumatic for her. My daughter! I had a daughter! Elizabeth. I'd always known that would be your name. But there was more. The birth had been physically devastating for me too. I had lost a lot of blood and was torn and cut. He said that it would take me a week or so to be well enough to get around. And then he broke the most devastating news of all, that it was unlikely I'd be able to have any more children. Mind you, at that moment, I didn't care much. I was battered and exhausted, and had just given birth to a baby that no one seemed to want but me. The implications of what he said didn't really hit me until years later.'

'How long was it before you finally saw me?'

'While the doctor was there, that kind nurse came in again. She asked him if it was all right to take me down in a wheelchair to see you, and he agreed. What a wonderful moment it was, when I first peered into that special little cot to look at you. You seemed to be smiling at a secret dream you were having as you lay there, helpless and tiny. They couldn't take you out of the incubator, but they let me put my finger in to touch you. I remember your perfect little fingers clasping mine, as if you were holding on to your very life. It was then, as I looked down at this amazing being Richard and I had created, that I knew I could never let you go.'

'How long was I in special care?'

'A few days. I went down to the ward for hours every day, just to watch you as you slept, holding you close to me when I could.'

'Did you feed me?'

Gwen smiled at her. 'Do you know, that was one of the things I longed to do? I remember crying my eyes out when they came to give me something to dry up my own milk. I was allowed to give you your bottle though, and as I held you your eyes were always fixed on mine as you drank. I used to talk to you then – all about me, where I went to school, who my friends were, about your grandparents. And I told you about your father, how handsome he was, and how much we loved each other. It was so important to me that you knew that.'

'Did you parents come up to see you – and me?'

'Just once. I was so excited. I felt sure that when Mum saw you, she'd love you as much as I did.' Gwen's head dropped as sobs began to choke her. 'After all, you were her first grandchild . . .'

'What did she say? How did she react when she saw me?'

'She didn't touch you. Wouldn't let herself. I begged her to pick you up, to see as I could her own colouring in the blue of your eyes, her expression in yours. But she kept her distance. She couldn't allow herself to feel anything.'

'But she must have seen how distressed you were.'

'My distress was my problem, and I'd caused that myself. There's no way she was going to let that problem land on her own doorstep.'

'No discussion.'

'None at all. She never came again. Instead, my dad rang the next morning to tell me that if I kept my daughter, I could never go home. They would wash their hands of me.'

Kate reached out to draw Gwen to her, and they both sat

in silence for a while, each dealing with the tangle of their own memories and emotions. It was Kate who spoke at last.

'How long were you able to keep me?'

'Three weeks. Three short weeks that flew by, but I was so close to you by then. Everything they say about the unique and powerful bond between mother and baby was true for me. I was overwhelmed by the strength of the love I felt you, and appalled at the thought of letting you go.'

'What did they tell you about the adoption? Did you know what sort of parents I would be going to?'

'Not much. I was told they lived on a farm, and they had no children of their own. The welfare lady tried to be kind. She knew I was heartbroken at the thought of losing you, but she kept telling me that you'd have a good life, with lots of good food and fresh air. I had to do what was best for you. That's what she said, and those words have haunted me every moment since.'

'Did you ever meet them?'

'No. I wanted to, but they told me it wasn't allowed. There was so much I needed to say to them, such a lot I wanted them to know – about Richard and me, that we might have been young and foolish, but we really did love each other. And I desperately wanted them to know it broke my heart to part with you, that if there had been any way on earth that I could have kept you with me, I would have done so. They could give you a better life than I could, I knew that. That was the only reason I could let you go. I longed to see what they were like so I could watch them with you and be sure that they would love you in the way you deserved. All these years, I've had no image of them, no idea whether they were affectionate and outgoing, or quiet and strict. Every day when I've thought of you, overwhelmed with guilt, I've wondered what your home was like, whether you were happy.'

'So how did the handover take place?'

'The child welfare lady came to take the two of us to an adoption centre in central London. By the time she arrived I'd been up for hours, washing and feeding you, putting you in the prettiest clothes I could borrow from what they had at the home. I barely remember the journey. I know we went in a taxi, and that the building had big steps at the front and a black door with very chipped paint. We went up to her office, and you were asleep in the carrycot beside me while I signed all the papers. The words seemed to dance in front of me. I wasn't crying. I was determined not to cry but I couldn't seem to see straight for the fog in my eyes. Then someone else came in, another social worker I think, to join my welfare lady. I remember grabbing you to me then, and you started to cry. Suddenly I knew the moment had come. They were going to take you from me! They were going to take you from me . . .'

Racking sobs jolted through Gwen's body as she spoke, her eyes fixed on the unseen image in her head.

'There were two of them, and only one of me. They tried to be kind as they prised you from my arms. One of them told me I was being silly and not making things any easier. I remember screaming at them. I screamed and screamed – and then you were gone, and I kept on screaming. I thumped my fists on the locked door and yelled until my lungs ached and my hands were red and bruised.'

'And no one came to you?'

'Not for a long time. I was in a heap on the floor by then, exhausted, beaten and beyond consolation. The welfare lady who'd brought me came to take me home. She was trying to be bright and businesslike, completely ignoring the state I was in. The carrycot was still there, with the little blanket that had covered you. I remember grabbing that to breathe in the smell of you. I still have that blanket. After all these years, I still have it.'

She broke down then, unable to speak, while Kate gently held and rocked her as if she were a child herself. In the gathering evening gloom, the two women sat clasping each other, shocked at the pain and brutality of the last time they had been this close. And in their embrace the long years fell away, mother and daughter together at last.

'I can't hear anything,' hissed Madge, drawing her bulky self back into the kitchen from where she ventured as far as she dared into the hallway. 'Do you think they're all right? Should we go in?'

'No,' was Martin's firm reply. 'They've got a lot to talk about. Let's give them a bit of space.'

Madge sighed dramatically as she perched heavily on the kitchen stool. 'They've had half an hour already, and it will be time for *Neighbours* soon. I never miss that.'

'Shall I make another cup of tea?'

'I didn't finish the last one.'

'A biscuit?'

Madge shook her head, fiddling petulantly at a loose bit of skin on her thumb. 'I'd rather open that new bottle of sherry.'

Martin grinned in agreement as the old lady looked up with a smile.

'Can I have a ciggie too?'

'It's your house.'

'Are you any good at crosswords?'

'Brilliant.'

'Really? Well, you've met your match in me! Pass me that paper before you open the bottle, and we'll let battle commence.'

'Mum and Dad welcomed me back as if nothing had happened.' Gwen's voice was low and lifeless as she began to speak again. 'But nothing was ever the same. They expected me to slip back into my life as a little schoolgirl, but too much had changed for me. The pain of losing you was like a raw, festering wound that woke me in panic and guilt in the middle of the night. I didn't even bother trying to talk to my mum about it because she made it clear that discussion was not invited. I remember my dad hugging me a lot, but he said nothing. He knew better than to cross Mum, and so did I. It simply wasn't worth it.

'Loneliness engulfed me. Who could I talk to? I had friends at school, of course, but when I went back at the start of term in September, they thought I'd had some kind of mental breakdown. I looked at them and saw schoolgirls, all giggly and full of nonsense that no longer held interest for me. I had grown up beyond my years, and they hadn't changed. I know I was distant. I know I was prickly and difficult to be near. I remember taking myself off to sob my heart out behind the coats in the cloakroom one afternoon, then looking up to see a girl I'd known since infant school staring at me with real fear in her eyes. She thought I'd completely lost my marbles. After that, the girls kept clear. I was aware of their whispers, felt their eyes on me, but I was too low and desperate to care. I realise now that I must have been deeply and clinically depressed. At the time, I just felt a failure who would never have a moment's happiness again.

'Worst of all, I couldn't see Richard. Or perhaps I should say that Richard wouldn't see me. Our parents had made a pact. We were not permitted to see each other again. The break was complete, and the pain unbearable. As he was a year older than me, he'd left school at the end of the summer term to take up a place at university in Birmingham in the autumn. I almost walked into him on the High Street one morning, and he actually stepped away to avoid meeting me. That was the first time I'd seen him in more than four months, and he crossed the road rather than face me.'

'What about your friend, Tricia, was it? She knew what you'd been through. Could you talk to her?'

'She was the only one, and I will never forget what a wonderful friend she was to me then. I was unreasonable and moody, but she took it all. A friend in a million, that's Tricia.'

'And her boyfriend? Did he go to university too?'

Gwen smiled. 'Mike was never much of an academic. He was good-looking and popular, always able to come up with the right words to persuade anyone to do anything. He became a car sales-man in the town, started wearing smart suits, and plainly earned far too much money for his own good. Tricia never stopped loving him though. They were married before she was twenty-one. Their kids are grown-up with children of their own now.'

Kate leaned forward to look directly into her mother's eyes. 'I didn't know about your note until a few weeks ago. Mum never told me. I suppose she was waiting for me to ask.'

'I was terrified that the welfare woman would search you,' said Gwen, 'and find where I'd hidden it, sewn into the back of your jersey so that it was between the layers of your clothes right up behind your shoulder blades. I begged them to let me send a letter openly, but they said that wasn't allowed. It had to be a complete break, which was probably better for you, but devastating for me. I didn't really expect to get away with hiding a note and photo for you, but I wrapped them in a hankie and sewed it in so that it wouldn't rustle and was almost invisible as long as you kept the jersey on. One of the nurses had taken a picture of me holding you when you were just two weeks old, so I sent that. And because I didn't have any proper paper, I just tore a sheet out of my exercise book to tell you how I felt about letting you go. I didn't put my full address because of how my mum would react, and besides I had no idea where I might end up in the future. But I gave you Richard's name, and told you that we both lived in Chesham in the hope that if ever you did decide to try and get in touch in the future, you'd have a chance of finding me. But the days went by, then weeks and months and years. Your birthday was the worst to bear, Christmas of course, and Mothering Sunday. Not a day passed when I didn't think of you, wondering where you were, what you were like, whether you were happy. Had I made the right decision? Had you been given all the love you deserved?

Did you feel an emptiness in your life to match the void in my own?'

Kate nodded. 'There was always something not quite right. I couldn't put my finger on exactly what was missing, but I was aware of feeling different from the people closest to me from a very early age. I never seemed to fit in as I should. My parents are dear and wonderful, the best ever – but they don't look or react like me. They love fresh air and being out of doors. I prefer to be tucked up with a good book, or a piano to play. They are hardworking, down-to-earth and practical, whereas I'm dreamy, with my mind full of complex thoughts and feelings. They're dark, and I'm blonde. They're shorter than me, and sturdily built. I'm tall and gangly. Their eyes are green and brown, mine are pale blue.'

'Did you ever talk to them about the way you felt?'

'Yes. I can picture myself as if it were yesterday, sitting at the kitchen table eating breakfast with my mum. I must have been about eight, I should think. How the subject came up, I'm not sure, but I know she told me then for the first time that I was adopted. She said she and Dad had been married for a long time before they accepted the fact that they were not going to be able to have children of their own. It took ages to go through the adoption process, and they'd almost given up hope when they heard that I had been born and needed a home. She cried, I remember that, when she spoke of their joy at having a child who needed their love and care at last. After that, I felt special and cherished. My parents had chosen me, and what could be better than that?'

'Did you grow up on a farm? That's what the welfare lady told me.'

'Yes, over in Essex, and they're still there. Dad's getting on a bit now, and it's really becoming too much for him, especially with prices desperately low. He's a dairy farmer, so it's up at the crack of dawn every morning, working flat out until it's dark. Mum worries about him, and so do I.'

'Were you happy?'

A warm smile spread instantly across Kate's face. 'Blissfully. It was an idyllic childhood with plenty of room to explore and play, good friends, and the kind of unworldly innocence that children in the cities can rarely have.' Her expression changed as she went on. 'But as I grew older, probably into my teenage years, the thought of having another mother, a *real* mother, obsessed me. I could never give up my own child, so why did she? I lay awake at night, wondering who you were, where you lived. Did you have other children that you loved enough to stay with? Did they know about me? Did you laugh and chat and get on with your life as if I didn't exist? Did you ever give me a thought, or was I just a guilty secret in your past, a memory to be buried and forgotten?'

'You must have despised me.'

Kate's gaze was cool as she considered her answer. 'With a vengeance, at least some of the time. But there was also curiosity. I wondered what you looked like, whether I got my build and colouring from you. I remember when I first learned to drive, wondering if you were a good driver, and whether my lousy sense of direction came from you. And who was my father? Did I have brothers and sisters through him? Did he even know that I'd been born?'

'Were you able to talk to your mother about your feelings?'

'Probably I could have done, but I didn't. I was her world. Her every thought and deed was for me. She couldn't have been a better mother, and I can't properly express the love and gratitude I feel for her. But ...'

'But there was something else,' prompted Gwen gently.

Kate nodded. 'Someone else. Another mother I didn't know. And although her blood flowed in my veins, and her personality shaped mine, I didn't know her — and I longed to. I didn't know if I wanted to hug you or shout at you. And the thought that you might have gone on to have other children you loved and cared for filled me with overwhelming jealousy. Stupid and unfair, I know, but that's how I felt.'

'What did your mother think about my letter and photo? Does she see me as a threat? Was she worrying year after year that one day I'd come back and claim you?'

Kate's expression softened as she thought of Margaret. 'You must meet my mum. She's very special, the sort who always stands at the back of the queue to let others go first. I know she worried, but she never said a word about it to me. She just wouldn't.'

'Does she know you're here now?'

'Yes, and all she did was hold me and wish me luck. I could see the apprehension in her eyes, the dreadful fear that she might have to compete with another woman who had more claim on me as a daughter than she feels she has herself.'

'That's ridiculous. She brought you up. She's made you what you are. I missed out on all of that.'

'Fear isn't rational though, is it? Our emotions override everything logic tells us.'

'I'm no threat to her, or her position in your life. You must tell her that.'

'I will. She won't believe it. I'm not sure that you do either.'

And for a moment the two women stared at each other, realising they'd started out along a path not knowing where it would lead, nor what hurts they'd unleash along the way.

'I'm starving,' moaned Madge. 'Doctor says I've got to eat regularly.'

'Oh?' queried Martin. 'Is that a medical condition? Diabetes or something?'

'No, he just says I've got to stay regular. Never missed a meal since.'

'What have you got? Anything in the cupboard I can rustle up?'

'Well, if you're hungry too, how about nipping down to the chip shop? It'll be open now, and they do a smashing steak and kidney pie. Mushy peas too, if we're lucky.'

Kate's husband hesitated, glancing towards the lounge with its firmly shut door.

'Don't worry about them. They're obviously set for the evening. While they've got things on their minds, there's nothing wrong with us taking care of our stomachs. Large chips, please, and don't spare on the vinegar. Mint sauce on the mushy peas too, if they've got them. And I like Coke with chips. Keep the rest of that sherry for later.'

Martin grinned. 'Don't you ever worry about your diet?'

'What diet?'

With a chuckle he headed for the front door.

'And a pickled egg!' His hand was on the latch as Madge barked out her last instruction. 'Or two!'

'It seems unbelievable after all you've told me that you and my father ever got back together again. How did that happen?'

'It was years later. I went back to school and took my A levels the following summer. Life at home was pretty unbearable. My mum didn't ever mention what had happened, but it hung in the air between us. I was stupid and irresponsible as far as she was concerned, and it was only her good management that had saved face for the family. We never had been close, but after that, the atmosphere between us was practically icy.'

'Was your dad more sympathetic?'

'He might have been if he'd been at home more often. Work at the office, clubs he belonged to, and of course the social life he led with a certain lady in Chesham Bois kept him away from the house more than my mum thought was decent. She was all right, though. She belonged to every charity organisation going, mostly as chairman or secretary.

She was always in the thick of some fund-raising venture or other.'

'How did things go at school? Did you eventually get on better with the other girls?'

'It was never the same again, mostly because I was so very different. That probably wasn't a bad thing because I just knuckled down to my studies, and kept myself to myself. Tricia was all the friend I needed.'

'So did you go away to university too?'

'As soon as possible. I chose to go as far away from Chesham as I could. I'd always liked Scotland when we'd been there on family holidays, so I applied to Edinburgh to study history, and much to my relief, got in.'

'How did you feel about meeting other lads then? Did you go out with anyone else?'

'No one at all. Some of them probably thought I was a bit stand-offish, but I didn't care. I had built a wall around myself, I recognise that now. Losing you had been so deeply painful, it was as if I put all my emotions into cold storage. I felt nothing, needed no one. At least, that's what I thought.'

'So what changed all that?'

'Four years later I had my degree, but didn't know exactly what I wanted to do with it. I planned to base myself in London, and start searching for jobs as an archivist, which I'd always really fancied. I'd got a few interviews lined up, and while I went through that process of job-hunting, decided to move back home for just a few weeks, no longer.'

'What did your mother think of that idea?'

'Actually she was relieved. It was in that year that she first discovered a lump in her breast. She was whipped into hospital for a mastectomy before we knew it, although, as it turned out, it was too little too late. By the time I came home she was over the operation, but the stuffing had been knocked out of her by the experience. What we didn't realise at the time was that the cancer was gradually spreading to her liver. It was no wonder she felt so dreadful. For someone who had always been at the centre of community life, it was surprising how few people took the trouble to visit regularly once she became virtually housebound. Mind you, she had always been a difficult woman at the best of times. During her illness she became unbearable: bad-tempered, impatient and bitter about everyone and everything.'

'So when everyone else faded away, you were the only one left.'

'Something like that. I did find a job as an archivist, but as it was in the west of London, it made sense for me to save money by living at home, initially at least. But then, as Mum's illness became more acute, there was no question of me leaving.'

'And your dad? How did he cope?'

'Badly. Illness always made him feel uncomfortable. He went through the motions of caring, but it was plain that all the love had long gone from their marriage. Mostly, he kept himself busy away from home, and although Mum moaned constantly about him, I don't think she really minded much. They had so little in common, nothing left to say.'

'Not much of a life for a young woman, stuck at home nursing a sick and bad-tempered mother?'

'Well, I was at work during the week, but for most of the weekend I was at her beck and call. Don't get me wrong. We might not have been very close, but I did love her. She was my mum, after all. The thought of losing her filled me with fear. I so much wanted her to feel better, but when it became clear that the cancer had taken too firm a grip, I was determined to make her last months as comfortable as I possibly could.'

'How long was it?'

'In the end, thankfully quick. I came home in September. Just before Christmas we lost her. I've never been able to get through the run-up to Christmas since then without having a cry over her. All these years, and it still fills me up.'

'So then you were free?'

'It didn't feel that way. Dad might not have had much time

for her in the last years of her life, but he seemed completely at sea once she died. I meant to leave, but somehow didn't quite manage it. And then, of course, there was Richard.'

'My father? How did he get back in touch?'

'He wrote to me. Because Mum had been such a queen bee in local charities, there was an article about her in the paper when she died. His mother pointed it out to him when he was home one weekend. I'm still surprised that she did that really, except that I suppose she was certain our friendship was completely over. After all, you must have been about five years old by then. It was old history for everyone except me. Anyway, his letter just dropped through the letterbox one morning. I can't tell you the emotions it churned up in me. I nearly didn't answer. I left it for several days, turning over in my mind the carefully worded note I should send in reply. I didn't have the courage to write to his home, but he'd given me his address in London. I actually got as far as sealing the envelope when, in a moment of decision I've never been able to understand since, I just picked up the phone and called him. When he answered I was so shocked I very nearly slammed the phone down.'

'But you didn't.'

'No.'

'He must have been surprised to hear from you.'

'Actually, he sounded pleased. It was as if nothing had happened between us, like old friends slipping back into the comfortable familiar relationship we'd always had.'

'Did he mention me?'

'No, not then. And when we finally met up a few days later and I tried to tell him how I was still haunted by the memory of giving away the baby I loved – *our* baby – he made it clear he didn't want to talk about it. Not then, and as it turned out, not ever.'

'You mean, you went on to marry this man, you loved him enough to commit yourself to a lifetime with him, even though he refused to talk about the child to whom you were both parents? How could I mean so little to him? To you?'

Gwen's eyes filled with fresh tears. 'He was a good man, decent, honest, hardworking. And he loved me. He always had. I had no doubts that he would make a good husband, and at least you weren't some dark secret that I might have had to keep from any other man I married.' Her shoulders began to tremble as her voice dropped to little more than a whisper. 'I thought he would change. He was beside me when I woke up crying for you in the night. He recognised my sadness, but simply wasn't able to cope with it. For him, the whole business of my pregnancy and your birth had been a nightmare best forgotten. He believed that in time I'd be able to forget too. He chose to ignore the hurt which festered away inside me. I remember mentioning to him that it was your fifth birthday. When he turned away as if I'd never spoken, it felt as if he'd slapped me hard across the face. It took a long time, and a lot of courage, before I ever mentioned you again.'

'But you didn't give up? You didn't let him just put me out of his mind, did you?'

Gwen turned towards her daughter until their foreheads rested together. 'I'm afraid I did. He just couldn't cope with the memory, and I wasn't able to handle the unhappiness of being dismissed every time I tried to tell him how I felt, the dull, gnawing ache of loss which overwhelmed me at some time in each day ever since the moment you were born. And when Susie came along . . .'

'Susie? That's your other daughter? My sister?'

Her mother nodded. 'She was nothing short of a miracle. Your birth had caused a lot of damage which the doctor said would prevent me from getting pregnant again. For years, I thought of that as a punishment for my wickedness in the past. Becoming pregnant with Susie was almost a medical impossibility. I think I must have held my breath for nine months, terrified of losing her as I had you. And then she was born. Beautiful, perfectly healthy, and ours to keep.'

A shadow passed over Kate's face. She said nothing.

'Looking down as Susie lay in my arms, I thought of you. You looked so different, of course. You were blonde from birth, while Susie was born with a shock of dark red hair. You had been placid and calm. She came out screaming, and has never stopped yelling for attention ever since.'

'And my father loved her?'

'To distraction. There was always a special bond between them. She was the centre of his world from the moment he first set eyes on her.'

'And he didn't want to know about me. I was as much his child as she is – and he never gave me a single thought, nor even allowed my existence to be mentioned.'

Gwen looked at Kate as if seeing her clearly for the first time since their painful conversation had begun.

'He would have loved you. I think he understood that, and that's why he couldn't cope with the thought that you were somewhere in the world without him knowing you. I believe he genuinely thought that by shutting out the very mention of you, he was helping us both to get over it. Perhaps for him it worked. For me, the knowledge that you were growing up in someone else's family was like a festering wound for the whole of my married life. Oh, Elizabeth, I can't tell you what it means to me to have found you again.'

'Kate. My name is Kate.'

'I'm sorry. I'll get used to it, I promise.'

'My parents named me Katherine after my dad's mother. Oddly enough, my middle name is Elizabeth. Now I know why.'

'And you're going to have a baby? When's it due? How are you feeling? Are you all right?'

'I'm fine.'

'Your husband, Martin, is it? He seems nice. I didn't have much chance to meet him.'

'He's wonderful. I'm very lucky.'

Gwen reached out to circle her daughter's face with her fingers. 'You look so like your father, you know. Your smile, the shape of your face, even the way you use your hands when you speak.' She sighed at the memory. 'He was simply the love of my life. We had just celebrated our twenty-fifth anniversary when he died so suddenly. I still can't believe he's gone. Even now, I half expect him to walk into this room at any second.'

'And I walked in instead.'

'Yes.' There was a catch in Gwen's voice as she spoke. 'You walked in, looking just like him – and pregnant with my first grandchild.'

Kate drew back abruptly, and got to her feet. 'Forgive me, but I've left Martin too long. It's best that I go now.'

'But you will come back? There's so much I want to know about you. You've hardly said a thing about yourself.'

'Another time.'

'There will be another time? I couldn't bear to lose you again.'

'I just need some space to take all this in. I didn't expect to discover so much this soon. I'm not sure I'm ready for all this. Just let me think things over for a while, and then I'll call you.'

Gwen clutched at her hand as she began to turn away towards the door. 'You will call, won't you? Please. I don't expect your forgiveness, not yet, but I beg for your understanding. You're expecting your own baby. Imagine how difficult it was for me to give away mine, when I felt exactly as you do now.'

Unable to reply, Kate managed a smile at her mother as she turned the handle on the living-room door. Moving through to the kitchen, the two women were greeted with the most unlikely vision. Martin and Madge were both perched on kitchen stools. With more of a grimace than a grin, Martin looked up from where he sat with his arm around the cumbersome, well-padded Madge, trying with limited success to stop her from sliding on to the floor. Not that she cared as she snored and whistled contentedly against his shoulder, her lips fluttering and nostrils flared.

Suddenly, as if aware of eyes upon her, she woke with a start. 'Good!' she said, as if the hour since she'd last spoken had never happened. 'You're finished. Does that mean it's teatime?'

Chapter Eight

Brian suspected the house was empty before his finger even touched the bell, but he rang all the same. It was so unlike her to miss the art class which plainly gave her pleasure. Gwen must be ill. That was the only explanation. Either that, or something was dreadfully wrong.

He stood back and gazed up at the silent house, his face creased with worry. It wasn't as if he could honestly say he knew her well. A chat or two over cups of coffee hardly constituted a relationship. They were friends though, of that he was certain, and as her friend he was concerned not only about her absence that afternoon, but the generally distracted air she had worn about her for a week or two. Something was worrying her, beyond her grief at the loss of her husband, and because he could remember only too well from his own bereavement what a lonely experience worry could be, he simply wanted to be there for her. Perhaps his concern would be viewed as an intrusion. Then again, perhaps what she needed most of all right now was a caring friend.

There was no reply. He'd guessed there wouldn't be. Should he leave a note? Hesitating on the doorstep, he finally rummaged in his pocket for a scrap of paper and a pencil, and in fine flowing letters wrote:

Gwen, where are you? Are you OK? Call me an old fusspot, but I was worried about you. Give me a ring if you'd like to. Brian

He eyed the note critically, inserting on impulse the word 'love' in front of his name, then hurriedly stuffed the paper through the letterbox before he could think better of it.

'Isn't she in? She's not at the library, so I thought she must be here.'

Brian turned to find an elegantly dressed woman walking through the gate. Her neat blonde haircut framed a pleasant oval face as she walked up to greet him, hand outstretched.

'Don't tell me, you're Brian! I recognise you from Gwen's description.'

'Really? Whatever did she say?'

'Oh, something about you having lovely hands, a nice grin and twinkly hazel eyes.'

'You can see my eyes in this light?' he laughed.

'No, but your beard gave you away.'

'Then you have an advantage over me. The fact you haven't got a beard gives me no clue as to who you are!'

'Tricia,' she replied, her expression lighting up with interest as she took in the length of his lean frame and tanned skin. 'Gwen and I went to school together.'

'Tricia. I remember now she mentioned you. Well, if you two have been friends for a while, you might know where she is. I certainly got the impression she meant to be at the art class this afternoon, so when she didn't turn up, I was a bit concerned.'

'You're not the only one. She's definitely been rather elusive lately. I've rung and left a message for her a couple of times, but she's not been in touch. That's very out of character, I'd say.'

'Do you think she's all right?'

Tricia looked at him thoughtfully for a moment. 'Tell you what,' she said at last, 'have you got a car here? My house is only in the next street. If you've got time to give me a lift home, why don't you come in for a cup of coffee and a chat? As we are both worried about our Gwen, I think we should join forces, don't you?'

'What do you mean, she's had a shock? What kind of shock?'

Celia's face was screwed up with curiosity as she leaned in as close as she dared to Madge's chair.

The old lady sniffed. 'I'm not saying another word, so don't ask.'

And with that Madge fell silent, apparently completely absorbed by the TV guide on her lap. Uncertain how to proceed, Celia waited a good minute before her next attempt to wheedle out further titbits of information.

'Poor Gwen, she's been through so much. And if she's in shock, that's hardly surprising with all the stress and worry she's gone through. Is she under the doctor? She should stay in bed. Plenty of liquids. Always does the trick with me.'

Madge turned the page of the TV guide, and pushed her glasses a little further up the bridge of her nose as she read. 'Good, *Casualty* is on tonight. I like that. I always try and guess which patient is going to be dead by the end of the show. It's usually the one who seems healthiest at the start.'

Celia shook her head and clucked sympathetically. 'Only, if she's in bed she'll need some shopping done. I'll pop in this afternoon and see what I can get for her.'

If she expected an answer from Madge, she was disappointed; but then, Celia was never one to give up easily.

'Besides, if she's under the weather, she won't miss that computer of Richard's for a few days, will she? Graham could make good use of that for the golf club minutes.'

'Don't you dare. She's got enough on her plate without you poking your nose in.' Madge peered more closely at a tiny photo on the television page. 'I wish my doctor looked like that one at Holby General.'

'So she's up and about then, is she? In pain, of course, but not physical, is that what you mean?'

'That dark one, the fella with the hair? He could feel my bumps any time.'

'More emotional, is it? A bit of a breakdown? Perhaps she needs anti-depressants. Graham was a new man on those.'

'Mind you, I reckon he's got an eye for that little nurse ...'

'Talking of a new man, Gwen hasn't got one, has she? It would be absolutely indecent, of course, with Richard hardly in his grave – but it's not man-trouble that's depressing her, is it?'

'... you know, the blonde one with the lisp ...'

'No, knowing Gwen, she'd hardly have men running after her, not at her age. Perhaps that's what's depressing her? Am I right? Is she upset because she hasn't got a man?'

'She's far too good for him, we all know that, but some people never learn.'

'I knew it! There is someone! And you don't approve? Why? Is he penniless? Gormless? After her money? Well, it certainly wouldn't be her body now, would it!'

Madge lifted her head slowly from the TV guide, and stared at Celia in puzzled disbelief.

'Do you know, Celia, you wear me out. Switch on that telly, there's a good girl – and if you're going to be quiet, you can stay. If not, take yourself off home and bother Graham instead.'

Susie's mobile phone didn't often ring in the evenings. Most friends knew her home number, so usually she switched the mobile off completely to save the battery. That was why when she heard the distant buzz of it ringing in her handbag she ignored it for several seconds before she worked out what it was. Flinging herself across the bed to grab her bag, then rummaging desperately into its dark depths to draw out the trilling con-traption, she was out of breath and laughing as she answered.

'You sound happy. Am I interrupting something?'

Shock shot through her. It was Paul. His voice was unmistakable.

'No. No, I just couldn't find the phone. It was buried . . .'

'Would it be better if I rang back another time?'

'No, this is fine.'

'Correct me if I'm wrong, but did you say you live in West Hampstead?'

'Just off Finchley Road.'

'That's what I thought. Well, in that case, what are you doing in about an hour's time? Fancy meeting up for a drink and perhaps a bite to eat at that new place by the overground station? Do you know it?'

'No.'

'No, you don't fancy it?'

She giggled. 'No, I don't know it, but yes, I do fancy it. An hour, you reckon?'

'I'll be sitting there waiting for you. Should I have a rose between my teeth so that you recognise me?'

'Might be an idea. Who is this, by the way?'

'Oh, you hurtful woman! I'll make you remember. It's an Italian restaurant. That should give you a clue.'

'Narrows it down to just half a dozen possibilities. If you're not the one I hope you are, I'll just turn round and leave.'

'Then I'd have to drink a bottle of your favourite red wine all by myself . . .'

'What a waste! I'll be there in an hour.' And without waiting for his reply, she put the phone down. For several stunned moments, she clasped her hands to her mouth in sheer disbelief that he had actually called her. Out of working hours too! However did he know her mobile number? He would have had it on the schedule for the Rome shoot, of course, but surely he hadn't kept it all this time?

Had he?

She glanced at her watch, then unclipped it, stripping off

the rest of her clothes as she rushed to the shower. One hour to soak, steam, curl, iron, spray, moisturise – and shave her legs.

Just in case!

The building was harder to find than she had imagined, but then thirty years was a very long time in a city which changed as quickly as London. It was almost seven o'clock as Gwen turned the car into the right road at last, narrowing her eyes as she peered at the dark houses, hoping to catch a glimpse of a street number. Ten, twelve, fourteen – this must be it. Number sixteen. As the trees parted either side of the drive, the silhouette of the imposing double-bayed house loomed into sight. She recognised it instantly. It looked smarter, with neat paintwork and lit windows through which she could glimpse office premises. Of its former role in the lives of so many distressed young women, there was no clue. ARMSTRONG AND DAVIS, CHARTERED SURVEYORS, read the large wooden sign to one side of the steps which led to the front door. At least the steps hadn't changed. She still recalled the time she had first walked up them, a frightened, pregnant young girl, a long way from home and filled with dread not just for her own future, but for that of the baby she carried inside her. Memories flooded into her mind as she sat in the shadowy driveway staring at the steps. She had walked down them with Elizabeth in her carrycot, both of them heading for the adoption centre. Closing her eyes for a moment, she swayed as the feelings of that day once again overwhelmed her, the despair, helplessness and guilt which had haunted her ever since. They had wrenched her baby from her arms. For the best, that's what they said. It was for the best.

Gwen rested her pounding head on her hands as they gripped the steering wheel. Well, they hadn't beaten her. They had underestimated the bond between a mother and daughter. They might have torn them apart, and broken two hearts in the process, but they had found each other again. Elizabeth – or Kate, as she now was – had found her. They were reunited. They might have lost their past, but oh, what a future they had.

How long she sat there Gwen was unsure, but finally she dabbed her tearstained face with a hankie, fumbling in her bag for a fresh coat of lipstick. Glancing in the rear-view mirror as she ran her fingers through her hair, she made a decision. It was time to talk to Susie. Heavens, there was so much to tell her. How happy she would be to know she had a sister, a beautiful sister who was lovely and clever and expecting her first baby. More than that, wonder of wonders, she looked so poignantly like dear Richard. Knowing of the special bond between Susie and her father, the sight of Kate would certainly bring Susie great comfort too, just as it had Gwen. After all the grief, here was the most unbelievable gift to give them hope. Susie would be delighted, absolutely thrilled, once the whole thing was explained properly to her. Wouldn't she?

Should she ring first, to let Susie know she was coming?

No need. Let it be a surprise. And what a surprise it would be!

She was late. Of course, she had never intended to be bang on time, but a quarter of an hour was probably stretching things a bit. At least he was there. She saw him immediately through the softly lit window, and her heart lurched. Self-consciously flattening her hair, and wiping her hot palms on the bottom of her jacket, Susie opened the restaurant door. He rose to greet her immediately, his face lighting up with pleasure as he gathered her to him in the warmest of hugs. All thoughts she'd had of playing it cool disappeared from her mind as she sank into the familiar, exhilarating feel of him.

He stood back from her, holding out a red rose. 'Seemed a waste to put this between my teeth! It's for you, with love.'

'Love?'

'And pasta. The food's great here. Make your choice before we start talking, or we'll never get round to eating.' Looking down at her, his expression softened. 'I'd forgotten how sweet you look. I've missed you, Susie.'

And as his arms went round her again, she felt her thumping heart might burst with happiness.

Gwen hurried up the stairs to Susie's flat with a skip in her step. Turning the corner at the second floor, she pressed her finger to the buzzer of number three. From within, she heard the sounds of someone walking down the hallway towards the front door. Good! Susie was in! How great it would feel to be open and honest at last about the daughter she'd lost but never forgotten.

The door opened and Gwen's face instantly fell as Rachel, Susie's flatmate, greeted her with surprise. 'Mrs Moreton! How nice to see you. Was Susie expecting you? Sorry, but she's out, I'm afraid. I've only just come in myself, so I'm not sure what time to expect her back.'

Disappointment engulfed Gwen as she forced a smile in reply. 'Oh, never mind. I only called in on the off-chance.'

'From Chesham?'

'Well, I had another call I needed to make in London.'

'Do you want to come in? We could give her mobile a ring.'

Gwen hesitated before shaking her head. 'No, I don't want to disturb her. Would you tell her that I called, and that I have some marvellous news for her?'

'Really? Anything I can pass on?'

'I think I really need to see her myself. Perhaps you could ask her to ring me urgently?'

'Of course.' And Rachel watched with bemusement as a plainly flustered Gwen disappeared into the shadows down the stairs.

*　　*　　*

When Paul smiled, his eyes sparkled with fun and his face creased with laughter lines which made him more dangerously attractive than ever. Susie watched in fascination as he regaled her with hilarious tales of the various shoots that had taken him away from London for most of the time since their trip to Rome two months earlier.

'It must be wonderful to travel the world as you do. You work in such exotic places.'

He shrugged. 'Yes, but it's all work, and the schedules are usually so tight that there's not enough time for sleep or meals, let alone sightseeing or relaxation. When I got back from that desert shoot last month, I felt as if I could sleep for a week.'

'Did you actually stay in the desert, or were you in some exclusive hotel round the corner?'

'In a tent, would you believe! All mod cons though, so I'm not complaining.'

'Have you been to the desert before?'

'Oh, many times. It's the clarity of the light there that makes it so unique. I've never found anything to match it.' He chuckled. 'I remember my first trip years ago. It was for a calendar, and we had a bevy of models with us, all breathtakingly beautiful, but in the case of one or two of them at least, not as bright as they could be. We had to get up at about four in the morning to make the most of the light, and I was shaving with my battery razor, listening to the BBC World Service, when one of the girls came up and asked me in a broad Cockney accent what I was doing. I explained I was listening to the news, and that it was a very sad day because Fred Astaire had died. "He was a bit young, wasn't he?" was her reply, and I was too puzzled by her reaction to bother to say any more. Anyway, she wandered off to the girls' make-up tent where I couldn't help overhearing as she walked in and announced to them all, "Guess what? That Freddie Starr's just snuffed it!"'

Susie roared with laughter.

'The worst thing,' Paul continued, laughing with her, 'was realising she was too young to know who Fred Astaire was. I was twenty-five then, a sophisticated man of the world, but I can tell you I felt like an old codger at that moment.'

Susie glanced down with surprise to see that their hands were clasped across the table. Play it cool, that's what she had promised herself before she came – but the sight of his strong tanned hand covering hers filled her with a thrilling buzz. He wasn't to be trusted, she knew that. He was a charming flirt. He had a long-term girlfriend; and not just any girlfriend, but Deborah McCann, who apart from being a stunning looker just happened to be Susie's boss as well. Deborah had made it quite clear in her short visit to Susie's desk the previous week that Paul was her own personal property. It would be a very foolhardy woman who crossed the formidable Deborah.

Susie looked up to find Paul gazing at her with warm admiration in his eyes, and knew that where he was concerned she would always be happily foolish. She should tell him about the abortion. She should dismiss him as irresponsible with the feelings of others. She should rise from this table and walk away, knowing she would never be in control of her life if she allowed herself to be picked up and dropped whenever it suited him.

Drawing her hand back, she took another sip from her glass of wine before asking, 'And Deborah? Did she manage to go with you on any of your travels?'

'No. Why should she?'

'Well, you've always said that you find your trips quite lonely. Too many cities, too many faceless hotel rooms. To have a companion with you must make it much more bearable.'

'Depends on the companion.'

'Deborah understands your work. She's always talking about you with such pride.'

'Does she now?'

'But surely that's only to be expected. How long have you been together now? At least a year, isn't it?'

'Deborah might think so. I'm afraid she's read a great deal more into our working relationship than I ever have.'

'Working relationship? Come on, Paul, she's always telling us about the weekends you've spent together, the places you've been. It's more than just a working relationship.'

'Look, we're friends. She's a lovely girl, and she's certainly been helpful in putting in a good word for me with new work clients.'

'That sounds as if you're using her.'

'If I have, I've done it openly and with her encouragement. She's been keen for me to get on, and I've been grateful for all her contacts. There's no denying she's been brilliant . . .'

'. . . because she loves you.'

'I'm not sure Miss McCann would know the meaning of that word,' smiled Paul wryly.

'She thinks you love her.'

'Then she thinks wrong. I'm fond of her. I'm grateful, of course I am. And I can't deny I've been glad of her company at the odd function or job. But Deborah loves herself too much to need love from anyone else. I've had my uses for her too, I know that. She's needed the right sort of man on her arm, and I've fitted the bill. But love? I could never love a woman who is as single-minded and ambitious as dear Deborah plainly is. She didn't become a director of the agency by being nice to people, believe me. She'd sell her own mother to get what she wants.'

Susie fell silent, suddenly unsure of her ground.

'Besides,' continued Paul, stretching out once again to take her hand in his, 'I've found myself rather preoccupied lately with a certain young woman who has a sweetness and sincerity Deborah could simply never fathom. I may have a flashy job, Susie, but I'm not a flashy person, really I'm not. I'm not good at relationships. I'm dreadful at timekeeping. I'm always exhausted and falling asleep at the wrong times. I forget important occasions. I'm insensitive and boring when my mind is full of work. I'm also hopeless at putting my feelings into words, especially when it really matters that I say it right.'

Hardly daring to breathe, Susie absent-mindedly stroked her thumb across his hand as he went on.

'It wasn't until I got back from our trip to Rome that I began to realise how special it was. You were so easy to talk to. I know you were hurting and sad about losing your father, and perhaps it was your vulnerability that made me want to share my own painful memories too. I found myself opening up to you in a way I've never been able to do before. Something happened for me on that trip that has stayed with me ever since.'

'But I've hardly heard from you. I thought you'd dismissed me as a silly, lovestruck little girl with whom you'd had a one-night stand while you were far away from home.'

'No, it was nothing like that. But it took me a while to recognise that my reluctance to call you was actually because I wanted to see you very much indeed. That's a new experience for me, Susie. I was out of my depth. My feelings about you were complicated and unclear, and I wasn't sure what I hoped would happen. I felt that I had already taken advantage of you at a time when you were bereaved and fragile. I didn't want to make things worse by being unsure of what I was asking. So I kept away. I'm sorry.'

'Paul, I—'

'Look, I can't expect you to think of me as a good bet. From your point of view I've treated you really shabbily. Tell me to push off, if you like. I wouldn't blame you.'

Susie's mind raced with her own thoughts. Would he blame her when she finally plucked up the courage to tell him about the baby she had aborted — *his* baby? With so many misunderstandings and secrets between them, what possible chance could they have of happiness together? And then there was Deborah. Paul might not think of them as a couple, but clearly Deborah did. Susie stared at him at him for several seconds before finally speaking

'Paul, I can't deny that the trip to Rome was unforgettable for me. Just having the responsibility for a major agency shoot for the first time was terrific enough, but the city itself was simply magical. And then there was you. I didn't expect you to be so kind to me, nor to choose my company as often as you did – but it was wonderful. And of course, that last night . . .'

'I shouldn't have done that. I overstepped the mark. It was all too soon.'

'That last night was the most perfect of my whole life. And it took two, Paul. It was what I wanted too.'

'I don't want to hurt you, Susie. I'm on unfamiliar territory here.'

'I'm a big girl, you know. And as you said, I can always tell you to push off.'

'Do you feel like pushing off out of this restaurant right now? I want to kiss you very, very much indeed, and I don't fancy an audience.'

With a slow smile and real certainty in her heart, Susie watched as he hurriedly paid the bill, then led the way through the restaurant door. No sooner were they outside than he swung her round to lean against the wall, holding her gaze for just a moment before kissing her with a passion and urgency which swept every thought and doubt from her mind. She loved him. That was all. And perhaps, just perhaps, he loved her a little too.

The phone was ringing as Gwen turned her key in the door. It was Tricia.

'Hello, stranger! Where have you been?'

'Trish, I've been meaning to call you. There's so much to tell you.'

'Oh? Anything to do with that very attractive art teacher of yours? You didn't tell me he was so dishy.'

'Brian? You've met him?'

'On your doorstep earlier today. In fact, he even came back here for a cup of coffee because we were both so concerned about you. You must admit you've been acting rather strangely lately.'

Gwen sighed. 'Have I?'

'You sure have.'

When her friend didn't reply, Tricia thought for a moment. 'Need a cup of tea?'

'You've no idea how much.'

'Now?'

'What time is it?'

'Half past nine. Is that too late?'

'Of course not. I'll put the kettle on.'

'I'll be there in two minutes.'

'Trish, did you say that Brian went to your house for a coffee today?'

'That's right. Stayed for more than an hour. What a lovely man.'

'Hmm, he is.'

'See you in a while then. Leave the door on the latch.'

As Gwen replaced the receiver, she wondered at her reaction to the news that two of her friends had met and liked each other. That was nice. She was pleased.

Wasn't she?

They talked long into the night. The years fell away as Gwen and Tricia remembered their last years at school – going out in a foursome with Mike and Richard, keeping the secret of Gwen and Richard's friendship from her parents, the awful trauma of her pregnancy, the awkwardness and alienation Gwen felt when she came back to school after having the baby, only a schoolgirl but already a woman.

'What's she like, this Kate?'

'Just beautiful, all I could ever wish for in a daughter. She's smart and lovely, with real warmth and compassion. And she's so like Richard. The way she uses her hands as she talks, that lopsided grin of his, the colour of his eyes — she's him all over again.'

'Be careful, Gwen. However much like him she may be physically, she's not a replacement for the husband you've lost. She's grown up with another mother and father in a world that doesn't include you. When you gave her away, you gave up your rights to have a place in her life.'

'But she came looking for me.'

'I know, love, and that's wonderful. But you must take things at her pace, not your own. You've suffered an enormous loss with the death of Richard, and I worry that you see the void in your life being filled by this new daughter.'

'And grandchild.'

'And her child. But Gwen, Kate's own mum and dad will be that child's grandparents. They deserve that. They've earned it. They are Kate's family now, and you can only be a part of that if they invite you to be.'

Gwen's expression was guarded and defensive. 'I know. I'm not trying to push anything.'

'Aren't you?'

'I'm not stupid, Trish. Emotional and overcome maybe, but never stupid.'

'How many times have you rung Kate since Sunday?'

'Only once or twice.'

'And you've written too?'

'I dug out some photos of Richard. I knew she'd like them.'

'And what about Susie? Does she know?'

'That's where I've been today. I set out this afternoon to go the library, then somehow found myself on the road into London. And I found it again, Trish! The mother and baby home. It's still there — or at least, the building is. It seems to be some kind of office now, but the outside hadn't changed that much. It brought it all back so clearly.'

Trish put her arm round her friend's shoulders.

'You should have told me. I'd have come with you. I don't like the thought of you going through all this on your own.'

'I knew you would react like that, and that's why I haven't been in touch. It was all so new and overwhelming, I simply haven't got my thoughts and feelings in any kind of order yet. I needed to do this alone. After all, I was very much on my own last time. This was a private pilgrimage for me.'

'And Susie? Did you see her?'

'I decided not to ring her, and just call in on the off-chance. She was out.'

'Is she coming home at the weekend?'

'I'm not sure. I hope so. I've left a message for her to call me.'

'And what do you think she'll make of all this?'

'She'll be delighted, of course she will. She was so close to her father. Seeing Kate is like having him in the room again. And Susie's often told me she hated being an only child. I just know they'll love each other.'

Trish shook her head. 'I hope so. I really do hope so.'

'Look, I know my Susie. It will be all right.'

'Perhaps, but just take care, dear Gwen. You're very excited about this, and after the unhappiness of recent months, I only wish better things for you. But nothing is straightforward, just remember that. Tread carefully, and don't expect too much of anyone, including yourself. Give Kate time, and Susie too. Would you like me to be there when you tell her?'

Gwen smiled gratefully. 'No, I'll be fine, but I will yell for help if I need it, promise.'

'Make sure you do.'

Gwen sat back, taking a gulp of her now-cold tea. 'And what about you? How's the new job?'

'Brilliant. David's great to work with, although he's rarely in the office. He's very well organised though, even when he's out on the road, and I really appreciate that. He was right about needing help with all the back-up work. He says that having me around to sort out the orders and make sure everything runs smoothly has allowed him to see twice as many clients each week, and almost doubled his income.'

'Great! I hope he passes on some of that profit to you.'

'He's very fair – and it's great to know I'm earning my own money, living on income I provide myself. I've been the little woman at home for so long. That was one of the things Mike constantly threw at me, that I had an easy life doing nothing more than running the house and bringing up the children while he had the much more important and difficult job of providing the money. He simply couldn't understand how exhausting and challenging it is to organise a home and family. He dismissed me as good for nothing more than housework and shopping, and I resented that every minute of my married life. He undermined my confidence. David's job has helped me find myself again.'

'Do you really think your marriage is over? You and Mike have been together for as long as I can remember. You've had two great kids, and how many grandchildren now? Three? Can you write all that off? He's looking wretched and miserable without you. Perhaps he's learned enough of a lesson to treat you as you'd like now?'

'I need be taken as an individual, a woman who is capable and strong and whose opinion matters. Mike's a chauvinist, always has been. Whatever he says, however wretched he feels now, I don't believe at heart he'll ever change. But I have. I want a job, a home, my own life.'

'Won't that be lonely? I'm on my own, Trish, and I'm the first to admit I'm incredibly lonely at times.'

'Because you and Richard had always loved each other when you lost him, and that love continues beyond death. But whatever I feel for Mike now, it isn't love. I feel pity, especially when he cries, because in all the time we were together I only ever saw him cry once, and that was when England lost some football cup or other. I feel compassion, because I hate to see him hurting. But to be honest, I find myself despising him because he's so weak and pathetic. If that sounds harsh, forgive me, because you know me well enough to know I haven't a harsh bone in my body. I've simply lost respect for Mike, probably because I realise now that in all those years together, he never treated me with any respect at all. I was invisible, a convenient, hardworking, uncomplaining asset. I've finally crawled out from under his shadow and now I've made it I'm not going back.'

'Well, I say the same to you as you did to me. Don't expect too much of yourself or of him. And just remember I'm here if you need me.'

'Thanks, Gwen, that means a lot.' Trish glanced at the clock on the mantelpiece. 'Heavens, is that the time? I'll be falling asleep over my desk tomorrow.'

At the door Trish turned to Gwen, her face thoughtful.

'That Brian? You're not interested in him, are you?'

'Whatever do you mean?'

'Well, you're not an item or anything?'

'Of course not. He's a friend, that's all, who's been absolutely wonderful over the past few weeks.'

'Only I think he's rather nice, so easy to talk to, and I've always had a penchant for men with beards.'

'Oh,' replied Gwen lamely.

'You wouldn't mind, would you, if I asked him for supper one evening? I get the impression he doesn't get round to much cooking for himself.'

'No, I don't think he does.'

'You could come too, of course, if you like.'

'And cramp your style? What sort of a friend would that make me?'

'A lovely one. You don't mind then? That's great.'

The two women hugged warmly, then as Trish disappeared

down the path towards her car Gwen closed the door quietly behind her.

It was good to see Trish getting on her feet. She seemed happy and positive, which was wonderful. And Trish needed friends, and they didn't come much better than Brian Hewitt. He'd be good for her.

Gwen wearily made her way up to bed. Sleep was elusive though, and for what seemed hours she tossed restlessly as she turned over in her mind the events of the past few days. And inexplicably it was Brian Hewitt's face which swam into her mind's eye before she finally sank into dreamless sleep.

Chapter Nine

'Mrs Davis?'

'Yes.'

'John Diggens from the bank. Your husband is expecting me.'

'He is?'

'He should be. We made this appointment two weeks ago.'

'But he's not here. He's gone over to the garden centre that sells his geraniums to sort out what they need next year.'

John Diggens picked up the briefcase which was at his feet. 'Mrs Davis, I think it would be best for us to have this discussion in the house. Your husband was under no illusion about the need for this visit, nor the urgency of his financial situation. If he has chosen to avoid this meeting rather than face hard facts, then I think it only right and proper that you, as joint owner of the farm, should be fully aware of the precarious position in which you now stand.'

Blood drained from her face as Margaret stepped back to allow the bank manager across the threshold.

'Tea?' she managed to offer at last.

'Not necessary. This won't take long.'

For a moment, Margaret thought of leading him through to the kitchen where they could sit at the table which had always been the place for discussions of every kind. Then a glance at the seriousness of his expression had her scuttling to open the parlour door where they took a seat at either end of the neat, cushioned settee.

'Are you aware of your financial standing at present?'

'Not exact details, but I know it's bad.'

'Your current account stands at ten thousand pounds over your agreed overdraft level. That means that you are in debt to the bank to the tune of more than eighteen thousand pounds.'

Margaret's mouth went dry as she reached out to take the bank statement from his hand.

'That is in addition, of course, to the loan already allocated for the farm three years ago. Do you know that payments have not been made on that loan for the past four months?'

'They haven't? I don't understand why.'

'And that insurance premiums were cancelled by your husband some weeks ago?'

'Mr Diggens, I don't need to tell you how hard it is for farmers at the moment. We can't be the only ones in this situation. You know as well as I do that things will get better. It's just a matter of allowing time and leeway for the situation to improve.'

'You've had time, Mrs Davis, and frankly the bank is of the opinion that the general challenges facing farmers are unlikely to change significantly in the foreseeable future.'

'What are you saying?'

'That unless constructive moves are put into place to repay this debt immediately, then the bank must call in the charge they have over the property. To put it simply, sort this out or you'll lose the farm.'

Margaret felt tears prick at the back of her eyes. She would not cry. In front of this officious, unfeeling young man, she would not break down. Taking a deep breath, she straightened her back, staring steadily at him as she spoke.

'Mr Diggens, this farm has been in my family for two

centuries – that's seven generations of farmers, all proud, hardworking, honest men just like my husband. There's more than money at stake here, although I don't expect you to understand that. We *will* deal with this situation. We *will* keep our home. And if you would kindly explain all the facts and figures to me clearly, right now, my husband and I will guarantee that we will come up with practical plans to improve this situation in exactly a month's time. We will take whatever action is necessary to sort out not only our liability to your bank, but our own future. Agreed?'

John Diggens eyed her thoughtfully. 'Can you think of any reason at all for the bank to allow you another month, when we've been waiting for a viable response from Mr Davis for more than half a year now?'

'I suggest you were talking to the wrong member of the Davis family, Mr Diggens. My husband is a wonderful farmer. When he's allowed to produce to capacity and sell at the price his work deserves, he is more than capable of supporting his farm and family. But he would be the first to admit that he has no business brain. And I would remind you, Mr Diggens, that this farm has always been my home, bequeathed to me when my father died. If there are financial decisions to be made that affect my property, then I am the person you should be dealing with. Give me just four weeks to work my way through this, and I promise you that one way or another I will come up with constructive plans to put things right. You have my word on it.'

The bank manager hesitated for a moment, eyeing up the determined expression of the woman in front of him. Finally, he nodded his head. 'All right, that's agreed, Mrs Davis, but I stress that this is absolutely your last chance. Your husband has been burying his head in the sand about all this. You mustn't make the same mistake, or the farm will no longer be yours.'

'I understand completely, so let's get down to business. I want you to explain the problem to me in minute detail, so that there can be no possible misunderstanding. Let's go through to the kitchen so that we can spread the papers out over the table. Now do you want that cup of tea?'

During the lunch break at school that day, Kate slipped Gwen's letter out of her bag so that she could have another look at the photograph of Richard. He had been a striking man with his tall, athletic frame, fair hair which matched her own colouring, and those blue eyes. Even she could see the likeness between them. It was almost uncanny, and certainly unnerving, that this man she had never known should have set the mould for her own build, looks and even her personality.

Would they have got along? Would there have been that special bond between them that other fathers and daughters so often mentioned? She thought for a moment about the way in which she had always felt different from Margaret and Roger. Of course she couldn't possibly have had a more loving mother and father, but in many ways she had felt apart from them, introspective, studious and artistic where they had been outdoor people, sturdy, strong and practical. Would she have felt more immediate empathy if her birth parents had brought her up? Did her love of music come from Richard? Her flair for languages too?

Once again, she became aware of irrational anger rising like bile within her. What might she have become with parents like that to encourage and guide her? They had loved each other so much that they had stayed together for the rest of their lives, yet never cared enough to fight for her right to be with them. And they had gone on to have another daughter: this Susie, who was plainly cherished and beloved as their only child. But she herself wasn't. They had two daughters. One they adored. One they abandoned.

Kate pulled out the photograph of Susie with her father taken at the twenty-fifth anniversary party just months before.

She didn't look like the kind of person Kate would normally come across. She was fashionably dressed with wild spiky auburn hair, and a collection of stud earrings decorating her ears. She was looking up at her father with undisguised affection as he hugged her close. A sudden pain stabbed in Kate's gut. Jealousy? Surely not, when her own upbringing had been full of comfort, warmth and unquestioning love. She had lacked for nothing.

Except her real parents. They hadn't wanted her.

And with that thought Kate buried her head in her hands, hating herself, hating them.

Because it was such a beautiful day, they chatted as they ambled through the local park. As soon as Gwen left the library earlier that afternoon she'd made her way over to Brian's studio, hesitating before she knocked on the glass panel to watch him as he worked with complete concentration on the oil painting which filled his easel. Pleasure and surprise crossed his face in equal proportions as he looked up to see her. Within minutes, he had grabbed his jacket and they had strolled companionably into the fresh air.

Once she started talking, she couldn't stop. Out it all poured about meeting Kate, and the events of the past which had not only brought about the birth of her first daughter but then torn mother and child apart. She spoke of the raw hurt within her because of that loss, a pain which surprisingly she had never been able to share with the husband she adored. For him, Kate's birth belonged to another life, another couple. Once he and Gwen had re-met and were planning their future together, he was adamant that the whole unhappy episode should be best dealt with by ignoring it. The subject was buried. Their baby was never mentioned. The problem disappeared — so he thought. For Gwen a lifetime of private agony followed, sharp stabs which gripped her when she least expected it. If Richard himself remembered, he never mentioned it. If he cared, it never showed. Their firstborn child was no longer a part of their lives. Gone. Forgotten.

Brian and Gwen sank on to a park bench where she sobbed with a mixture of sadness at her loss, and relief at being able to speak openly at last. She cried for Kate. She cried for Richard. Most of all, she cried for herself, huge tears of release from years of longing which had drained her emotions and dulled her senses. And when she could cry no more, she leaned against his shoulder until her racking sobs subsided and her body was still. He was wise enough to say nothing, holding her quietly.

Margaret had always been a good sleeper, but in the days following Mr Diggens's visit sleep eluded her. Figures swam before her eyes as she tussled with the awful and unchangeable fact that they owed too much, earned too little, and had nothing left on which to draw. Her confidence in the face of the bank manager's inflexibility was fading fast as she acknowledged what her dear husband, even without a head for figures, had known instinctively all along. They were broke, with little collateral, few prospects and no obvious ideas worth investigating.

At first Roger had denied all knowledge of the bank manager's appointment. It took firm words then gentle encouragement to draw out the truth from her proud, independent husband. He was beaten and deeply ashamed, crushed with the disgrace of knowing that he was no longer able to provide for his family. Margaret saw little point in recrimination, and hurt pride was neither productive nor helpful. They simply had to look at their current situation, search their meagre assets for possible salvation, and make the best possible plan for the future.

'Perhaps,' said Margaret, as the two of them sat together at the kitchen table with papers strewn around them, 'we should talk to Kate and Martin about this.'

Roger stiffened, and Margaret reached out to cover her husband's rough, calloused hand. 'They're part of our family, love. The farm will be Kate's one day, so we're all in this together.'

'Whatever will she think of me, getting into a mess like this? Just when she's finding out about her birth parents and how wonderful they apparently are, what's she going to think about her old dad now?'

'She'll love you for it. She'll always love you. She's a bright girl, our Kate. She may be able to think of something we can't.'

Roger said nothing, but his sigh of resignation sounded more like a snort of frustration. Instead he rose from his chair and made his way over to the Aga where he filled up his half-empty cup from the huge enamel teapot which in their house was never empty and always hot. They sat in silence for a while, she poring over the papers yet again as if hoping to find a new clue hidden somewhere within them, he deep in his own thoughts.

'I forgot to tell you,' he said at last, taking a gulp from his cup before he continued, '"Marvellous Maggie" went down well.'

She looked at him blankly.

'That new strain of perennial geranium. I told you about it.'

'Those cuttings in the greenhouse, do you mean?'

'You remember last year? The lacy chaps with dark purple petals tinged with golden edges. "Marvellous Maggie", I called them.'

She smiled. 'I never knew about the name. And the garden centre liked them?'

'More than that. That manager, Gordon, got quite excited. Well, it's the colour, you see. People have come up with variations on the magenta colour for years, but this is the first time that anyone has managed to breed in an orange tinge around the edge of the deep magenta petals. To get any shade of yellow in the flowers has proved tricky – and I've done it! Then, of course, the leaves are a bit special too, with their silvery sheen.'

'That's wonderful! You and your green fingers! Plants just love you.'

'When they said it couldn't be done, it was like a red rag to a bull. I just had to prove them wrong.'

'And? How many do they want?'

'All I've got at the moment. They'll sell the lot. They're putting it in their catalogue, so he says.'

'But that's just marvellous! Will they pay? Proper rates, I mean, not just the pocket money they've been giving you up till now?'

'We haven't discussed money in detail.'

'Right! Then we'll go and see Gordon as soon as we can, and I'll come with you.'

'There's no need. Geraniums are my hobby. I'd just like to cover my costs. I'm not in it to make money.'

'You are now! When it comes to horticulture, Roger Davis, you are a very clever man, so don't sell yourself short. You leave the talking to me. You grow the blooming flowers – and I'll sell 'em!'

The phone was ringing as she reached her desk. Susie grabbed for it, smiling at the sound of Paul's deep, familiar voice.

'It's raining, so we've abandoned the shoot for a few minutes, just long enough for me to ring you.'

'That's Manchester for you, always raining! How's it going? Is that model behaving herself?'

'Like a lamb. I think I scare her!'

'Well, you know how frightening you are . . .'

'Me? Scare you, do I?'

'The only thing that scares me is that I'll wake up and find this is all a dream.'

'No chance.'

Susie felt a warm glow spread through her body and colour her cheeks.

'You're not back until late this weekend, are you?' she said at last. 'Only I forgot to tell you I've arranged to go up and see Mum on Sunday. She's hot under the collar about something, sounded quite desperate really, but she won't say much on the phone.'

'Well, it's not that long since your dad's death, is it? It's hardly surprising that her moods are up and down.'

'This sounds different. I can't put my finger on it. She's not depressed, in fact, quite the opposite. It's as if she's really excited about something one minute, then tearful the next.'

'Then I'm glad you're going to see her this weekend. In fact, that might work out quite well.'

'Why?'

'Because Deborah rang me last night. I've been summoned.'

Susie felt a chill drain through her.

'Look, love, I've got to see her some time. Debs and I have been friends for ages. I owe her the truth.'

'She won't like it.'

'That's up to her. If she's the friend she says she is, she'll be glad for me.'

'Don't hold your breath.'

'I'll just explain how I feel about you. She's got to understand.'

'Oh heck . . .'

'Susie, don't worry. You don't know Debs. She's got a good heart, really she has.'

'She never stops breathing down my neck these days. She hates me. I can feel it.'

'Of course she doesn't hate you.'

'You know what they say about a woman scorned.'

'She can say and do what she likes. I will never feel about

her as I do for you. That's a fact. Now stop worrying, and leave Deborah to me.'

'Where are you meeting her?'

'She's coming round to the flat.'

'Sounds cosy.'

'Not at all. She won't be staying long. Sue, don't worry. It's all right.'

'OK.'

'Hey, it's stopped raining. Must go. I'll ring later.'

'Paul?'

''Bye!'

The phone went dead.

'I love you,' she whispered as the dialling tone buzzed in her ear.

Until now Kate had always found it easy to talk to Margaret. There was so much she wanted to share with the woman who had been her mother for as long as she could remember, but she hesitated, knowing that Margaret's natural generosity would make her hide her true feelings about the impact on them all of the new birth family Kate had just discovered. The two women pottered around the kitchen together as they prepared the evening meal that Saturday, avoiding delicate areas of discussion.

'Are you all right?' asked Margaret at last, busying herself with basting the lamb joint so that she need not look her daughter in the eye.

'Well, you know, up and down.'

'How are you feeling? That grandchild of mine behaving?'

They were on safer territory here.

'Going to be a footballer, no doubt about it. And he's a night owl, always on the move when I'm trying to sleep!'

'Not long to go now. The last two months always fly by, so they tell me.'

'Can't come soon enough for me. I feel like a barrage balloon already.'

'When do you leave your job at school?'

'Two weeks' time. It will be easier for me when I haven't got to do that trip in and out of the city twice a day.'

'Oh, I nearly forgot. I've something for you.'

Wiping her hands on her apron as she walked out of the kitchen, Margaret returned a minute later with a package loosely covered in white tissue paper. 'Here, this is for you. Or at least, for that footballer grandson of mine.'

Kate gave a small gasp as she drew back the soft layers to reveal an exquisitely crocheted shawl.

'Mum, it's beautiful, even lovelier than it looked on the pattern. It must have taken you ages.'

'Well, I'm a bit out of practice with the crochet needle. I enjoyed it though. Just don't have another baby without giving me at least two years' notice!'

Kate drew Margaret to her, hugging her tightly, voice muffled as she buried her head against the well-upholstered shoulder. 'Thanks, Mum. You're the very best. You do know that?'

Margaret didn't reply, but her eyes were suspiciously shiny as she drew back to pull a hankie out of her cardigan sleeve and blow her nose.

'You look tired. Are you all right?'

When Margaret didn't answer, Kate stared in surprise as the older woman's face creased in distress.

'This is my fault, isn't it? I've done this.'

'No, love, it's not that.'

'Look, no one will ever take your place. I shouldn't have started this business with the Moretons, when it would obviously bring nothing but trouble. I can stop it right now. I don't need to be in touch with her ...'

Margaret stopped Kate mid-flow. 'Really, it's not that. I understand your need to know. Please don't think for one minute I blame you. I don't.'

'Then what is it? Are you unwell?'

Margaret sighed, straightening an imaginary crease on the front of her apron.

'The bank manager was here.'

'Why?'

'Well, I've known Dad has been worried about money for months, but I never realised how bad it's become.'

'What do you mean? Bad?'

'They're talking about taking the farm from us if we don't come up with a proper business plan in a month's time.'

Kate's hand shot to her mouth, her eyes wide. 'Oh, Mum.'

'Your dad's a good man but he just didn't tell me, and the bank manager said he's ignored letters and avoided phone calls for months.'

'Can Martin and I help? If we went to see the bank ...'

'That's kind of you, love, but what can you do?'

'But this house has been in the family for generations. They can't simply take it away from you.'

'They will, and they have every right, because a couple of years back we agreed that the house should be used as a guarantee for our overdraft.'

'And they now want you to pay that overdraft back?'

Margaret nodded. 'Ten thousand pounds, plus another eight beyond that. And there's a loan too, do you remember, for the milking-shed roof?'

'Well, Martin and I have got a bit put by. It's only a couple of thousand, but if it will help?'

'No, dear, you have a baby on the way. You'll need that for your own family. Dad and I must sort this out on our own. We'll come up with something, don't you worry.'

'Mum, we're in this together. Martin's full of good ideas. Let's discuss it properly over lunch.'

'No, don't. Your dad wouldn't like that.'

'But that's the problem. He *must* face facts. He can't do this alone, and you plainly can't take any more.'

'I appreciate your concern, really I do, but we need to do this our own way.'

'All right, but you must promise to keep me in the picture. Don't shut me out, Mum, please.'

'Never.' Margaret's voice was husky. 'How could I ever do that? You're my own dear daughter, aren't you?'

Long into the night, Martin and Kate lay awake in bed talking over the problems facing Margaret and Roger.

'The worst thing is that they won't discuss it with us openly,' said Martin. 'This would be so much easier if we could all just get round a table and come up with a few ideas.'

'Dad would hate that. He'd be mortified to think we all felt he'd failed in some way.'

'Then all farmers have failed. It's the conditions facing farmers generally at the moment that are to blame, not Roger himself.'

'Try telling him that.'

'I can't help thinking,' said Martin thoughtfully, 'that the answer lies not in what they've always made money from in the past, but in some sort of new product for the future.'

'Like what?'

'That's the problem. I'm not sure.'

They both fell silent, each deep in their own thoughts, before Martin spoke again.

'What about his geraniums? He was buzzing this morning about that new variety he's developed. "Marvellous Maggie", isn't that what it's called?'

'He's always dabbled with those plants of his. They're just a hobby. He might make a bob or two out of them through the local garden centre and the occasional craft show, that's all.'

'But people buy them?'

'They seem to. I get the impression he can sell as many as he grows.'

Conversation faltered again, and Kate could feel her eyes dropping with tiredness when suddenly Martin sat up in bed.

'Do you know, I might just have thought of something!'

Kate was too sleepy to reply until she realised he was tossing back the covers and heading across the room.

'Where's that good camera of yours? In the wardrobe? Can I borrow it?'

'Of course, but why?'

'If my idea works, I'll tell you in a day or two. Go back to sleep, love. That footballer baby of ours will be kicking you in the ribs soon enough.'

'Brian, how nice that you're in!'

Brian smiled as he recognised Tricia's voice when he picked up the phone. 'Well, hello yourself! It's good to hear from you.'

'I know you and Gwen have talked. How do you feel she is?'

'Delicate. Confused. Relieved. A jumble of different emotions.'

'I remember so well that dreadful time years ago when she first got pregnant. It was really frightening for her, and Richard too.'

'I never knew her husband, of course . . .'

'Lovely man.'

'. . . but I just can't understand why, in all those years together, he didn't recognise her need to deal with the loss of their child. What that must have done to her, to keep that hurt bottled up inside for so long!'

'Richard was one of those people who was always organised. On time, never in a panic, a place for everything and everything in its place.'

'And the place for that painful memory was firmly in the past? Poor Gwen, how hard that must have been.'

'She was always able to talk to me about their baby, of course.'

'Well, thank goodness she could. She certainly needed a friend like you.'

There was a slight pause while Tricia smiled to herself, then gently brought up the subject which had prompted her to ring.

'Do you know, I'm so glad our paths crossed, even if the circumstances weren't ideal. Now that we've got to know each other, I wondered if you might like to pop round for supper one evening? Nothing formal, of course, just a plate of pasta and a bottle of wine.'

'What a great idea! That will do Gwen good.'

There was a barely noticeable pause before Tricia answered. 'Well, of course, it goes without saying that Gwen's invited too.'

'Have you an evening in mind?'

'You decide. I know how busy you are with art classes. I'd love to see your work sometime, by the way. Do you allow visitors in your studio?'

'Not usually. I'm always very defensive about my work until I'm absolutely sure it's finished to my satisfaction.'

'You know, I have an empty wall or two around the house now Mike has gone. Perhaps I could commission something?'

'Well, I'm not one to turn work away. Pop round to the studio any time. Give me a ring first, just to make sure I'm there.'

'Tell you what, you invite me. When you ring back to let me know what evening you'd like to come to supper, you can invite me over to look at your work then. You know my number?'

'You did give it to me, but I'm not sure I could lay my hands on it.'

'It's 642457. I'll look forward to hearing from you then. Goodbye.'

As she replaced the receiver, Tricia found herself thinking of

Richard who could always lay his hand on things that mattered. Pity Brian wasn't a bit more like him. Still, she could work on that!

Susie knew there was something different about her mother the moment she arrived at the house. Gwen was nervous, moving things unnecessarily around the kitchen, asking the same question twice, and finally dropping a teacup.

'Right, that's it,' said Susie, 'what's up? I've never seen you so on edge.'

'Well,' began Gwen, obviously choosing her words carefully, 'I've got something I must tell you.'

'Snap! So have I,' smiled Susie, thinking of Paul and how glad her mother would be to know that he was back in her life. 'Who's going first?'

'Me, because we should have had this conversation years ago.' Susie's smile slipped as she noticed for the first time the strain in her mother's expression.

'For heaven's sake, Mum, you're spooking me.'

Gwen cleared her throat and looked down at her fidgeting hands.

'It's about your sister.'

Susie's mouth fell open.

'The baby that I gave birth to when I was sixteen and still at school.'

'You . . . you had a baby?'

'I named her Elizabeth, and not a day has gone by from that day to this when I've not thought of her. Well, last week she came back. She's called Kate now. She's beautiful and clever, and I just know you're going to love her.'

'For heaven's sake! You expect me to love someone I don't know, a woman from nowhere you now tell me is my sister. What about Dad? Did he know about this? Would he have married you if he had?'

Gwen smiled. 'Oh yes, he knew all about Elizabeth. He was her father just as much as he was yours.'

Seeing Susie was speechless with shock, Gwen reached out to touch her as she went on. 'I'm sorry, Sue, I know this is a lot for you to take in. I should have told you before, I realise that now — but I'd given up on the thought that I would ever hear from her again. And when she wrote to Madge—'

'What do you mean, Dad was her father just as much as he was mine?'

'When Dad and I first dated, we were both at school – and I got pregnant. It's not something I'm proud of. Our parents were all furious. My mother practically disowned me. They split us up and I was sent away to a mother and baby home in London.'

'I don't believe you. If my dad knew you were pregnant, he would have stood by you. He never ran away from anything, ever!'

'Susie, he was just a schoolkid. We both were. We thought we were so grown up and independent, but we weren't. In the end our parents were in control of our lives, mine blaming him for getting me pregnant, his blaming me for being no better than I should be. We were frightened and ashamed, and we did as we were told. We had no choice.'

'And this baby? What happened to it?'

'It was arranged that Elizabeth should be adopted, but she was with me for three whole weeks before the handover was arranged. For three weeks I fed and dressed her, walked the corridors rocking her to sleep. I grew to love her, Susie. She was my own flesh and blood, my daughter, as dear to me as you are. And I had to give her away.'

If Susie noticed the tears which now flowed freely down her mother's cheek, she showed nothing, sitting stiffly, her hands so tightly clasped that her knuckles glowed white through the taut skin.

'Dad didn't abandon you. He married you.'

'That was much later. We had both been to university by then, so we were out of touch for more than four years.'

'And you had another daughter, a replacement for the one you really wanted. How very convenient.'

'Susie, we loved you. You always meant the world to us.'

'But not a day went by when you didn't think of her, that's what you said. This Elizabeth, or Kate, whoever she is – it was her you were thinking of all the time.'

'How could I forget, Susie? How could I?'

'Why didn't you search for her? Dad would have wanted that.'

'He didn't, Sue. He felt that she belonged to another life, a past which was better left where it belonged. Because of the complications of that first pregnancy, having you was very difficult for me. We were told that to have more children was out of the question. Your dad was over the moon once you came along, because for him our family was complete. But I always regretted that you were an only child. A brother or sister would have been nice.'

'But I did have a sister, didn't I? And you never told me. In all these years, you never thought to mention it.'

'Susie, I . . .'

'Why didn't you have an abortion?'

'I just couldn't. I never even considered it as a possibility.'

'Why not, Mum? You made me get rid of my baby, didn't you? When I was in exactly the same position as you were, you came with me to the hospital to make sure I had an abortion. Why didn't you suggest adoption for my baby? Perhaps because you knew what havoc it would cause when my child tried to force its way back into our lives.'

'I didn't make you do anything you didn't choose for yourself.'

'But you brought your own baggage, didn't you! And I never knew! You never told me that when it came to us facing the same problem, there was one right for you, and another for me!'

'You don't understand.'

But Gwen was talking to herself. The whole house shook as Susie slammed the front door shut behind her.

Chapter Ten

Tricia had not long been in when she heard the bell ring. Expecting no one in particular, she opened the door with curiosity. Scarcely visible behind the huge bunch of flowers which greeted her was Mike.

'Peace offering.'

'Are we are war?'

'I'm not sure. I hope not. I just thought these might help to warm the atmosphere a bit.'

She took them without comment, burying her nose in the sweet-smelling blooms.

'Can I come in?'

'Best not.'

'Trish, I'm not here to argue, quite the opposite, in fact. I know we're finished. The sooner we put this marriage behind us the better as far as I'm concerned. But we don't need to fight all the time, do we? We could save a lot of money on solicitors if we agree amicably on how to settle the details. What do you think?'

Tricia eyed him with suspicion for a second or two, then stood back to allow him through the door, noting how much better he looked than the last time she'd seen him. He was smartly dressed, the gaunt expression gone from his eyes.

Nevertheless, she didn't offer tea or a drink. He wouldn't be staying long.

'You'll sell this house, I presume.' Mike was strolling around the room reacquainting himself with pictures and photographs as he spoke.

'I haven't decided yet. I might.'

'Probably best. I know you'll want the division of our assets to be fair for both of us, and I can't buy a new place if I'm not able to take any of the profit out of this one.'

She made no reply.

'Anyway,' he went on, 'you won't want to stay here with all its memories of our dreadful marriage, will you? You'll want a new place for your new life. I know that's how I feel.'

Still no reply.

'I never got round to finishing that conservatory, did I? Do you think it should be completed before we put the house on the market?'

She turned to straighten the cushions before she sat down carefully on the settee.

'I haven't given it any thought.'

'Well, I know one of the things which annoyed you most about me was that I never finished jobs I started around the house. I'm not surprised that drove you mad. Just to show there are no hard feelings, I'll finish it for you now, if you like. It's up to you, but the offer's there.'

'I don't think that's a good idea, Mike. Besides, the state of the conservatory is hardly going to matter much to someone who falls in love with the house. It's a nice place.'

His expression softened as he sat down beside her.

'It's lovely, a credit to you. You always kept a good home. That's another thing I've realised since all this happened.'

'What do you want, Mike?'

'Nothing. Well, a lot probably, but it's all too late for both of us. I just don't want us to argue any more. I was wrong, Trish. I made a mess of our marriage, and I'm prepared to pay the price and move on. I know you have. How is the new boyfriend, by the way?'

She stiffened. 'Who I see and what I do is no longer any of your business.'

'That's right. I only ask as a friend. We still are friends, aren't we?'

She hesitated before answering, eyeing him with distrust.

'Aren't we, Trish? I'm tired of fighting. I understand your reasons for wanting a divorce, and wish you well. I love you. I always will. I don't want us to be married any longer, just as you don't, but it must be possible for us to organise our individual futures without continually swiping each other.'

She nodded slowly. 'That would certainly be an improvement.'

'Agreed. So as your friend, I'd like to finish that conservatory for you. Call it a gesture of apology. I owe it to you, Trish. Let me pay my dues. Please?'

'How long would it take?'

He shrugged. 'A week, perhaps two. If I can get one of the lads from the garage to come and give me a hand, it shouldn't take long. I won't get in your way, honestly. I'll do it when you're not here, if you prefer.'

She stood up. 'I'll think about it. Can I let you know?'

'Fine. Well, I must be off.' He looked at his watch. 'My, is that the time? I'm picking up a friend at eight.'

He walked briskly towards the front door, turning almost as an afterthought to peck her cheek.

''Bye then.'

And as he disappeared down the garden path without a backward glance, Trish was struck by the odd thought that, in all their meetings since the separation, it had been she who walked away. This time it was Mike who called a halt – and was calling the tune.

*   *   *

'Coo-ee! Anyone home?'

Margaret was upstairs changing the bed linen when she heard Gillian's voice hailing her from the kitchen door.

'I'll be right down! Help yourself to a cuppa. The kettle's hot!'

Minutes later, Margaret appeared in the kitchen, her arms laden with sheets and pillowcases which she stuffed straight into the washing machine. Gillian was already settled at the table drinking from a steaming cup as she glanced through the morning paper.

'It's a fine day.'

'Isn't it?' Margaret eyed Gillian's well-worn sweatshirt and jodhpurs. 'Have you just come from the stable block?'

'Why on earth did I decide to keep horses? On mornings like this, I forget.'

'Because you love them. You always have.'

Gillian smiled. 'I'd have to, wouldn't I? In fact, I'm amazed at how well the whole venture is going. I picked up another six new pupils for riding lessons on just one day last week. And I've got more requests than I know what to do with from people who need stabling for their own ponies and horses. I never expected it to take off like this.'

'That's great news. Hard work for you though.'

'True, but there are always a few keen teenagers around who enjoy spending their time at stables. I have to pay them, mind, but my handful of regulars are a good bunch. I know I can rely on them, and that's all that matters.'

'Did I see another pony arriving yesterday morning? How many does that make now?'

'Enough for me to ask if you and Roger would mind if I opened up more stables on the other side of the block. I know he and Simon talked about that possibility when we were first planning this, but I didn't expect to need extra space quite so soon.'

'We'd be delighted to see that building put to good use after all these years. Mind you ...'

Gillian looked up as Margaret stopped mid-sentence.

'What?'

The older woman pulled out a kitchen chair and sat down heavily. 'I was just thinking that it's probably not a good idea to plan anything too far in advance at the moment.'

'Why ever not?'

Margaret's expression clouded as she considered how much she should say.

'Strictly between ourselves?'

'Of course. I'm not interested in gossip. Never have been.'

'Well, I'm not sure how long we're going to be able to hold on to the farm.'

Gillian gasped. 'Don't tell me Roger's planning to retire?'

'Not exactly.'

'What then?'

Margaret sighed. 'The bank are making noises. They say that if we don't come up with a viable plan for paying back our loan and overdraft, they'll call in their charge over the farm.'

'No! They can't do that! This is your home.'

'They can, and I'm afraid they will if we don't find the right answers.'

'What does Roger say?'

'He's out of his depth, Gillian. He's a wonderful farmer, but he's got no head for business. No, I've got to sort this out for him. I need to come up with a new way of making money from this place, and I've got to do it fast.'

'And suppose you don't? What happens then?'

'They take over the farm and house, I suppose, then sell off whatever they can. If we're lucky, there may be enough money left in the pot for us to pick up another little place.

If not . . .' She smiled. 'If not, then I suppose we'll be looking to rent some of that stable block back from you.'

'Isn't there part of you that might welcome a change, though? Farming has never been an easy job, and you and Roger work such long hours. Wouldn't you like to put your feet up a bit?'

Margaret traced the line of the wood grain in the table with her finger as she spoke. 'It's not so much the land I'd miss, but this house. I've lived here all my life, just like my parents and grandparents before me. I was even born in that front room upstairs. We belong together, this house and me. It would break my heart to move.'

'And Roger? How's he taking this?'

'He thinks he's failed, and that's hard for a proud man to bear.'

'So when does the bank need an answer?'

'Four weeks – even less than that now.'

'Then we've got to get cracking!'

'We?'

Slipping her arm around the older woman's shoulder, Gillian smiled. 'That's right, we. What are friends for?'

Gwen soon got the message that Susie was not going to answer her calls. Her mobile rang for just a few seconds before being instantly switched off as if Susie registered it was Gwen calling, and even at work someone else always seemed to pick up her extension. This estrangement with her daughter was not only deeply painful, but had come as something of a shock. In her own happiness at rediscovering Kate, Gwen had assumed that everyone else would be delighted too. It hadn't occurred to her that Susie would reject out of hand the idea of finding an unknown sister. Of course, Susie's reaction to being told that her own mother had given birth to a baby when she was young and unmarried would inevitably be coloured by her own recent abortion. Why hadn't Gwen thought of that? How insensitive she had been! Insensitive and selfish in her own happiness.

She became aware of a shadow at her shoulder. Brian looked down at the sketchpad she was supposed to be filling, and saw only a page of melancholy doodles. Kneeling down so that their conversation could not be overhead by the rest of the class, his voice was soothing as he spoke.

'Are you all right?'

'Probably not.'

'Need a chat?'

'A stiff talking-to, that's what I need.'

'About everything in general, or something in particular?'

'Very particular. I've been a fool, and I've hurt someone I love very much.'

'Hmm. Sounds serious. Might need two cups of tea and a cream cake to fix that.'

'You're laughing at me.'

'Never – but if anyone even needed a bit of tender loving care, it's you today. Chin up, dear Gwen, and we'll grab a quiet corner in the café straight after the class. Right?'

She smiled at him gratefully. 'Right.'

Since the conversation with her mother, Susie's mind had been racing. She couldn't even put her finger on exactly what she felt. Anger? Perhaps, but a sense of betrayal too. All these years, she'd thought she'd known her parents, especially her dad to whom she had felt so close. Yet it had all been a lie.

From the moment she stormed out of the house, tears were never far away. She didn't even know why she was crying, and she hated herself for her weakness and confusion. If only Paul weren't away again! How she longed to talk to him – except, how could she? How could she explain the complexity of her feelings when so far she hadn't even managed to find the right moment to tell him about their baby? And when he realised what she'd done, how could he possibly go on loving her? She had made a decision to abort his child without taking his feelings or rights into account. All his declarations at the moment, the caring gestures and affectionate words, would count for nothing when he knew the truth about her. She was heartless and uncaring. She was hurting her mother, but couldn't help herself. She hated what she was discovering about her father. And in the end, Paul would despise her.

Reluctant to leave the sanctuary of the ladies' room on their office floor, she bent down to splash cold water over her burning face. Straightening up again, she was dabbing her cheeks with rough paper towels when she became aware of another face staring back at her in the mirror. Deborah.

'You're quite a plain little thing really, aren't you? Look at yourself! Do you think for one moment that a man like Paul could really be interested in a nobody like you?'

'Go away, Deborah. I'm not in the mood for this.'

'He's only after one thing, you know, and when he gets bored he'll come right over to my place and we'll have a good laugh about it as usual. You know, in all the time we've been together, I've watched with some amusement as he picks up one little groupie after another. Well, so many of them throw themselves at him, and he's only human after all.'

'I've got work to do. Excuse me.'

But Deborah was in full flow, blocking Susie's exit.

'Seems a shame to wreck your career over something as trivial as this – but if you continue with this affair, I will not have you working here.'

Susie's eyes flashed, cold and disbelieving. 'Are you saying that if Paul chooses my company rather than yours, you'll make sure I lose my job?'

'Sounds good to me.'

'And it sounds to me as if you're scared to fight for him fair and square. Paul doesn't *belong* to you, or anyone else for that matter. You can't just demand love and loyalty. You have to earn it. If you try putting the spoke in for me, you'll not only lose him, but his friendship too.'

Deborah snorted dismissively. 'My, you have a very inflated idea of your own importance, don't you? And believe me, it won't be me who loses you your job. I'll leave you to do that all by yourself. One false move, one piece of work that's not up to scratch, and the first thing you'll hear will be the sound of the door banging behind you!'

'Then, as I said at the very start of this extremely enlightening conversation, I have work to do. Excuse me.' And with all the dignity she could muster, Susie hoped her hands didn't shake too noticeably as she pushed Deborah aside and left the room.

'Look, she's written to me again.' Kate handed Gwen's letter across to Martin. He read it quickly, then sat back to look closely at her.

'Nice letter.'

'Very nice.'

'What do you think? Are you going to see her?'

'Should I?'

'Do you want to?'

'Yes, probably I do.'

'Where? Here?'

'Is that a good idea? I mean, I'd like her to see me on home territory. I want to her know what I am, what I've become. I'd like her to look at the books on my shelves, admire my photos, taste my cooking . . .'

'That will be an experience for her.'

'More than that, I want her to see what's she's missed, how well I've done in spite of her giving me away.'

'That's understandable.'

'Is it?'

'Of course.'

'What about Mum and Dad though? Do you think they'll mind?'

'Do they have to know?'

'I wouldn't like to keep anything from them.'

'But they have got rather a lot on their own plates at the moment.'

'And the last thing I'd want is to give them something else to worry about.'

'I think they understand that having found your birth mother, the chances are that the two of you will want to meet again. That's only natural. You have a great deal of catching up to do.'

'I just don't want to undermine them in any way. I owe them so much. Nothing will ever alter my love for them, but ...'

'You're drawn to Gwen, I can see that.'

'I feel so disloyal.'

'You didn't create this situation, my love. You've simply lived it out. That's all you're doing now.'

'So should I write back then? Suggest she comes here?'

'Fine. When?'

'A couple of weeks' time, I think, when I've left work to have the baby.'

'Do you want me to be here?'

Kate smiled. 'Always – but I'm happy to see her on my own.'

'Are you sure? You were very emotional after the last visit. That could happen again.'

'It might, but I'll be more prepared this time. I've done a lot of thinking since I met her. All the questions I'd like to ask, so much I need to know.'

'I bet she has too.'

She grinned at him. 'What a wise and lovely fella you are.'

'Perfect in every way! That's why you married me.'

'It wasn't for your body and intellect then?'

'Well, yes, and you made the mistake of thinking I had a bob or two.'

'That's right, I remember now.'

And she leaned forward to plant a long, adoring kiss on his willing lips.

Once a fortnight, Madge went for Sunday tea with Celia and Graham. Graham had always been Madge's favourite nephew, although she had never been able to decide exactly what it was she liked about him. Now in his late forties, with a tall portly frame and almost hairless head, he looked back on a life which had been comfortably unchallenging. His work as a senior financial assistant with the local council was hardly taxing. His social life revolved around the local pub, the golf club and his monthly Rotary meetings. He was popular and easy-going with no daunting ambitions or heartfelt regrets. Except perhaps for one. Given another chance, he would not have married Celia.

Mind you, as far as Madge could recall, there hadn't exactly been a queue of ladies interested in Graham even in his heyday. He had always been the lanky, unassuming, unimpressive young man at the back of the crowd, especially as his hair had started to recede by the time he was eighteen, and his style of spectacles had never been much of a fashion accessory even in the late sixties.

Madge's fondness for Graham dated back to his very youngest days, when it became clear early on that his brother Richard was not only quicker and smarter, but worst of all, older. Try as hard as he might, Graham never quite managed to crawl out from under his big brother's shadow. Where Richard shone, Graham was never more than almost average. Richard was good at sport. Graham had two left feet. For Richard, studying was a way of life. Graham was sick of school by the time he was thirteen. Richard was an academic with university potential.

Graham was simply aiming for a local job with regular wages and a quiet life.

Madge's sister, Elsie, despaired of her younger son. With her upwardly mobile husband doing well as an accountant, and her own ambitions of grandeur, Graham was a permanent disappointment. That's probably why Madge liked him so much. She knew how it felt never quite to come up to the expectations of those around her. And just like him, she didn't care one bit.

She had never forgotten the first time Graham brought Celia along to meet her. With one look at the tight-lipped, plain-looking girl, clutching Graham's hand possessively as she stood beside him with her neat suit and carefully curled hair, Madge had taken an instant dislike to her. Graham, however, was hooked. A couple of years after leaving school Celia marched him up the aisle, and had been marching all over him ever since.

The table, as usual, was well spread. If Celia had one saving grace, it was that she could cook. That Sunday she had excelled herself by not only coming up with sausage rolls, which were a particular favourite for Madge, but chocolate cup cakes too. And even if she did use that awful marge stuff instead of real butter in the sandwiches, the ham was nice and the jam homemade. That alone made the visit worthwhile.

'So she just came out with it,' Graham was saying, disregarding Celia's disapproving look as he spoke with his mouth full. 'Quite a shock really. You know, I don't remember any of that. I had no idea that Gwen had got herself pregnant while she was still at school. In fact, I didn't even know that she and Richard knew each other then. I always thought they got together after university, about a year before they married. I must say, I'm surprised she had it in her! She was so prim and proper, don't you remember?'

'You never were a very good judge of character, but I was always suspicious of her.' Celia was still smarting to discover she was the last to hear of the recent revelations in Gwen's life.

'And your mother disapproved of her, that was quite clear! I knew there was something about her. I *knew!*'

Madge sniffed, leaning forward to extricate a particularly large sandwich from the bottom of the pile. 'You seem to forget that Gwen didn't "get herself" pregnant. Richard played his part, and if there's any blame, then he must take his fair share.'

'Richard was always naïve. Never had his head out of his books long enough to recognise a scheming girl when he met one.'

'Oh, I don't know,' said Graham evenly, 'he never really got involved with anyone but Gwen. And they had a very happy marriage, anyone could see that.'

One glance at the challenging look on Madge's face decided Celia against replying. Instead she sat back in her seat with the martyred, knowing expression of someone who had a lot to say but had chosen to keep her thoughts to herself, for the time being at least. Minutes ticked by as the trio continued to eat in silence.

'I wonder why she's come back now, that daughter of hers?' Graham finally mused aloud.

'Probably heard that Richard had died, and wondered if there might be money in it for her.' Celia couldn't resist the jibe.

'Hardly,' Madge retorted. 'She didn't know who her parents were, let alone that her father had recently died, until I told her.'

'And she's pregnant, did you say?' Celia spoke the word as if to be pregnant was a deliberate act of vandalism. 'She's after something then. Gwen ought to take great care. She's extremely vulnerable now, anyone can see that. We must make sure that she doesn't give this young woman anything until we're all absolutely sure of her credentials and motives.'

Graham and Madge exchanged an exasperated glance

which ended in a shared smile of disbelief. Unfortunately, Celia saw them.

'Right!' she said, standing up abruptly. 'I've got a committee meeting tonight, so if you want a lift home, Madge, you'd better get your jacket on quick. And I will just say one last word on Gwen's situation. No good will come of it. Don't turn round and tell me I didn't warn you.'

The moment she'd disappeared through the door, Madge and Graham grinned at each other, the understanding smile of long-time fellow-sufferers and confidantes.

'I've got a box of liqueurs for you in my briefcase. I shouldn't, I know ...'

'... but you did anyway!'

Left on her own for a few moments, Madge took one last lingering look at the tea table. Then she opened her large shopping bag, scooping two sausage rolls and three cup cakes inside until a flash of movement made her look up sharply.

'You forgot something,' said Graham, winking at her as he pushed the plate of ham sandwiches in her direction.

'So I did,' agreed Madge. 'They'll go down a treat with a nice chocolate liqueur.'

Kate left it until she and Margaret were washing up after their evening meal before she raised the subject of Gwen's imminent visit.

'I'm not sure how you feel about her coming, but it seemed only fair to tell you.'

'Look, love,' said Margaret, her attention apparently totally focused on the soapy water in front of her. 'Of course you'd like her to see your home. That's only natural.'

'And you don't mind?'

Her mother didn't answer immediately as she fished about in the bottom of the bowl for a wayward spoon. 'Mind?' she replied at last, 'Why should I mind?'

'It's just that I'd hate you to feel ...'

'... threatened? Replaced?'

'Exactly! That's just what I'm worried about.'

Margaret sighed, turning to wipe her hands on a nearby teatowel. 'Honestly, Kate, I don't know how I feel about anything these days. So much has happened. This business with the farm. The way your dad looks absolutely exhausted all the time. And you finding your real mother.'

'My *birth* mother. You're my real mum. You always will be.'

'Your birth mother then. Of course I've thought about it. I'd be lying if I didn't admit to several sleepless nights over it. But I can never do more than my best. I've always tried to be the right sort of mum to you, and in the future, all I ever wish for you is the best. If that comes from someone else rather than me ...'

'She could never replace you. That's never been my intention. I just need to know about her and my father. I need to know why they didn't fight for me. I want to hear about their life together, the life I might have had.'

'If you hadn't come to live with Dad and me.'

Kate nodded. 'If I hadn't been lucky enough to be chosen by the two of you. You've given me so much, and I can never truly express the love and gratitude I feel for you.'

'But you still need to know.'

'Yes, I do. I'm sorry if that hurts you.'

'Kate, I understand. Just don't expect too much from me, not at the moment. Now where have those men got to? That tea's ready to pour.'

Out in the greenhouse, Martin and Roger had finished their rounds of the geranium cuttings.

'Well?' asked Martin, 'What do you think? Is it worth a try?'

Roger's grunt was non-committal.

'Seems an odd way to go about things to me. Do you really think people will respond?'

'Absolutely certain. Look, Dad, you've got a darned good range of product here. And that new strain, "Marvellous Maggie", is a real winner. I've done my homework over the past couple of days, and the professional opinion is that you've come up with something quite revolutionary in that little hybrid. All we need is a bit of publicity for it in the trade press, and we're in business. Now, are you quite sure you can meet the demand?'

Roger looked thoughtful for a moment, glancing along the neat rows of pots in the greenhouse and in the beds beyond.

'Depends, I suppose. I never bothered to produce extra but it's no trouble to pot up a lot more. If there's likely to be a big demand, I'll get cracking on new cuttings.'

'Lots of them!'

'Do you really think they'll sell?'

'No doubt at all. We've just got to let people know what you have here, and how they can buy direct from you. If you concentrate on coming up with as many plants as you possibly can, I'll handle the ordering and packaging side of the operation. Frankly, I think I'll enjoy that challenge.'

'And the photos you took? What exactly are you going to do with them? I've got no time for computers.'

'I'm still putting the whole thing together, but if you come over next weekend I'll have plenty to show you.'

'Newfangled ideas,' muttered Roger, pushing back his cap to scratch the front of his head. 'Can't get my mind round them.'

'You leave the technology to me, I'll leave the horticulture to you. But believe me, the world is your marketplace when you've got a unique product to sell – and I reckon the internet is your gateway not just to new customers, but very possibly to saving your farm too.'

✳   ✳   ✳

Susie's heart skipped a beat as she pulled back the curtain to peer down on his car when she heard it draw up. Paul glanced up to wave at her as he locked the car door. Seconds later she was down the stairs and in his arms.

It was some time later as they lay curled up together on the battered settee in Susie's rented flat that Deborah's name was first mentioned.

'Did you see her?'

'Yes.'

'And?'

'And I told her that I was seeing you.'

'That much I gathered. I had a very interesting chat with her in the ladies' loo — a meeting of minds, I think you could say. She gave me a piece of her mind, and I made up mine to scarper before I said something I'd regret.'

He groaned. 'She was a bit upset.'

'So was I when she told me you'd joke about this later. That you always had groupies running after you, and you'd go back to her in the end when you'd finished with me.'

He laughed. 'Oh, is that what she said!'

'Paul, it's not funny, not if there's even one ounce of truth in it. Are you and she an item? Do you always go running back to her? I couldn't bear to be just a diversion from the relationship you really want. I'd feel humiliated and pathetic to care so much and matter so little.'

He stopped her with a kiss. 'Don't let her rile you. She's offended rather than hurt. She's not used to losing out.'

'But you still do care for her?'

'She's been good to me. I don't want to hurt her, because she doesn't deserve that.'

'She said she'd make sure I lose my job if I carry on seeing you.'

'Can she do that?'

'I don't know. Probably. I wouldn't like to find out.'

'Shall I have a word with her?'

'No, I'll deal with it. I just need to be sure that I'm not deluding myself about all this.'

'You think I'm not sincere?'

'I think you've played the field for years, and that there are dozens of glamorous and beautiful girls you could choose. Why me? Why are you here with ordinary, inexperienced me?'

As he tilted her face up towards his, she was surprised to glimpse a raw vulnerability in his eyes. 'Because glamour is skin-deep and true beauty is revealed in what you are, rather than the way you look. What I see in you is an honesty and warmth that I want to cherish and protect. I know the death of your father hurt you, and I don't want to be the one to add to that hurt.'

'You might not feel that way when I tell you what's happened. You know I went to see my mum over the weekend?'

'And she'd been rather mysterious about whatever it was she wanted to discuss with you?'

'Right. Well, it turned out to be quite a revelation – and I don't think I handled myself very well at all.'

'Oh dear,' said Paul. 'This sounds serious. Tell me more.'

'Come in! Supper's almost ready!'

Brian handed Tricia a bottle of Chablis as he made his way through from the hallway to join her in the kitchen.

'Smells great. What's cooking?'

'Oh, just an old chicken thing I threw together. Nothing fancy, but I hope you'll like it.'

'I like anything I don't have to cook myself. If it's not simple, I don't waste time trying to make it. I'm a dab hand at omelettes though and my pasta's not bad, so I'm told.'

Tricia smiled as she handed him a brimming wine glass. 'Well, it's nice to feed a man who enjoys his food.'

'I'll drink to that!' They beamed at each other over the rims of their glasses.

'I suppose,' continued Brian, breaking their gaze, 'that I don't bother to cook because it hardly seems worth the effort for one person.'

'I know just what you mean. Since Mike left, I often forget to eat. That's why tonight is such a treat. Meals are so much better if they're shared, don't you think?'

'Absolutely. And who are we sharing with tonight? Is Gwen here yet?'

'Gwen's not coming.'

'But I thought . . .'

'I was going to ask her, of course, until she mentioned that she had a prior engagement this evening. A family thing, I think.'

'Oh.'

'And I haven't been organised enough to ask anyone else, so I'm afraid it's just you and me. I hope you don't mind.'

Brian caught a whiff of her musky scent as she leaned towards him to remove a minuscule piece of fluff from the shoulder of his jacket.

'Of course not,' he said, swallowing hard. 'I don't mind at all.'

'Your poor mum.' Paul spoke softly, his face resting against Susie's auburn spikes. 'She was really young to go through all that on her own, in a place she didn't know far from home.

'Sixteen, nearly seventeen.'

'Times have changed though, haven't they? Don't you think our generation is much more worldly-wise than hers?'

'Maybe.'

'And can you imagine how dreadful it must have been to

give her child away? To grow to love the baby she'd given birth to, and then have to hand her over to total strangers? You could never do that, so just think what a nightmare it must have been for her.'

Susie didn't answer.

'And then the families keeping your parents apart! Thank goodness they found each other again, otherwise they'd never have had you – and that's the worst thought of all.'

Susie felt a coldness drain through her body.

'What I can't understand,' he went on, 'is why you've reacted so badly to this? Surely to discover you have a sister is wonderful news. It must have made your mum so happy to have found the daughter she thought was lost forever. What a pity your father wasn't able to meet her too.'

At that, Susie got up abruptly. 'I'm sorry, Paul, I feel a bit under the weather. Would you mind if I called it a night?'

Puzzled, he unfolded his long legs and got up painfully from the sagging settee. Lightly placing his hands on her shoulders, he peered at her closely.

'What's up? Have I said something wrong?'

'Of course not. I'm just bushed.'

'Come on, Susie, spit it out.'

This is the moment, she thought. This is when I should tell him. The reason I'm so confused about my own mum having a baby that I never knew about is because I nearly had a baby too. *Your* baby – and I killed it. What do you think of me now?

But she said nothing, her eyes tightly closed to shut out the hurt in his expression. Finally he stepped back with a sigh.

'I don't know what's bugging you. I'm just sad that you can't talk to me about it. I thought we trusted one another, that it's because we can be open with each other that this thing between us is so special.'

'I'm sorry. Paul, I'm sorry . . .'

He reached out to wipe away a shiny tear which was making its slow way down her cheek.

'Look, don't cry. I'll call you tomorrow. All right?'

She nodded dumbly, feeling the brush of his lips on her hair as he turned to leave.

Chapter Eleven

Even though Kate had been watching the clock for at least half an hour as she waited for Gwen to arrive, there was an awkwardness between the two women when they finally stood on either side of the doorstep staring each other. Should they hug? Shake hands? Instead, Kate stepped back to allow Gwen through into the hall, where they exchanged stilted pleasantries about the weather and the dreadful state of the M25.

'I've made lunch.'

'You shouldn't have.'

'Nothing special, just cold chicken and salad.'

'That's kind, thank you.'

'Would you like a glass of wine?'

'I'm driving ...'

'Oh, of course. Coffee then – or tea?'

'Either will be fine.'

'Tea might be best, I think. Or perhaps coffee would be better at this time in the morning?'

Suddenly Kate laughed. 'This is awful, being polite to each other. We're such strangers, I don't even know if you take sugar!'

'No, I don't. And I'm relieved you're nervous too. I was petrified as I drove here.'

'Me too. I've been pacing the floor all morning.'

They stood at opposite ends of the small kitchen, grinning at each other. Finally it was Gwen who spoke.

'Shall we just throw a couple of teabags in cups, forget about lunch, and settle down somewhere comfortable so that I can show you the photographs I've brought with me?'

Half an hour later, conversation flowed easily between them as they sat surrounded by albums, cuttings and faded photographs spanning thirty years.

Kate stared hard at the good-looking, fair-haired young man who stood at Gwen's side in one of the older pictures.

'Even I can see the likeness between us. It's uncanny. What a strange thought that I actually am the spitting image of a father I've never met.'

'You'd have liked him, Kate. And he'd have loved you.'

'What sort of man was he? Was there more similarity between us than just our looks?'

Gwen reached out to cover her daughter's hand, her expression softening as she thought of Richard. 'He was very handsome — well, I always thought so — but he never seemed to be aware of his good looks. I suppose his natural shyness meant that he was happy with his own company, or for just the two of us to be together. We were very happy, Kate. Twenty-five years of marriage, and I don't remember one cross word between us.'

'He was an accountant?'

'By profession, yes, but I often wondered why he chose to work with figures when he had such a natural flair for languages.'

'And now I'm head teacher in a language department. Was it just French that he spoke?'

'That was what he was best at, but he could make a passable stab at German too. And he never learned Italian, but always managed to make himself understood.'

'I majored in French for my degree.'

'He'd have been so proud of you. Envious too, I think.

It seemed to me that he often wished he'd taken languages instead of economics at university.'

'And music? Did he enjoy that too?' asked Kate picking up another larger photo. 'He's playing the piano here.'

'He was very gifted. Could play anything without knowing a note of music.'

Kate smiled, nodding over in the direction of the upright which stood in a sunny corner of the room.

'Do you know I had lessons for years? Went right up to Grade Eight, playing all the classical pieces. But I was never happier than when I just sat down at the piano and played by ear. Mum used to despair of me because I'd be playing music I'd heard on the radio and popular songs rather than practising the Chopin and scales I was supposed to be tackling.'

Gwen's face was suddenly serious. 'I worry about your mother. How has she taken this?'

Kate shifted uncomfortably. 'Well, she's got a lot on her mind at the moment. Things are very hard for farmers, as you probably know.'

'How old is your father? Will he be thinking about retirement soon?'

'Farming is a difficult job to retire from, especially when your work place is also your home.'

'But who could take over the farm if they retired? Do you have any brothers?'

'No, they never had children of their own. That's why my adoption meant so much to them.'

'Were you lonely then, living on a farm without other youngsters around?'

'I had lots of friends in the village, and the farm was always busy. The funny thing was that I never needed a great deal of company. I'd spend hours up in my room reading books, or penning some great tome or another.'

Gwen smiled. 'I remember feeling just like that when I was a kid, only I would be painting rather than writing.'

'Do you still paint?'

'Not for years, but I've just taken it up again. I hadn't thought about it at all until Richard died, and then I realised what a release it was to be able to pour out my thoughts and impressions on to canvas.'

'I envy you that. I've always wished I could draw.'

'Susie can. She has a wonderfully visual eye, not just for art, but any kind of fashion or design. You should see her cartoons. She captures expressions perfectly.'

'Does she live near you?'

'No, she shares a flat in London with a girl who seems to stay with her boyfriend most of the time.'

'So she works?'

'In a job she loves with an advertising agency. She has a few accounts of her own to look after now. It's the perfect job for her. She even went off to Rome for a photographic shoot a couple of months ago.'

'Would we get on, do you think?'

'I hope so. To look at, you couldn't be more different, but then Sue's more like me, legs too short, body too long, hair definitely too red. A free spirit, that's our Susie.'

'Were you always close?'

'Richard used to say that we were too alike to get along well. My daughter and I have always had an abrasive relationship, with high emotions and hot tempers to go with our fiery colouring.'

'Her father's death must have hit her hard.'

'It did. She adored him. We both did.'

'Were you able to grieve together, help each other through?'

'That was the one bright spot during that whole dreadful business. I couldn't have got through it without her presence and support. I think we both saw each other in a new light. I finally recognised her as the lovely mature young woman she's become and she acknowledged that I'm just a fallible human being trying hard and failing often. Kids are inclined to think of parents as super-beings who are simply there to make things happen for them. She had always been such a demanding child, and it infuriated me when Richard gave in to her all the time. She used to play us off against each other to get what she wanted. I could see it so clearly, even if he couldn't.'

'And sharing the shock of her father's death helped her to view you as a friend, a person rather than just a parent. Do you still see a lot of each other?'

A shadow fell across Gwen's face.

'Does she know about me?' Kate's voice was gently insistent.

'I tried to tell her.'

'And she didn't want to hear?'

'She was so angry. I didn't expect that from her. I thought she'd be as delighted as I was to have found you.'

'But is her reaction so unreasonable? She's been an only child for years, and then in losing her father she finds a new depth of understanding with her mother only to find that she may have to share you from now on.'

'But my feelings for her will never change. Surely she must know that!'

'I only know what an emotional tussle I've been through since I found you. It was hard to discover that the mother and father who created me went on to spend a lifetime together – without me, but with another daughter. I'm not surprised Susie should find it equally unsettling that that same couple, her parents, had a past they never chose to share with her.'

'Or even with each other.'

Why was he like that? Why would my father never let you speak of me?'

'Because you were part of such a painful time that was long gone. You didn't belong in the life he made for us.'

'But should I belong now? Would it be better – for Susie, for my parents – if having met and talked, we just let this go?

In our compulsion to fill in the years we've lost, are we hurting the people we love most?'

Gwen studied her daughter's face for a moment. 'Honestly, I don't know if there is a right and wrong to this. I just feel that after all these years of longing, now that I've found you, I couldn't bear to lose you again.'

'Then I must meet Susie. Do you think that would help?'

'It might, but Sue can be stubborn, and she said some very bitter things. I've not managed to speak to her since she stormed out, although I've written and rung several times.'

'Perhaps I should write to her too? What do you think?'

Gwen hesitated. 'Well, you can try. I'm not sure how she'll react.'

'Can you give me her address?'

As Gwen dug into her bag for a pen and piece of paper it crossed her mind that if ever she hoped to mend the rift between herself and Susie, then handing on her address to Kate might be the worst possible idea.

Paul did try and speak to Susie the next day as he promised he would, but her answerphone was always on and her mobile switched off. He felt sure she would ring him. She didn't.

Because of that, he wasn't able to warn Susie that he would be calling in to the agency the following morning. His meeting with the directors about the major magazine campaign they were working on was the culmination of weeks of work. All the top brass were there, including, of course, the manager of the account, Deborah McCann.

Paul had to admit she looked stunning as she walked out to reception to meet him. Her golden hair fell in soft folds on to her shoulders, framing her flawlessly made-up face. Enormous blue eyes greeted him as he arrived, never leaving his face as they teased and flirted one minute, teetering dangerously near to tears the next.

The only time she wasn't at his side was when she was directly in his eyeline whispering provocatively to some other man, her fingers brushing sleeves and shoulders as she spoke. When the group settled themselves at the huge boardroom table, she took the seat beside him. And as the meeting progressed, her expression didn't falter once, while out of sight under the table her thigh rubbed sensuously against his.

It was when they came out of the boardroom, as a few of them went to look at the display of designs around Deborah's desk, that Paul finally spotted Susie. From the other end of the open-plan office, her eyes burned into his, taking in the sight of Deborah holding court in the midst of the group of executives, with Paul standing closest of all. Suddenly Deborah said something witty that raised a round of laughter, and giggling, she placed a casually possessive hand on Paul's arm. As he turned to smile back at her, Deborah looked not at him, but straight down the office directly at Susie. This display was for her benefit, Susie knew that. But did Paul have to look so happy about it? Was it really necessary for him to stand close enough for Deborah to keep her arm on his, marking out her territory for all to see?

The discussion continued for some time before Paul was finally able to extricate himself not only from the conversation but from Deborah's clutches. Then one look in the direction of Susie's desk told him the damage had already been done. She was nowhere to be seen.

'What's he doing here?' whispered Gwen as soon as she and Tricia were out of earshot. 'I thought you were never going to let him in the house again!'

Tricia closed the kitchen door behind them so that there was no danger of being overheard by Mike and his colleague, who were busily assembling a complex wooden construction in the garden. 'I thought I told you, he offered to finish the conservatory so that we can put the house on the market.'

'Is that really necessary?'

'He said it would put up the value, and I must admit it did look a bit of a mess as it was.'

Gwen's eyes narrowed suspiciously. 'Any strings attached? It's not like Mike to do something for nothing.'

'That's the worst part of it. I don't know. He was absolutely charming when he offered. He even apologised for being difficult to live with all these years.'

'Perhaps I've known Mike too long. Perhaps it's just that I've seen him sell too many shady cars in the past. Either way, I don't trust him. Do you?'

Tricia sighed. 'Probably not – but then I thought, why not? He's paying for all the materials. He's even got one of the lads from the garage to help in his spare time. What have I got to lose?'

'Your privacy? It means he's back in your home again. Have you got anything here you'd rather he didn't see?'

'Well, yes, I have tucked a few bits and pieces out of sight. The trouble is that he knows both me and this house so well, he'd probably know where I'm likely to hide things better than I would.'

'Does he ask questions?'

'Not really. Mostly he just makes sweeping statements about what I must be feeling, and what I should be doing. He's really pushing for the house sale now, because he's obviously got plans of his own, and needs money to buy a new place. I think he might even have a girlfriend.'

'Really? Who?'

'No idea. In fact, he's not said anything concrete. It's just that he's constantly looking at his watch because he's meeting someone, and mustn't be late. And he never seems to be off his mobile. All very mysterious.'

'How do you feel about that? Would you want to know if there's another woman in his life?'

Tricia thought for a moment. 'No. Yes. I suppose it depends who it is.'

'You're not jealous?'

'I'm not sure if jealous is the right word. After all the years when he's had illicit affairs, the thought that someone other than me should be legitimately on his arm for all to see is ...'

'Humiliating?'

'Unsettling. That's how I feel. As if my feathers are ruffled, but I can't do a thing about it.'

Gwen stared closely at her old friend. 'Because we've known each other forever, and because I care about you very much, can I say something?'

Tricia nodded.

'I think you still love him. That's why your feathers are ruffled, because you can't bear the thought of someone openly sharing his life, his home, his bed.'

'But I'd had enough, Gwen. I know I don't want to go back to what we had before.'

'Do you have to? Don't you think you've both changed through this? Could there be enough love left for you to talk about a new basis for your relationship? A partnership where there are a few more rules on both sides?'

'I'm not sure. I don't feel I've given myself enough chance to stand alone, find out what I would like from life. To go back to Mike now would be admitting defeat.'

'Then you must accept that he is already moving on, and that because of the sort of man he is, he couldn't live without a woman alongside him.'

'Then he must accept I'm moving on too. I started going out with Mike when I was fourteen years old. I've never been with any other man, and right now I regret that. I want to find out what love could be like with someone else, a man who is sensitive and caring.'

Gwen grinned. 'They're a bit thin on the ground.'

'Are they? I'm not so sure. Take my boss, David Abbott, for example. He adores his wife, Wendy. He's romantic and affectionate, can't do enough for her, even though they've been married for more than twenty years. Marriage doesn't have to be the drudge it became for Mike and me. And if there's a chance of discovering that kind of happiness with someone else before my teeth fall out and gravity takes its toll on my interesting bits, then I'm going to find it.'

'Good for you! Where are you going to start looking?'

'Well,' said Tricia as a secret smile crept across her face, 'I think I might have hit the bull's-eye straight away.'

'You have?'

'And it's all thanks to you really. Brian! He called round for supper the other evening, and I haven't come down from cloud nine ever since.'

Gwen felt herself going very still. No reaction. No coherent thoughts at all. Not that Tricia seemed to notice.

'He is just so *gorgeous*, those lovely hazel eyes, and you know how I've always had a soft spot for men with beards. And he's really interesting. Well, he's an artist, isn't he, so he's in touch with his sensitive side. And he's available! I mean, it's tragic that he's lost his wife, but I do think he's over that now, and ready to consider sharing his life again.'

'And you think that could be with you?'

Tricia's grin was conspiratorial. 'Well, it's early days yet, of course, but I think he likes me. He certainly likes my cooking, and it was nearly midnight before he left so he must have been enjoying my company, mustn't he? Well, what do you think? You're his friend, and he obviously rates your opinion because he talks about you so much. Do you think I have a chance with him? I could make him happy, I'm sure I could.'

'Are you planning to see each other again?'

'Nothing definite, but it was sort of understood between us. If he doesn't ring me in a day or two, I'll call in and see him. He's a bit disorganised, as I'm sure you know. Well, artists are supposed to be free spirits, so I like that about him. He can just leave all the organising to me. I expect it will be quite a relief really.'

'Perhaps.'

'Anyway, enough of me. What about you? You went to see Kate the other day? How did that go? I want to hear every little detail!'

And as Gwen started to speak, she was aware of a dull ache inside her. Probably, she thought, I'm going down with a cold.

Susie couldn't sleep. She hadn't slept for nights, ever since that awful evening with Paul when his reaction to her mother's news had been such a shock to her. He simply hadn't responded as she thought he would She had expected, if not complete understanding, then at least sympathy and support. It was unbelievable enough that her mother had wanted her to be pleased at the devastating news. It was simply incomprehensible that Paul should react the same way.

She thumped the pillow angrily, throwing herself over to lie on her other side. How could two people, who both professed to love her, get her so wrong?

She heard the local church clock strike three, then the quarter-hour, and when it sounded again fifteen minutes later she threw back the covers and lay spread-eagled on the bed, hot and exhausted, her eyes pricking with tears.

The image of her father's face swam into her mind, but her thoughts about him were no longer totally loving. In the end, she had known him so little. In fact she hadn't known her parents at all, because they'd not allowed her to. It was unbelievable to think they had had another child together, and even though that child was living somewhere in the world without them, made no effort to get in touch. What if all had not been well with her? Suppose she had been mistreated, or ill? How could they bear not to know? More than that, how could they bear not to talk about it, to each other, to her? Didn't she have a right to be included? She had always thought she was an only child, holding an unique and cherished place in her parents' lives. Now her beloved father had died, just like the image she held of him. She had looked up to him, trusted his judgement, respected his principles. Now she knew he had had none. He had feet of clay and she could never trust anything again.

And her mother! After everything they'd been through during those dreadful months following Dad's death! Susie buried her face in the pillow as she thought of the new closeness she had been starting to discover with Gwen. In spite of all their difficult, volatile years together, finally her mother and she were able to talk to each other with a degree of warmth, drawing strength to cope with their shared grief. Then she thought of the baby, her baby – the child Gwen had persuaded her to have aborted. Her mother had gone through that with her, been at her bedside for the abortion, held her through the tangle of emotions that followed.

And all the time Gwen had known that when she was faced with the same decision, she didn't choose abortion. She chose to give her baby life. She decided to give her child away to people she didn't even know. Then for years she said nothing, closing her mind until this Kate came back to haunt them. And what hurt Susie most of all was the depth of joy and love she glimpsed in her mum as she spoke of this long-lost daughter. How come this Kate, who had played no part in her mother's life, could claim Gwen's love in a way that Susie had never been able to herself?

And what of her own baby? What of that little scrap she had aborted, not daring to think who that child might have become? She could have loved that baby. Oh, it wasn't the right time for her to be pregnant, and without a father, what chance would they have had – but reluctantly Susie allowed herself to acknowledge the fiercely protective maternal feeling which kept creeping up on her, the regret, guilt, the overwhelming longing for this tiny being who might have meant so much to her.

What sort of woman kills her own child? Only a woman unworthy of love. Of course Paul could not love her. Who could?

The vision of Paul and Deborah together at the office stabbed its painful way into her thoughts. Deborah had been right. He had simply been playing with her, and having tired of the game he'd gone back where he belonged.

She didn't know she'd fallen asleep until she woke with a start with the alarm clock buzzing insistently in her ear. Groping across to silence it, she blinked at the pencils of cool light streaming round the edge of the curtains. With a groan, she pulled the duvet up over her head. It was Monday morning. A work day. She had to get going.

Half an hour later, after a shower and two cups of strong black coffee, she finally spotted the letter on the doormat. It was a thick, pale blue envelope addressed to her in a neat, sophisticated hand which she didn't immediately recognise. It wasn't until she spotted the Colchester postmark that she felt a chill of unease.

'Just the person I was hoping to see!'

Margaret was walking back from the milking shed when she heard Gillian call her. Smiling in return, she led the way over to the back door and into the kitchen, where the two women warmed up in front of the ever-comforting Aga.

Gillian was excited about something, Margaret could see, but it wasn't until they were both sitting with steaming cups in front of them that, with a flourish, she produced a brown folder which she slapped purposefully down on the kitchen table.

'I think I might have come up with something!'

'You have?'

'Something that could be very good news for you as well as me.'

'For me?'

'How do you feel about going into business?'

Margaret smiled ruefully. 'Look, I've been a home bird all my life. I would have thought our current situation might tell you a lot about the kind of business sense I have. All I've ever known is the farm and this house.'

'Precisely!' Gillian's expression was triumphant. 'Just take a look at this.'

Out of the folder she drew a shiny magazine on the cover of which Margaret was dimly aware of a picture of a horse. But Gillian turned to the back, opening at a page of tightly listed adverts. 'Look at that lot! Look at how popular they are. It's such a fast-growing market, that's absolutely certain. I've done my sums, and I'm convinced that if I'm going to expand, this is the way forward. And I can't possibly do it without your help. You have both the facilities and the ability that I need – *we* need! From now on, we're going to be more than friends. We'll be partners!'

At work that day, Susie read and re-read Kate's letter. It barely covered one sheet of paper, but she suspected that much thought and time had gone into its writing because the words were carefully chosen to say enough, but not too much. No assumptions were made. No gushing sentiment. No demands. It was formal, wary – and kind.

In spite of herself, Susie found herself warming to the writer. It had taken courage to get in touch – more courage, and definitely more interest, than she had herself. For the first time she wondered what it must have been like to grow up in a family where one day you learned your parents were not really your own. And how would you feel to know that somewhere in the world there was another woman who had held you first, perhaps even loved you, a mother who had given birth then handed you away? Of course you'd be curious. Of course you'd have a longing to know who that woman was, a wish to find her in the hope that she could fill in the jigsaw puzzle of your own life?

But it was the photo that fascinated Susie most, bringing out in her intensely conflicting emotions. There was curiosity as she stared at the image of a smiling young woman with straight blonde hair and a ready smile, her shoulders encircled by the arm of a tall, serious-looking man with glasses. But her overriding reaction was one of shock. As Susie gazed at the picture of Kate, what stared back at her was her own father's face.

Once they discovered that they both had Tuesday afternoon free from the library and art classes, the thought that they should take their sketchpads and find a quiet corner of countryside was irresistible. When Brian's car drew up outside Gwen's gate she ran out immediately, her bag bulging not only with art materials, but with sandwiches and a bottle of wine which she thought might help the afternoon pass more pleasantly.

He knew the perfect spot, and they settled down under a shady tree in companionable silence. Here he was no longer her teacher. He didn't comment on or criticise her work. They worked for themselves, each lost in the challenge of their own chosen picture. Gwen was dimly aware of her shoulders dropping an inch as her taut muscles relaxed and her mind emptied of the jumble of thoughts and worries that cluttered it. Bees hummed. Far-off sounds of town life faded. Leaves rustled in the soft breeze that occasionally lifted her paper as well as her spirits. Hours passed and tension eased, seeping away through her pencil as she created line and contour of hill, branch and farmhouse.

Just as she felt she could add no more to the sketch that had absorbed her for quite a while, he sat back stiffly and stretched.

'Lunch?' she smiled.

He glanced at his watch. 'More like tea. No wonder I'm peckish.'

They delved into the sandwiches and bread sticks, drinking warm white wine from plastic cups. At last, her voice carefully casual, Gwen asked, 'I hear you had a meal with Tricia?'

'Yes, the other night.'

'She's such a lovely person.'

'Oh yes!'

'And a great cook. She always has been ever since I've known her, and that's a good few years. Richard always loved going over to their house because he knew the dinner would be wonderful.'

He laughed. 'How hurtful. Was he trying to say something about your cooking then?'

'Actually he enjoyed cooking much more than I ever did. He would often push me out of the kitchen and take over – and of course, I never minded a bit.'

'Did you and Richard spend a lot of time with Tricia and her husband?'

'We were friends from school days. There's been a lot of water under the bridge of friendship we shared.'

'You must miss that now, with Richard gone and Mike ...'

'Mike almost gone? I still can't quite believe they're breaking up. But then he's led Trish a merry dance for years with all his dalliances and affairs. I don't blame her for deciding she's had enough, although judging from my own experience of how hard it is to adapt to single life after years of marriage, I just hope she understands how lonely that can be. I'm inclined to think that however cold a marriage is, it's a great deal chillier outside, only you don't realise that until it's too late, do you?'

Brian smiled to himself. 'Oh, I think she's adapting to single life very well. In fact, I don't think she plans to remain single for long.'

For some reason, Gwen couldn't think of a suitable answer, so reached out for her cup of wine instead.

'How are things with you?' he asked quietly. 'Heard from Susie yet?'

A bleakness crept over her. 'No. I've rung and even written, but she's not made contact at all. I just don't know what to do next.'

'Go and see her?'

'Finding her in would be the problem. And if she were busy or just pushed me away, I'm not sure I could cope.'

'Would you like me to come with you? I could stay in the car, be around if you need me.'

Her smile was grateful, but didn't quite reach her eyes. 'I've handled this all wrong, Brian. I've hurt Susie with my thoughtlessness. I wish she could understand that for years I've carried around the burden of my guilt at giving my baby away, and the relief of knowing that she's happy and healthy fills me with such unbelievable joy.'

'Especially after the shock of losing Richard.'

'How I wish he'd met her. I wish he could have seen how much she's like him. He would have been so proud.'

'Perhaps if he had been alive, Susie would have taken his lead and found it easier to accept a new sister. At the moment, she's frightened and confused because the foundation of her life has shifted and changed. Her father has gone, and now she finds out that neither of her parents was quite what she thought they were.'

'In many ways, she's still very young.'

'In fact, she's a modern young woman who is judging you on a decision you made more than thirty years ago when you were barely more than a child. The choice you made then to give Kate away was the only loving, practical solution available to you. You did what you thought was best – for both you and your baby. And perhaps if Susie gives Kate a chance, she may come to think that through getting to know and love her sister, the best is yet to come for her too.'

Wordlessly, she leaned against him as his arm went round her shoulders, his woollen jersey smelling faintly of paint and white spirit as it brushed roughly against her cheek. Sinking closer towards the solid comfort of his chest, she could feel his heart beating, his breath brushing a warmth across her faded red hair. For minutes they rested against each other, until she felt him pull back his head to look down at her. For one heart-stopping moment she thought he might kiss her. Gently he traced the line of her cheek with his thumb, their eyes locked, lips close, so close. Then just as she realised how very much she wanted to stretch up until her mouth met his, she pulled back appalled at herself.

With Richard, the true love of her life, only a few months in his grave, whatever was she thinking of? What sort of woman could care so little, be that disloyal?

Ashamed, she looked at Brian expecting to see perhaps disappointment, even derision. Hardly daring to breathe, she saw he was smiling.

'It's all right, Gwen, it's all right.'

She stared at him, sensing the care in him, the reassurance of his arms around her. And because she knew it really was all right, she exhaled a slow sigh of relief as she relaxed against him.

Paul's letter arrived at her office the following morning. Susie recognised his artistic scrawl instantly, but didn't immediately tear open the envelope, choosing instead to slip it into the top drawer of her desk until she had a quiet, private moment in which to read it properly. At lunchtime, when the office emptied, she took out the envelope and laid it in front of her.

She wondered why she hesitated to discover the actual contents of the letter when she already knew what it would say. He would be finishing with her, of course. He would have found her odd and illogical, immature and unworldly. Perhaps Deborah was right. When he had the choice between someone as confident and glamorous as she undoubtedly was, why would he choose a girl who proved herself to be gauche and inexperienced?

Finally, she could bear the suspense no longer. So if this was the end, so what?

My dear Susie,

I am posting this at Heathrow on my way over to New York. You know about the major magazine campaign the top brass at your place all seem to be working on? I was in for the big meeting on that the other day, but when I came to find you, you'd scuttled away. Anyway, I hope to get this part of the job finished in about eight days, which means I'll be back on Tuesday, maybe Wednesday, next week — and hoping to see you as soon as you can manage after that.

I so much want to talk to you. I've hurt you, I know that, but honestly I'm not sure how. This isn't about Deborah, is it? Don't you trust me? I thought we knew each other better. From the start, I felt a real connection between us, and for me trust was at the heart of that. Don't you feel it too? Have we really got each other so wrong?

Is there something you're not telling me. Susie? Someone else? I'd rather know.

My mobile should work over in the States, so ring me if you'd like to. It would be good to hear your voice.

Take care.

With love,

Paul

Susie dropped the letter, and buried her head in her hands. 'Is there someone else?' he asked.

Well, there might have been if she'd only been honest from the start. If she'd told him she was pregnant before she decided on the abortion, then perhaps that tiny being might have had a chance of life. And as the familiar sense of guilt and loss overwhelmed her, she knew that because Paul was a decent man, he would never be able to forgive her for being stupid enough to get pregnant, for keeping silent, and most of all, for killing his baby.

'I've done your washing up. Could you *try* and keep that down a bit? There was mildew at the bottom of one cup.' Celia's lips narrowed into a tight line of indignation. 'You'll poison yourself if you carry on like this.'

'Well, at least that would make your day!'

'I beg your pardon?'

'I said I don't find enough time in the day to do things like washing up.' Madge's face was a picture of innocence.

'You find plenty of time for eating. Do you have to take absolutely every pot and plate out of your cupboards rather than wash up the ones you've already used?'

'Yes. It's more hygienic. You've already told me I'll kill myself if I use any of that lot piled up in the sink. Besides, you know my legs. I can't stand for more than a few minutes at a time.'

'Unless you're cooking or getting yourself another glass of sherry. You manage all right then.'

'Yes, that's a blessing, isn't it? The doctor says I should keep my strength up by eating well.'

'And that's the only bit of advice you ever remember from that doctor. You conveniently forget the bit about watching your weight, or getting exercise and fresh air now and then.

And I see your pills are on the kitchen table. Have you taken them yet today?'

'Are they the blue ones?'

'Yes.'

'Oh, I can't swallow them. Great big dry gobstoppers, they are. No, I prefer the pink ones, so I take double rations of them instead.'

Celia looked appalled. 'You don't!'

'No, I don't – and if you stop talking to me as if I'm a five-year-old, I'll stop answering like one.'

'I've had enough of this. Just remember how much I do for you, Madge Moreton. I don't have to come here, you know!'

'Quite right, you don't. It just makes you feel important to have a poor old lady to boss about.'

'How dare you!'

'I just did. Now, pass me that glass before you go. I'm thirsty.'

'You're not having a sherry at half past ten in the morning!'

'In my own house, I'll have exactly what I choose.'

'Then you get it yourself!'

Madge glared defiantly back at her, then turned away towards the huge pile of newspapers that doubled as a side table by her chair to pick up a huge shapeless piece of grey knitting.

'I've nearly finished this.'

'What is it?'

'I don't know yet. I'll know when it's done.'

Huffily Celia gathered up her shopping bag and began to fish for her car keys. 'I'm going to the supermarket. Do you need anything special this week?'

'If they're selling tall, dark, sexy millionaires, I'll have one. And I'd like another packet of those cream doughnuts. They were nice.'

'Right. I'll be back in about half an hour.'

'And a newspaper.' Celia stopped in her tracks as she marched out the living-room door.

'A newspaper. Are you sure there's nothing else?'

Madge thought for a moment, then shrugged non-committally. With a sigh of exasperation, Celia continued through the door.

'Loo rolls!'

A stormy-faced Celia poked her head back into the room again.

'And loo rolls. Is that it?'

Madge smiled sweetly. Without another backward glance Celia strode to the front door, slamming it hard behind her.

'Yes! A civil goodbye would be nice!'

And reaching behind her armchair for a glass and a half-empty bottle of sherry, the old lady chuckled out loud as she began to pour.

Chapter Twelve

Just over a week later, exhausted after several sleepless nights, Susie came to two decisions.

Before she had time to change her mind, she got cracking on the first one. With shaking fingers, she rang Paul's home number. From the office, she had heard that he was due home later that morning. Her own attempts to ring him on his mobile in New York had proved futile. Mostly the number was simply unobtainable. On the one occasion when it had rung, she had slammed down the receiver in a panic.

Suddenly she heard the familiar voice on his home answerphone. 'Hi! This is Paul Armitage. I check this machine often, so please do leave a message.'

Her heart pounded as she listened to the series of tape rewinds and beeps while the machine reset itself for her to speak.

'Paul, it's me. Thank you for your letter which was – it was – well, it almost made me cry. It's certainly helped me do a lot of thinking. I must speak to you – to explain – and to – well, I just need to talk to you, that's all. Don't ring me at work, because I've booked myself off today. I'll tell you all about that later. I can't wait to see you.' She paused, uncertain how to sign off. 'Oh yes, welcome home! And this is Susie, by the way ...' Abruptly, she was cut off by the beep.

She grimaced as she replaced the receiver. That must have sounded ridiculous, but then he couldn't think much worse of her than he probably did already.

Glancing at her watch, she set about putting her second decision into action. Reaching for her handbag, a road map and her keys, she pulled on her jacket and headed for the car.

'Are you sure you'll be all right? Mum's not that far away, if you need anything. It's only for a few days.'

Kate smiled at her husband. 'Martin, I'm feeling much better now. I'm sure last night was just a fluke.'

'But if your blood pressure is up, shouldn't you arrange to see the doctor, just to be on the safe side?'

'Look, it's only a bit of a headache.'

'But you've been feeling so uncomfortable lately. If you had to sleep beside you, you'd know what I mean! I don't think you dropped off for more than a few minutes at a time last night. Is that normal?'

'Perfectly. And I promise if I have any doubts, I'll ring the doctor straight away.'

'And you'll ring me? Call me if you're worried about anything.'

'It's you who's worrying.'

'Perhaps I shouldn't go.'

'Darling, this trip is important to you. You and the team have been building up to the signing of this contract for months.'

'But with only three weeks to go until the baby comes ...'

'Yes, three whole weeks – and you'll be back in three days.'

'I love you.'

'I know you do.'

'If anything happened to you ...'

'... which it won't ...'

'I'd never forgive myself if I weren't here with you.'

'And your company won't forgive you if you chicken out on this contract. Martin, from now on you're the hunter-gatherer in this family. If you don't bring home the bacon, this sprog and I will starve! Now stop fussing over me.'

'I like fussing.'

'I'm not that fragile.'

'Love and cherish in sickness and in health, that's what I promised.'

'I'm not sick, I'm pregnant. And I'll cherish your love all the more if you get on that plane!'

'I'll miss you.' He stroked her tummy affectionately. 'Both of you.'

She put her arms round him, drawing him as close as her bulging tummy allowed. 'And we love you too. Just come back safe, sound – and as soon as possible.'

'Well, what do you think? Simon and I have been over all the figures, and we're in complete agreement over this.'

Roger and Margaret sat on one side of the kitchen table as Gillian enthused to them from the other, barely drawing breath in her eagerness to tell all.

'Now the girls are almost off our hands I need something to occupy my time, and if it makes a bit of profit into the bargain, all the better. The livery and stabling is going great guns. I seem to have hit on a hole in the market in this area. And if I'm going to ask you for more buildings and land to expand the stables and paddocks, then I might just as well go the whole hog. Riding holidays! That's where the money is. These pony magazines are full of them, and having done my market research, I know the well-run ones are doing very nicely, thank you.'

'Who goes on holidays like that?' said Roger.

'Youngsters mostly, all keen horse-riders who fancy combining a holiday away from home with their passion for horses.'

'How young?'

'I would say the average age is about twelve, but a few could be younger. Teenagers come too, and then there are adult parties who enjoy getting away from the stresses of their everyday lives on horseback. And the corporate market can be quite lucrative too – you know, when a group of people from one company all spend a riding holiday together?'

'Are these holidays just during the summer months?'

'Oh no! All the year round, if we want it to be.'

'But where would they stay?'

Gillian smiled brightly, fixing her eyes on Margaret. 'Here!'

'Here on the farm?'

'Here in this house.'

Roger almost choked on the cup of tea he was sipping. 'Hang on a minute! This house is not for sale. We may have hit hard times, but this is our home.'

'And it's a home from home that these folk are hoping to find. Just think! The countryside round here is as good as you'll find anywhere in England, yet it's within easy travelling distance from London. And the farm, of course, is traditional and pretty.'

'Huh!' snorted Roger.

'And its crowning glory is this house – centuries old, cosy and welcoming. People would *love* to stay here.'

'As guests, do you mean?'

'I mean that the house remains your property, but you turn it into a business where you provide accommodation and traditional catering for parties of visitors who come here for riding holidays. You're a wonderful cook, Margaret, and I've never known anyone have a more motherly way with children. They'll never want to go home!'

'And you'd need to expand the horse and pony facilities to achieve this idea?'

'Quite significantly. I'd like to find at least another twenty animals, and they'd all need paddock and grazing pasture. Then we'd have to set up hacking routes, and another field – perhaps that one beyond the stable block – for a school.'

Speechless, Roger and Margaret stared at each other in disbelief.

'And it would be important to have an indoor school too, so that we can carry on with lessons during the winter months.'

'An indoor school?' asked Margaret, plainly bemused.

'Oh, just a huge barn affair enclosing an indoor arena. In fact, if you didn't have the herd, that old cowshed of yours would do a treat.'

'Didn't have cows?' interrupted Roger. 'I'm a farmer. Farmers have cows.'

'But these days farmers don't make much money out of having cows, do they? This is a practical suggestion to help you make this farm pay. It will be a steep learning curve for all of us, but I know this could work.'

Margaret looked at her husband, covering his gnarled hand with her own. 'What do you think, Roger? Is it worth considering?'

'What about the land? Would it stay ours?'

'Yes, if that's what you'd prefer. Or Simon and I are more than willing to give you a fair price for the land we need, which would be most of the south part of the farm. That would leave you with all the fields in the immediate vicinity of the house.'

'We keep that.'

Gillian beamed across at Margaret. 'This is your home, Margaret, and always will be as long as I have any say in the matter. And how many times have you told me that this house comes to life with children? Wouldn't it be nice to have it filled by young people with all their noise and bustle? You'd have to plan their meals, and sort out rooms for them – and remember these are youngsters who are away from their parents for a few days, so they might be a bit homesick until they settle in. You'd be brilliant at all that. I can think of no one better.'

'And this would be a proper business partnership?' asked Roger.

'Hall Farm Stables, proprietors Margaret Davis and Gillian Bawdon.'

Roger's busy eyebrow shot up. 'Just the wives?'

'Well, we'll be doing all the work, and taking the responsibility. Simon is happy to put the money up and reassure your bank manager about his backing of this new use of the farm, but he's not interested in getting involved on a day-to-day basis. And honestly, Roger, are you?'

The old farmer narrowed his eyes thoughtfully.

'What about the farm and all the livestock?'

'Well, that's for you two to decide. The fields here near the house would still be available, so perhaps you could size down your operation to suit. Or maybe you could come up with some other use for that area.'

Margaret glanced with curiosity at Roger as a sudden gleam appeared in his eye.

'Right!' he said, pushing back his chair and standing up abruptly. 'Leave us to talk this over, and we'll get back to you. Shall we say Friday evening? You and Simon could come over and sample Margaret's cooking, seeing as you keep waxing lyrical about it.'

Gathering up her papers, and with a wink in Margaret's direction, Gillian got up to leave, crossing her fingers at them both as she pulled on her wellies and disappeared out into the yard.

It was late morning, when Kate opened the front door to bring in the milk bottles, that she noticed the car. In fact it was the driver who first drew her eye, or rather the mass of striking auburn hair which made the woman so distinctive. For a moment Kate could have sworn she was looking directly at their house; except that when she peered more closely the woman's head was down, apparently absorbed with something inside the car. Thinking no more of it, Kate went back indoors.

But half an hour later when her neighbour called round to return the garden shears she'd borrowed, Kate spotted the woman again. This time she was out of the car, standing on the other side of the road, staring at her with open curiosity.

Unsettled, Kate slipped the safety chain across when she shut the front door, then made her way up to the bedroom from where she could watch the woman without fear of being seen.

There was no doubt that she was watching the house. No other home seemed to interest her. She was gazing straight at it, sometimes pacing a few steps in one direction or another to get a better view.

Kate's palms became hot and clammy? Should she ring her neighbour? Martin? The police?

Then it happened. Kate found she couldn't stop herself moving towards the window as the woman looked directly up at her. With urgent fascination, they held each other's gaze – and in that moment, rooted to the floor as a cold chill rippled its way through her body, Kate knew exactly who the woman was.

'How soon do you finish? Fancy a cup of coffee?' Gwen turned from the shelf where she was stacking library books to find a smiling Tricia waiting for her at the desk.

'Ten minutes, and I can't think of anything nicer. I could do with a natter.'

'Great! Even better if Brian could join us. His Wednesday class finishes around now, doesn't it?'

'They're out on a field trip today.'

Tricia's face fell. 'What a shame. I was hoping to see him.'

'He'll be sorry he missed you.'

'Will he? Do you really think so?'

'Of course. Brian appreciates friends. He'd be the first to admit he's been a bit reclusive in the years since his wife died.'

'Oh, I plan to be his friend. His very good friend!'

Gwen turned back to the shelf without comment.

'Gwen, I really like him. Brian is the first man I've met for years that I think I could fall for.'

'There's such a lot going on in your life at the moment, Trish. You're very vulnerable.'

'I'm lonely. I've been lonely in my marriage for years. I want some romance. Is that such a bad thing?'

'Of course not, and I hope you find it. But at the right time, and with the right person.'

'You don't think Brian's right for me?'

'I didn't say that.'

'Then you don't think I'm right for him. Why not? He's lonely too, that's easy to see.'

With great precision and concentration, Gwen placed another book in the correct place on the shelf.

'And he's not involved with anyone else, is he?' With a dismissive shrug of her shoulders, Gwen went on with her shelf-filling.

Staring at her friend with curiosity, Trish was silent for a while before reaching out to turn Gwen to face her.

'Oh, I see! I'm not the only one who's lonely and in need of a little romance.'

'No, Trish, you don't understand ...'

'Yes, I do. I've known you long enough to understand perfectly.'

'It's nothing – really.'

'Nothing short of wonderful! You've been sad for long enough, dearest Gwen, and if Brian can put that flush back in your cheeks and some love in your life, no one deserves it more.'

And ignoring the stares of other library users, Tricia threw her arms around an obviously embarrassed Gwen and hugged her soundly.

There are moments in all our lives which are so significant that nothing is ever quite the same again. For Susie, such a moment came when she first locked eyes with Kate, standing pale and disbelieving in the bedroom window. She was only dimly aware of the modern estate house, the neatly turfed garden, the heavily pregnant young woman who gazed at her at first with suspicion, then with growing comprehension. But for Susie everything faded into the background except for one staggering reality. This stranger had her dead father's face. Younger, softer, but unmistakable. There could be no doubt that this was Richard's daughter. And that meant that she was Susie's . . .

She couldn't frame the word, not even in her mind. And she couldn't think, couldn't see. Words with no meaning reached lips with no sound. Acrid bile burned her throat, fingers fumbled, knees buckled as the world swam giddily around her. Groping wildly, she found what was probably the bonnet of her car, and sat back heavily, flushed and clammy, heart thumping in her chest.

Suddenly there was a voice at her side. She felt herself being gently propelled across the road, through the garden, and into the house at which she had spent so long staring. She meant to protest, meant to say that she didn't belong here, but the words never came. She was aware of being carefully lowered on to a soft seat, offered a sip of water. Then finally the fog cleared and her eyes focused on the concerned face of the woman beside her. For a while they stared openly at each other, devouring what they saw — expression, shape, colour — blue eyes, red hair, curve of the mouth, movement of a hand that echoed the parents they shared.

'I can't believe you came.'

'To be honest, neither can I.'

'That was quite an entrance.'

'Sorry I keeled over.'

'Don't be.'

'But to see you so soon after Dad's death ...'

'I know.'

Conversation faltered, neither sure how to continue. At last, able to bear it no longer, Susie tried to get up.

'I'd better go.'

'Why?'

'I don't belong here.'

'But you do. We belong together. Neither of us knew it, but the truth is that we should always have been together, you and I. Isn't that why you came?'

'I didn't mean to speak to you. I don't really know what I meant to do. Just look, I suppose. Then condemn. Dismiss.'

Kate didn't reply. Instead, she shifted herself back into the seat to try and get more comfortable.

'When's the baby due?'

'Three weeks.'

'It's you who should be having the vapours then, not me.'

'After this, I think having a baby will be a piece of cake.'

'You could do without nasty shocks like mad women turning up and fainting on your doorstep.'

'As shocks go, this is the best I could ever have.'

Susie smiled. She couldn't help herself. Unexpected. Unbelievable. Especially when she looked up to see that Kate was smiling too.

As time slipped away, so did the barrier of past history and unfamiliarity which stood between them. To the surprise of both, conversation, although stilted at times and accusing

at others, was more free-flowing than either of them had
dared hope as memories were unearthed, longings confided
and fears faced.

'I just needed to fill in the gaps, that's all,' Kate was
saying. 'I've known about being adopted for years, but it's
only now when I'm going to become a mum myself that I've
felt this compulsion to know what really happened. Who was
my mother? Why did she abandon me? And I had a father
too. To learn now that they not only stayed together, but I
missed meeting him by no more than a matter of weeks is
very hard to take in.'

'You'd have liked him. Everyone did. He was ...'

'... kind. I can tell that from his photo. And sensitive.
Gwen tells me he loved music.'

'He was always popular at get-togethers. He could play
anything.'

'By ear. You'll never believe this, but I can do that too.'

'You can?'

'And you're an artist?'

'I wouldn't exactly say that.'

'Gwen told me you have great talent.'

'Did she?'

'She's very proud of you.'

Susie looked sceptical. 'Really?'

'Immensely. She told me all about your job in London.
Rome, didn't she say? That's such a fantastic city.'

'I don't travel often. Not yet anyway.'

'How I envy you! I love to travel, probably because of
learning all those languages.'

'Dad was the same ...'

'I'm a teacher, did you know? French and Spanish.'

'You must love children then. Just as well in your present
condition.'

'I like other people's children, but then I can give them
back. Not so sure about having one of my own.'

'Are you scared?'

'Honestly? Yes, I am a bit. I feel so enormous. How is this huge baby ever going to make its way into daylight?'

'No stopping it now!'

'That's what worries me. Let this be a lesson to you! Don't ever get pregnant!'

A shadow fell like a shutter across Susie's face. Peering at her closely, Kate stretched out to touch her hand.

'Susie?'

No reply.

'Have I said something wrong?'

'It doesn't matter.'

'It does to me.'

Susie shrugged. 'It's over now. Gone.'

'A baby? You had a baby?'

'Never got that far. I had an abortion.'

Kate nodded. 'When?'

'About two months ago. I told you. It's over.' She stopped, staring at Kate. 'I can't believe I'm telling you this. It's behind me. I've forgotten it.'

'Have you?'

Susie bit down on her bottom lip to stop it shaking.

'You'll never forget.' Kate's voice was soft as she continued. 'And you'll always grieve for the baby you never knew.'

'But everybody has abortions these days. It's no big deal.'

'Do you really believe that?'

'I thought the hardest part would be making the decision. After that, it would just be a minor operation, a technical adjustment ...'

'But your emotions couldn't adjust at the same rate?'

Susie nodded dumbly.

'And the father? Is he still around?'

'Sort of.'

'But he wasn't there to help you through this?'

'It wasn't like that. I didn't tell him.'

'Why not?'

'Because I felt it was my fault. There's no excuse for girls getting pregnant by accident, not in this day and age.'

'Girls shouldn't have to take all the responsibility either.'

'He would have thought me inexperienced and ...'

'... not cool?'

Susie almost grinned. 'Definitely not cool.'

'But you never gave yourself – or him – a chance to find out what his reaction would be. Does he know now?'

Susie shook her head.

'Is he still in your life?'

'That's a good question. We've got very close again recently.'

'And you don't want to ruin it by telling him you had an abortion without asking him?'

'It was different when I thought I'd never see him again. But now – well, I just can't imagine how he could ever care about someone who got rid of his child without even mentioning it to him.'

'Do you think that if he'd known, if you had confided in him while you were still pregnant, that his decision would have been any different from yours? You weren't ready to settle down and have a baby. Was he?'

Susie fell silent while she considered this.

'Is it possible that it was the wrong time and situation, but he's still the right man?'

'Perhaps.'

'Then he'll understand, won't he? If he is the right person, he'll see what a dreadful dilemma it was for you, and love you anyway.' Kate paused for a moment, rubbing her back painfully before shuffling back into the seat to find a more comfortable position.

'Are you all right?'

'Just need another cushion.'

But an hour and several cushions later, it became clear to

Susie that Kate was far from well. She shifted her weight restlessly, dragging herself up every now and then to get the blood flowing into her legs. Then she would lower herself heavily, occasionally clasping her stomach, or cupping her forehead in her hand.

'Kate, is this normal? Can I get you something? A glass of water? Aspirin?'

'Can't take anything while I'm pregnant.'

'Have you got a headache?'

Kate's eyes closed tightly as she grimaced with pain. 'A thumper. Like a migraine, I suppose, except I never have those.'

'Why now then?'

'My blood pressure is up. I've had real problems with it over the past few weeks, and they've been monitoring me quite closely.' She took a sharp intake of breath as another spasm gripped her stomach. Her face became a mask of intense pain, until a few seconds later she relaxed back against the settee, pale and worn.

Susie watched in alarm. 'For heaven's sake, Kate, you're not about to have this baby, are you? You don't know me well enough, so I'll admit right now that I'm a useless blob in an emergency.'

When Kate didn't answer, Susie shot to her feet. 'That's it. I'm calling your doctor. Where's the number?'

'In the kitchen.' Kate's voice was barely audible. 'There's a list on the wall above the phone. Dr Knapton.'

Finding the number was the easy part. Getting an answer was impossible. After a quarter of an hour of trying, during which the line was permanently engaged, Susie returned to the living room to check once more on Kate. She sat slumped, face deathly pale, too worn down by pain to be able to speak, or even open her eyes.

It took just one look to decide Susie. Marching into the kitchen again, she picked up the receiver and dialled 999.

✳   ✳   ✳

It was Roger who picked up the phone. He had just come back into the house from milking when it rang, and because he was prising off his boots, he ignored it at first, thinking Margaret would get it as usual. Then he remembered it was Wednesday. Women's Institute night. His dinner was in the oven, and Margaret was gone.

'Mr Davis?'

It was not a voice he recognised.

'That's right.'

'I'm ringing about Kate. She's in hospital. She asked me to tell you.'

Roger felt himself go cold, his socked feet rooted to the floor.

'Is she all right?'

'I'm not sure. The doctor's with her now.'

'She's not having the baby. She can't be. She's got nearly a month to go yet.'

'Well, she's very unwell, that's for sure. And her husband is away, is that right?'

'Martin's in France. Doesn't come back till the end of the week.'

'Did he leave you a contact number?'

Roger scratched his chin thoughtfully. 'We've only got his usual mobile number. What did Kate say?'

'She's not really in a state to say much. Just asked me to ring you.'

'Where is she? The hospital in Colchester, is it?'

'In the Maternity Ward. Do you know where that is?'

'Can't say I do, but I dare say we'll find it. Mind you, I'll have to find her mum first. She's out tonight.'

'Well, I'm not sure whether Kate will be able to see anyone for a while. She just wanted you to know.'

'Thank you, Nurse. We'll definitely come down in case she needs anything. With her husband away, I wouldn't like to think of her going through this all alone.'

'Oh, she's not alone, Mr Davis. I'm with her. And I'm not a nurse. I'm her sister. See you when you arrive then. I'll keep an eye out for you. 'Bye!'

And as the line went dead, Roger's mouth dropped open.

'I got through to your father. He needs to track down your mum, but after that they'll be on their way.'

Beads of sweat lay across Kate's ashen forehead as she watched Susie return to her bedside.

'I wish Martin was here.'

'What about his work colleagues? Are they likely to have a hotel contact for him?'

'During the working day, yes. What's the time now?'

'Nearly half past seven.'

'He's probably trying to ring me at home. He'll wonder where I am.'

'And if he puts two and two together, what would he do then? Ring the farm?'

'Where he'll get no reply either.'

Susie reached out to touch Kate's shoulder. 'Look, don't worry. I'll find him if it kills me. What did the doctor say, by the way?'

'It's pre-eclampsia. That's why I've been feeling so wretched. They're obviously quite worried about the baby.'

'Oh Kate . . .'

'They're talking about inducing me tonight. I don't want to do this on my own. I'm scared, and Martin should be here. He promised. I need Martin.'

At that moment, a nurse appeared at the end of the bed. Susie squeezed Kate's hand encouragingly.

'Don't let them bully you. Tell them they'll have your hot-tempered sister to deal with if they do! I'm going to have another go at finding Martin. I'll be out in the car using the mobile.'

'But you will come back?'

Susie smiled down at her. 'Try keeping me away!'

Once in the car she re-tried Martin's mobile number just in case. Nothing. Time to try tracing him through his company. But first, Susie peered at the mobile in the darkness, and dialled her mother's home.

Tricia watched with curiosity as Gwen took the phone call, noting the flush of tension that slid across her friend's face, her fingers drumming taut on the side table as she asked short urgent questions. Trish could tell it was bad news, but the few details she could gather didn't make sense. It sounded as if it was Susie on the other end of the phone, but then there was talk of some sort of emergency with a baby being born early. That couldn't be right, because as far as Trish knew the only person in Gwen's life who was expecting a baby was Kate – and there was no way that Susie would be anywhere near her.

At last it was over, and Gwen turned round, plainly worried.

'I should go. Or should I? I'd so much like to be there for her, but what will the others think?'

'Hang on a minute, slow down! Who? Where?'

'Colchester. Kate's been taken in as an emergency. She's suffering from pre-eclampsia, and it looks as if they're anxious the baby is delivered as soon as possible. Susie says they're talking about inducing her any time now.'

'Susie?' repeated Tricia in amazement. 'I thought she wasn't speaking to you, let alone Kate! I don't understand.'

'Apparently they've spent the afternoon together. I can't believe it either, but thank goodness she was there when Kate needed someone.'

'What about her husband? Surely he's with her?'

'Apparently not, and that's what's worrying Sue most

at the moment. He's away in Europe on business, and can't be found. She's trying desperately to locate someone from his company who may have another number for him.'

'And Kate's parents?'

'Not there either.'

'So you feel you should go?'

'I want to. I remember how scared I was when I gave birth to her with no one around me but strangers.'

'Would you like me to come with you?'

Gwen hesitated.

'Do you know the way to the hospital?' asked Trish.

'Not really. Kate's house is in a village on the outskirts, and I had a devil of a job finding it. I'm not familiar with Colchester at all.'

'Neither am I.' Trish paused to look at her friend for a moment, before coming to a decision.

'You nip upstairs and get yourself together. I've got an idea.'

Once Gwen had disappeared, Trish punched another number into the phone. Brian answered almost immediately.

'How well do you know Colchester?' She didn't bother with niceties or preamble.

'Reasonably. We used to live not far from there.'

'Do you know where the hospital is?'

'Of course.'

'Then drop whatever you're doing, and get round here to Gwen's. She needs you.'

He arrived within minutes. No fuss. Few questions. There would be time for those later. When Gwen came downstairs, her surprise at seeing him was pushed aside by her obvious relief. And before the clock on the mantelpiece struck eight they were on the road.

✲　　✲　　✲

For Susie, the next half-hour was particularly ineffectual. She managed at last to find Martin's company number, only to be faced with a suspicious, unhelpful security officer who needed a great deal of persuading that she wasn't an absolute nutcase. Finally, with great reluctance, he took all the details, then agreed that he would try to locate one of Martin's work colleagues, in which case she should stay by her phone and wait for his call.

She waited. Ten minutes became fifteen, and still no call came. In desperation she picked up the phone again. The security officer's line was engaged. Without thinking she thumped in another number, feeling her shoulders drop a notch at the sound of Paul's voice. So he was still not home! Disappointment mingled with frustration as his answerphone beeped, inviting her to leave a message.

'Oh, Paul, I wish you were there to pick up this phone. I'm at Colchester Hospital with Kate — you remember I told you about the sister I've just discovered I have? It's a long story, but so much of what you said stayed with me, and today I decided to act on my instincts and come to see her. She was — is — great, but we both ended up in an ambulance because she became so dreadfully ill, and now they're talking about inducing her tonight — and her husband is abroad and I can't find him! I'm sorry, I know I'm rambling, but I wish I wasn't on my own trying to sort this lot out. I just miss you, and wish you were here because you'd know what to do. And there's so much more I need to tell—'

She stopped mid-flow as the machine cut her off. Well, that was it. Another stupid phone message she'd left him, When he finally got round to hearing her on his machine, he'd probably think he'd had a lucky escape.

She jumped as the phone shrilled. Eureka! The man on the line this time was not only sane and understanding, he was also Martin's immediate boss. Yes, of course he had a note of the hotel number and he'd already left a message for Martin to tell him about his wife's condition the minute he arrived. And yes, he'd left Martin details of both Susie's mobile number and the ward itself in case he wanted to get in touch direct.

Susie could have kissed him if he had been near enough. Instead she thanked him profusely and made her way back into the Maternity Ward, where she was shocked to see how much Kate's condition had deteriorated.

'Have you found him?' she croaked, staring at Susie with panicked glassy eyes in a face which was flushed and blotchy.

'I think so. I certainly found his boss who's left a message at Martin's hotel. He'll come, Kate, I'm sure of that, but even if he leaves almost immediately I doubt he'll get here much before morning.'

Disappointed tears coursed down Kate's face as she gripped tightly at Susie's hand. 'Stay with me, Susie, please! I feel so awful. I'm sure something's wrong. I just need to know the baby's all right.'

Susie stroked her hot damp forehead. 'I'm not going anywhere. Hang on, Kate. Look, the doctor's coming again. You'll both be fine, I'm sure of it.'

And with all her being, Susie hoped that she didn't show in her face the cold fear which lurked in her heart.

If only they hadn't had a special Women's Institute meeting booked for that night – a fashion show at a local hotel – Roger might have found Margaret more quickly. As it was, when he arrived at the darkened village hall, his heart fell. Where the devil were they? He racked his brain trying to think who would know, who he could ask. Everyone he could think of would be at the mystery location themselves.

The third door he knocked on was the vicarage. It was quite a surprise to find that Christopher, who looked after no fewer that five churches in the area, was actually in. His wife was also at the meeting, so, of course, he knew exactly where they were because he had been roped in to transport carloads of clothes there earlier that afternoon. With his parting quip that they would no doubt be planning a baptism in a few months' time, the vicar waved cheerily in the doorway as Roger sped off.

It took ten minutes to reach the hotel, but twice that long to track down Margaret who was nowhere to be seen in the crowd of one hundred or so women who had gathered for the special evening. Eventually, he discovered her where he should have thought of looking in the first place – in a nearby room laying out plates of sandwiches, cups and saucers. He had hardly got through his first sentence explaining that Kate was in hospital before she'd got her pinny off, grabbed her coat and was running towards the door.

Margaret's mind was racing as their old Land Rover puffed its way towards the hospital. Why had Kate needed an ambulance to take her in? How much of an emergency was this? Were she and the baby in danger? Too much time had been wasted while Roger raced round to find her. Why hadn't she made her plans more clear before she'd left that evening?

They hadn't gone directly to the hospital from the hotel because Margaret realised that if Kate had been taken in very quickly, she probably hadn't had time to pack a bag. She would need a nightie, slippers, toothpaste, perhaps some fruit or a drink. Ever practical, she insisted that Roger take her back to the farm where she hurriedly collected together anything useful she could lay her hands on.

Finally Roger set off again, travelling at his usual sedate pace which never varied whether or not time was of the essence. Margaret knew better than to ask him to put his foot down. He wouldn't. The car couldn't.

She watched the clock tick round for endless minutes until at last they pulled up in the crowded hospital car park. There was a queue at the information desk, and when they were finally told where they should look for her, they set off down a confusing maze of corridors. At last they reached Maternity, where the station nurse finished her telephone call before looking up at them with a smile.

'Mrs Gordon please, Kate Gordon? I'm her mother.'

'Oh?' replied the nurse, looking slightly puzzled. 'I thought her mother was already with her.'

Chapter Thirteen

Gwen sensed rather than saw Margaret's arrival. Sitting with Kate's hand in hers on one side of the bed while Susie did exactly the same on the other, neither heard the door open. It was only the warmth of recognition which flicked across Kate's exhausted face that made it clear who had come into the room. For a split second Gwen couldn't move, half in dread, half in anticipation of finally facing this woman she had envied, thanked and even hated at times over the years.

She turned just quickly enough to catch the panic in Margaret's eyes before the man who followed her in took his place solidly beside her. For heartstopping seconds the four stared at each other in horrified fascination until suddenly Susie got to her feet.

'Mum and I will wait outside. Yell if you need us.' Kate smiled weakly as Susie brushed an affectionate hand across her forehead. 'We'll be here.'

There was an awkwardness as Roger and Margaret moved aside just far enough to allow Gwen and Susie to get through the door. Eyes were lowered, nothing said. Then, as the door finally swung closed, Margaret moved quickly to take Gwen's seat beside the bed.

'How are you, love? What does the doctor say?'

'They're worried that the baby is in distress. Apparently he's

not turned, and his feet are where his head should be. They plan
to induce me immediately.' Kate's voice was barely a whisper, her
eyes brimming with pain-filled tears as she spoke.

'Don't you worry. Your dad and I are right here for you
now. Would you like anything? I've brought you some things
I thought you might need.'

Margaret bent down to put her bag on the floor only to
find that Gwen had already left a bag of her own. In it were
almost identical items: fresh orange juice rather than the squash
Margaret had brought, a creamy white embroidered towel where
Margaret's was striped and obviously well used, a silk dressing
gown in place of the bed jacket she had quickly grabbed.

Sitting up abruptly, Margaret's hand cupped her mouth as
she gulped back shocked, tearless, silent sobs.

To Susie's surprise Gwen, although clearly shaken, didn't collapse the moment she got outside the door. Instead she walked
across the corridor to the relatives' waiting room straight into
the arms of a tall, bearded, pleasant-faced stranger who stood to
greet her. For a while they clung together, Gwen plainly drawing
comfort from his quiet strength, while Susie sank heavily on to
a nearby chair staring in sheer disbelief.

At last, Gwen turned. 'Susie, you haven't met Brian Hewitt,
who is not only my art teacher, but my very dear friend.'

'I can see that. No wonder you were always so keen to get to
your art classes. And I thought it was the painting you loved!'

'Don't, Susie. Haven't we got enough to face this evening
without fighting each other?'

'Who's fighting? I'm simply trying to catch up. Just how
long has Mr Hewitt been "your very dear friend"? Did you wait
more than a week or two after my father died? Let's see! Over
the past three months, you've landed me with a sister you never
even mentioned, you've tried to destroy my father's character
and memory, you've made me abort my own baby – but that's

all right because your first-born child, the one you pretended you never had, is in there right now giving birth to your first grandchild. And now you top it all by openly embracing your "very dear friend" in front of me when I've never even clapped eyes on him before!'

'That's not fair.'

But Susie didn't wait to hear more. Avoiding her mother's outstretched arm, she barged out of the room and disappeared down the corridor.

Brian searched the ground floor of the hospital for ages before he finally found her huddled up almost out of sight on a bench behind the drinks machine. Beside her was a cold cup of coffee, untouched. When Susie saw him approaching she deliberately looked away, cursing under her breath as he went up to the vending machine to get a fresh brew for them both. Then very casually he sat down on the bench, holding out the cup to her which she doggedly ignored.

Placing the cup carefully on the floor in front of her, he gave a good-natured shrug, then fished into his pocket to pull out a sketchpad and pencil. For a couple of minutes he worked away, finally laying the open pad down on the bench between them.

Curiosity got the better of her. It was a cartoon showing Susie and her mother facing each other like boxers, both with their eyes shut as they threw ineffectual punches at each other. Between them was a much smaller picture of Brian, terrified and cowering as he dodged the blows.

Susie's expression didn't change as she stretched out to pick up the pad herself. Turning away from him so that he couldn't see, the pencil worked furiously for a while, before she too laid down the pad on the bench between them. It was a picture of Susie with her arm round Gwen as the two of them stood beside Richard's grave. On the other side of the sheet was a caricature of Brian dressed like the villain in a Victorian melodrama as he cast a greedy eye in Gwen's direction.

Nodding acknowledgement, Brian reclaimed the pad, dropping it casually back on to the bench several minutes later when he'd finished. This time the sheet was covered in a series of drawings. Firstly there was Gwen creeping nervously into the art class where Brian was obviously the teacher. Then there was a view from the back of the class where all the students had drawn light, airy pictures of trees and flowers, while Gwen's paper was covered in gloomy, depressing doodles. Following that were three cartoons of Brian encouraging Gwen as they painted still life, human models and finally countryside scenes together, and in each picture Gwen's expression became more absorbed and content. Finally, there was a picture of the whole class applauding Gwen as her work was displayed.

Without a word Susie took the pencil from his hand and picked up the pad. The cartoon she quickly sketched showed a vulnerable, frightened Gwen, with Susie standing in front of her challenging Brian. What do you want of my mother, her expression seemed to ask.

In reply Brian drew two pictures, one of him watching quietly as tears slid down Gwen's cheek, and another of him putting a comforting arm round her shoulder, bringing the start of a smile to her face.

Susie immediately snatched up the pad and began drawing again, slapping the book down on the bench when she'd finished. It showed Susie and Gwen trying to cling together as Brian forced his way in between them.

Taking his turn, Brian replied with a picture of mother and daughter, their hands lightly clasped, looking at each other with an expression of love and understanding, while his smiling bearded figure stood way back watching.

Susie hesitated before picking up the pad again. Then on one side of the sheet she drew a picture of herself looking across at Brian who stood opposite her. For the first time her expression was more curious than threatening.

Locking eyes with her as he accepted the pad, Brian drew quickly. His picture showed Susie looking almost exactly as she had done in her previous cartoon, standing on one side – but he had moved himself into the centre, where he stood with his hand outstretched in a conciliatory gesture of friendship.

Susie almost grinned when she saw it. Then she picked up the pencil again, finally laying the finished picture on the bench between them. In it Susie had moved into the centre of the sheet too, where she and Brian were tentatively shaking hands.

Brian looked up from the cartoon to find Susie staring directly at him, unspoken acceptance if not understanding acknowledged between them. And when with a slight nod of farewell Brian got up from the bench, they both knew he was going off in search of Gwen.

As soon as Brian had left Gwen had taken herself off to the ladies, where she splashed her burning face with cold water. Susie's attack had left her shaking with frustrated indignation. How could her own daughter get so much so wrong? How could she demand high standards of support and understanding from others, when she was completely dismissive and insensitive to the needs of anyone but herself?

Because she's been adored and cherished from the moment she was born, came the answer. Susie had been doubly cosseted by parents who idolised and indulged her, never admitting even to each other the obvious reason behind it. Kate was the reason. They had lost Kate, and the guilt of that had eaten away like a septic sore in them both, a hurt they neither aired nor shared. Their hurt made Susie what she had become, a young woman who had never felt a second's real pain in her whole life until her father died. From that moment pain was heaped upon her – the grief of bereavement, the frightening reality of pregnancy, the emotion and guilt of abortion, the shock of learning that her trusted and adoring parents had simply been human beings with their own feet of clay.

Gwen stared at the wretched face which gazed back at her from the mirror, and in her mind's eye saw a different image. She remembered how Susie and she had clung to one another at Richard's funeral when their shock and grief had united them in their need for one another. And she remembered too Susie's pale face as she lay on the bed after the abortion, her eyes wide with a mixture of remorse and relief.

They needed each other then. And if only Susie would allow it, they needed each other now.

Gwen took a deep breath, straightening her shoulders as she gazed in the mirror. She must pull herself together. After years of absence, she had to be here for Kate now. A daughter needed her mum at a time like this. She must be strong for her.

Pulling a comb through the tangle of her hair, she touched up her lipstick, pinching her cheeks to give them colour. Then, smoothing down her jersey and brushing off her slacks, she tiptoed down to the door of Kate's room, where she peered cautiously through the glass panel.

'Best not disturb her, doctor said.'

Gwen spun round to find herself facing the man who had stood so resolutely beside Margaret when they first arrived. This was plainly a man for whom fresh air and hard work were a way of life. His face was ruddy and weatherbeaten, with pale green eyes encircled by a network of deep lines. His hair was thinning, greying, and as she took the hand he stretched out to her, she could feel hard, calloused skin against the softness of her own fingers.

'Roger Davis. And you're Mrs Moreton.'

For a second or two they stood with their hands clasped, unsure what to say. Finally it was Roger who broke away, moving to stand beside Gwen as they both looked through the glass window.

'Margaret's with her.'

Gwen nodded, too choked to articulate the feelings of helplessness and envy which engulfed her as she saw the obvious closeness between mother and daughter.

'She loves her mum.'

Gwen nodded dumbly.

'She'll be needing her now – until Martin comes.'

Gwen swallowed hard, her eyes fixed on Kate's face as Margaret sat beside her stroking her forehead. When she spoke, it was with her back to Roger.

'I should go then.'

'Perhaps best.'

Dragging herself from the scene inside the room, Gwen turned slowly, straightening her shoulders as she started to move.

'Thank you.' His voice stopped her in her tracks. 'For Kate. Thank you. She's been our whole world, our life.'

She stared at him, eyes glassy, unable to speak. Then, with the slightest nod of her head, she held his gaze for just a second before she walked sadly away.

The clock above the lifts said nearly midnight as Susie spotted her mother coming out of the ward. Brian, who had been waiting by the lift for Gwen, glanced anxiously at her pale face as she announced, 'We should leave.'

'Well, I'm not,' retorted Susie, coming over to join them. 'I promised Kate I'd stay, and I will.'

'Kate is too ill and definitely too busy to know who's here at the moment. And her mum's with her. I think she simply needs her family right now.'

Susie registered surprise as she stared at Gwen. 'I think,' she said quietly, 'she's not the only one. Me too.'

Gwen reached out to grab her hand. 'So do I, Susie. Oh, so do I!'

And falling gratefully into her daughter's arms, Gwen hugged her close before the two women followed Brian out of the building towards their cars.

Susie turned the radio up full blast on the long journey back to her West Hampstead flat as a wave of weariness washed over her. She dimly remembered that this endless night had come after several others where sleep had eluded her. How long ago that morning seemed, when she had decided to go and see where this new sister of hers lived.

Kate. Her sister. Susie found herself smiling. How often during her growing years had she wished for company, longing to have siblings as her school friends did. Yet the reality of discovering the existence of a sister of her own had filled her with fear and resentment. She had made that visit expecting to despise Kate, meaning simply to make it clear that her mother was too vulnerable after her father's death to cope with another emotional upheaval. And then she met her. There was something about Kate, a calmness combined with warmth and sensitivity, which was disarming. Conversation had been surprisingly easy between them, rapport immediate, as if an invisible cord of belonging entwined the two of them. And her father's image which haunted the features of Kate's face in a way which had been such a shock to Susie at first, were already becoming dear and reassuring. In Kate, she glimpsed the same quiet intelligence she had always admired in her father, a counterbalance to the fiery temperament she herself had inherited from her mother.

In her mind's eye she pictured Gwen as she left the hospital, exhausted at the end of what had been the most extraordinary night. She still found it unbelievable that for years Gwen, who had been an almost smothering mother, had been able to hold to herself the guilty secret of Kate's existence. What a burden that must have been! And how lonely if she had not been allowed to share it with the husband who knew only too well what she had been through. And what of Richard who had always been such a loving, protective father to her? Was he ever truly able to bury the thought that another daughter existed somewhere? His pain might have been private, but pain it surely was. How tragic to think how nearly he met her. If he'd just lived a few more months. If only he'd had the chance to see Kate for himself . . .

At last she was there. Turning the car into the start of her road, Susie made for the piece of waste land on which she always parked, only to find that someone had got there first. Cursing softly under her breath she drove past – then stamped on the brakes a few seconds later. Peering back into the darkness she slowly reversed until she was alongside the car. It was Paul's.

Jumping out, she ran to pull open the driver's door – and there he was, stretched out in the seat sound asleep. His eyes flickered dreamily as he grinned sheepishly at her.

'I thought you might need a hug.'

'Oh, Paul,' she whispered, falling into his arms, 'you have no idea how much!'

Gwen never slept late. The first shaft of light round the edge of the curtains had always acted like a built-in alarm clock for her. Not that day, though. Once Brian had seen her inside the front door in the early hours of the morning she had mounted the stairs, left her clothes where they dropped, and fallen into bed. And so as she fumbled to pick up the telephone when it rang beside her, she was astonished to find that it was nearly ten o'clock.

'Is that Mrs Moreton? Gwen?'

The voice at the other end of the phone was hesitant, as if the caller were unsure of the reaction they would receive.

'Yes,' she mumbled, trying to gather her thoughts, 'Gwen Moreton here.'

'This is Kate's mum.' There was a pause. 'Margaret Davis. I hope you don't mind me ringing.'

'No – no, of course not!'

'Only I thought you'd like to know it's a girl. Kate had a little girl about an hour ago.'

'Oh!' Gwen was wide awake now. 'How is she? She looked so ill when I left.'

'Her blood pressure was a real problem, and the baby was lying in an awkward position which worried the doctor. They even called in the consultant because they were so concerned about her.'

'Poor Kate!'

'The baby was born feet first in the end. Martin said she's putting her foot in it already.'

Gwen laughed out loud. She knew she was going to like Martin.

'He arrived then! What time did he get there?'

'Not until seven o'clock this morning, just in time to be with Kate when it mattered. She burst into tears when she saw him.'

'She needed him, that was plain.'

'Well, he loves her very much. We all do.'

'I know that – and I'm glad.'

Margaret hesitated for a moment before continuing. 'About last night. I'm sorry, I didn't mean to be rude. It was just such a shock to see you there.'

'I know. I felt the same. I shouldn't have come, I know now.'

'Don't think that. We have so much to thank you for. Without you, we wouldn't have had our lovely daughter. She has brought real joy into our lives. I'm only sorry that your family weren't able to know her as we have.'

'Richard would have been proud of her.'

'I was sorry to hear about your husband.'

Gwen's voice shook as she replied. 'Thank you. It's especially sad that he never had the chance to meet Kate.'

'Sad for her too.'

Gwen couldn't answer.

'I want you to know you're welcome here.'

'You don't have to say that ...'

'I mean it. Roger and I both feel the same. I don't suppose the years have been easy for you without Kate. We heard you, you know, that morning at the adoption centre when they first brought her in to us. You must have been in the room next door because I heard them wrenching her from your arms. The pain of your cry was like the howl of a wounded animal, and that sound has haunted me from that day to this. I couldn't comfort you then, but perhaps in some small way I can now. There's so much to tell you that I think you've longed to know. I have photos and school reports and stories to share. One day, when you feel ready, come and visit. You're welcome here.'

'Thank you,' whispered Gwen, 'thank you.'

'Well, I'll go then.'

'It was kind of you to ring.'

'Come and see the baby. Kate would like that.'

'I will. By the way, has she got a name yet?'

'Yes, Kate knew the moment she saw her. Her name's Elizabeth.'

Chapter Fourteen

Elizabeth had fallen asleep in her buggy on the way back from the shops, so rather than wake her Kate wheeled her into the lounge where she could keep a watchful eye as she got on with the invitations. Careful not to wake the sleeping baby, she drew the invitation cards out of the shopping tray beneath the buggy, then arranged everything she needed on the dining table. Address book, notepad, a silver pen to make her copper-plate writing look really special – she was ready.

They had intended to arrange Elizabeth's baptism long before this, but with Martin so busy not just with his own work but also getting Roger's new business up and running, combined with all the comings and goings at the farm, she'd not quite got round to organising the event. She glanced across at the baby who slept with her head of golden hair resting gently against the seat, cheeks delicately flushed, rosebud lips slightly parted as she took quick shallow breaths.

Well, thought Kate with a smile, at ten months Elizabeth wouldn't fit into the christening gown which had been an heirloom in the Davis family for centuries, but she would look beautiful just the same. Their baby simply *was* beautiful, a blessing and gift which had transformed their lives and fulfilled their marriage.

The service would take place at their local church near the

farm, where Kate herself and generations of the family before her had been baptised. And the farm would be perfect for the reception afterwards. In spite of all the renovations and building work, the worst was over and the house which had been her home for so many years would come into its own not just to welcome the little newcomer, but to mark its own regeneration and new life.

It had been quite a year. Kate sat for a moment, pen poised in mid-air, thinking back over the highs and lows: the money problems, the emotional turmoil which had engulfed them all and changed them forever. Images flashed into her mind, like cartoons retelling the story – the exhaustion of daily grind in her father's face as he came out of the milking shed, her mum's worried expression when she talked about the bank manager's visit, Martin's hand tightly clutching hers as their baby was born.

Then there was Gwen. This year had brought Gwen into their lives. Funny how Kate had never been able to think of her as 'mother'. Of course not. Margaret was the only mother she would ever need.

With flowing italic letters, Kate addressed the first envelope to Mrs Gwen Moreton, adding a note on the invitation card that she hoped Brian would be able to come too. They all liked Brian, with his quiet warmth and dry wit. Kate had no idea how close he and Gwen were, especially as Richard's death had happened only just over a year before, but Brian was good for her, of that Kate was certain.

Next came the invitation for Graham and Celia. Kate had only met them on a couple of occasions, but she recognised that it would be a mistake to exclude them from such a family occasion. Celia could be a gushing and supportive ally. Heaven help anyone who made an enemy of her!

Just before she sealed Madge's envelope Kate scribbled a note on the back of the latest photograph of Elizabeth, sitting in her high chair, face and hands completely coated in chocolate pudding, her grin of delight stretching from ear to ear. Madge would love that photo because she adored Elizabeth. Kate chuckled. The old aunt would probably like the chocolate pudding too! She must remember to have some of Madge's favourite sweets on the menu for the christening lunch.

Next came Susie's invitation, and as Kate pulled out her book to make sure she'd got the new address right, she wondered how she could define her feelings for her recently found sister. They were very different. Susie was volatile, unpredictable and prickly. She was also artistic, sensitive and generous to a fault. In the short months during which they had been getting to know each other, they had shouted and cried and held each other as if their lives depended on it. From its shaky start, the relationship between them had grown until Kate dared now to think that the best way to describe it was 'love'. Not that either of them would ever use the word. To give it a name was unnecessary. It was simply a wonderful, surprising, heart-warming fact.

A sudden movement caught her attention as Elizabeth stirred in her sleep. Kate glanced at her watch. If she got cracking, these could catch the one o'clock post. Checking that she could find the book of first-class stamps, she drew out a sheet of paper. She and Martin had a special request to make of Susie. She chose her words carefully, checking and re-reading several times before she was finally satisfied Then, with a final flourish, she crossed her fingers and sealed the envelope.

Susie recognised the writing as soon as she spotted the letter on the hall mat. Smiling, she tore it open, placing the invitation in prime position on the kitchen shelf. She was on the point of throwing away the envelope when she noticed the other sheet of paper folded inside.

My dear Susie, (wrote Kate)

This year has brought so many miracles. Elizabeth, of course – Gwen, and you. Both you and I grew up believing each of us was an only child. The joy of finding that I have a sister as terrific as you is impossible to put into words. I know you understand, and share the feeling.

Because we have lost so many years of family life, Martin and I want to make sure you are very much part of our family from now on. Will you do us the great honour of agreeing to become Elizabeth's godmother? It would be wonderful for us if you say yes – a tie of love to bind us together from now on.

Think about it and let me know.

With fondest love,

Kate and Martin

Touched and delighted, Susie laid the letter beside the invitation card addressed to both her and Paul. She would show it to him when he got home. How she was longing to see him! This time he'd been away for only two days, but since they'd moved into their new home together a few weeks earlier, she found herself missing him more than ever when work took him away.

Susie looked around her, taking in the bare walls and the packing boxes which were stashed neatly about the room waiting for shelves to be put up and cupboard units finished. This Victorian school building in Kensington had been a real find with its large airy rooms, and the hall which would eventually be just perfect as a studio for Paul. Their office had been the first room they'd worked on, stripping and varnishing the old pine floor, painting the lofty walls a warm cream which was at once welcoming and elegant against the renovated architrave and coving. Best of all had been the rediscovery of the fireplace, with its original tiles still intact, their rich blues and greens gleaming now after hours of scraping and polishing.

Getting the office organised had been one thing. Dealing with their burgeoning workload was quite another. Neither of them had expected their decision to set up their own advertising agency to be received with such interest. Of course Paul's reputation helped considerably, but as they worked their way through his little black book of contacts, they found that the reaction to Susie's fresh approach and imaginative ideas was reassuringly enthusiastic too. It was early days, but the future looked promising with several contracts already in progress, and others falling into place for the weeks ahead.

The decision to leave the agency which had brought them together had become inevitable in view of Deborah's vitriol towards Susie. Deborah was not used to losing her man. Men left her life only when she had tired of them. She was far from finished with Paul, who had always remained tantalisingly elusive whenever she tried to pin him down. To see him ensnared by a red-haired little upstart like Susie was pathetic of him, and infuriating for her. She set out with cold determination to show him the error of his ways. She flirted and niggled and ignored and finally cried all over him – but from the warmth in his eyes whenever he spoke of Susie, Deborah finally accepted with disbelief that he was hooked. From then on she turned the full glare of her anger on to Susie, undermining her at every level, criticising her to anyone who'd listen. Fortunately Susie's work spoke for itself, and most colleagues and clients recognised Deborah's bitchiness for what it was. When Susie finally handed in her notice no one was really surprised, although when she and Paul announced that they were going into partnership with a business which could in time rival their own, astonishment was soon replaced by a distinct ripple of concern around the office.

In fact, Paul and she had found themselves to be very compatible work partners, and when Susie tried to analyse why their partnership worked, she could only put it down to communication. Conversation between them had always been easy, whether the discussion was personal or work-related. Neither seemed to feel the need to better the other, so that if one came up with the start of an idea, the other would enthuse, debate and constructively criticise until the inspiration became a plan worth selling with confidence to clients. The combination of Paul's visual eye and photographic skill and Susie's artistic flair and persuasive sales talk had clients intrigued enough to listen to what they had to offer. And so far, what they offered was proving to be a very successful package indeed.

But Susie was only too well aware of the fact that at the heart of their working partnership was a deep loving friendship which simply got better and better. That in itself was amazing when she considered its very uncertain start. The time when it all changed would be etched forever in her mind.

She had arrived back from the hospital utterly drained, and there he was, dozing in his car outside her flat. Between them hovered the spectre of misunderstanding and half-truths. He was jet-lagged and worn out by his trip to the States, his eyes circled by dark shadows of fatigue, knowing little of the events which had taken her to the hospital that night, nor the emotional rollercoaster she had been on.

With so much to talk about and little energy, they opted for saying nothing. Arm in arm they climbed the stairs, falling instantly asleep as they collapsed entwined and exhausted on the bed.

Waking the next morning, warm, tousled and cuddled together, conversation had been natural and easy, helped by the depth of need and love they glimpsed in each other. Overwhelmed with wonder and relief that this unique and talented man should not only love her, but want her to be a central part of his life, Susie found the courage to share with him the secrets she had kept tightly to herself. She told him of her delight at their time in Rome which turned to dread when she discovered she was pregnant; her shame that he would think her naïve and unworldly, which she probably was; her reticence to explain the situation to him in case he believed she was simply trying to trap him. Paul held her tightly, watching her face as she described her despair trying to decide what she should do. Her naturally protective feelings towards their unborn child fought with her clear understanding that a baby would be wrong for them both – especially as at that time Paul was hardly part of her life at all, although he clearly remained attached to the delectable Deborah.

Unaware of her tears which fell softly on to his shoulder, Susie told him about her mum, and the relief she felt once she'd shared with her the dilemma of the pregnancy. She spoke of her visit to the clinic, and her final decision to go ahead with the abortion. And Paul's arm tightened around her as he heard about the day of the operation, the emotion, the guilt, the trauma which had haunted her ever since.

On and on she went, unable to stop once the unburdening had begun. She described again the new and cherished closeness with her mother after the prickly distance of their previous years together, the shock of discovering her parents had had a daughter earlier on in their lives, a usurper who threatened to demand her mother's love just as, for the first time, Susie truly discovered that love for herself. Then she told of the sense of betrayal which led to her decision to confront Kate, to warn her off, dismiss her as irrelevant – an ambition which dissipated in the face of Kate's sensitivity, and then her illness.

Finally Susie described the events of the previous night: being at Kate's bedside, all the while desperately trying to locate Martin, the brother-in-law she'd never met. She spoke of the tension when Kate's adoptive parents arrived to find her and Gwen at Kate's side, and the shock of seeing her mother in the arms of 'her very dear friend, Brian'. Out it all tumbled, incoherent, wretched and tearful, while Paul held her close.

And then it was over. She lay spent and exhausted, purged of secrets, exposed by the truth. Paul buried his face in the softness of her red hair, his voice barely more than a whisper.

'Susie, I'm sorry. Sorry for all you've been through, sorry for my part in the hurt you've had to face alone. But see the love around you. See me. Know my love is here for you always.'

And so it was. That's how it had been ever since. No blame or recriminations. No distrust or accusations. No question too difficult to ask, nor memory too raw to face. Just ten months of growing closeness, easing out of each other the pains of the past which held and ensnared them.

And no need to discuss the future, because with their ghosts laid, whatever came they would face together.

'Well, are you going?'

'To Paris? I shouldn't think so.'

Tricia sat down heavily on the settee, peering over her cup of coffee to watch Gwen as she stood at the ironing board.

'But you've always loved Paris.'

'Because of Richard. He made it special.'

'And Brian will make it special too, in his own way. You've always said how much you wanted to visit the galleries there, and let's face it, galleries never held the remotest interest for Richard, did they?'

'We went there on honeymoon. He died just as we were about to leave for Paris to celebrate our twenty-fifth wedding anniversary. Paris was *our* place. I wouldn't dream of going there with someone else.'

'Would you go with me?'

Gwen stood the iron on its end as she thought about that question. 'Probably, yes.'

'So what's the difference? You've always said that Brian is just a friend.'

'He is, the best possible friend. But I would feel disloyal going with a man other than Richard.'

'Depends on what he has in mind besides visits to art galleries.'

Gwen thumped the iron along the length of the sleeve of the blouse which covered the board.

'Would you have your own room?'

'Of course.'

'And he'd stay in his? No *après*-gallery cups of coffee, no croissants on the balcony overlooking the rooftops?'

The iron stopped as Gwen glared across towards her friend. 'But I'm not going, Trish.'

'No moonlit walks along the banks of the Seine, no dancing cheek to cheek on the *bateau mouche*?'

'Look, I've made my decision, and that's that.'

'You're burning that sleeve.'

Jumping in alarm, Gwen snatched the iron away from the board.

'It just seems a shame,' continued Tricia, her eyes sparkling with amusement, 'when you have the obvious devotion of a lovely chap like Brian, to keep pushing him away.'

'Richard was the love of my life. His death is too recent. I can't, I simply can't.'

'Can't what? Be happy? Why ever not?'

'It's not right.'

'Really? Wouldn't Richard want you to be happy again?'

'Yes, I'm sure he would, but ...'

'... it's not decent. It would be all right if you went on interesting trips with the companionship of another woman, me for instance.'

'That would be fine.'

'But to find the same pleasure in the company of a man wouldn't be?'

Gwen sighed. 'You know what people would say.'

'Does it matter what other people think?'

'Of course.'

'Really, Gwen, does it? If you've found someone who makes you very happy – and honestly, in all the years I've known you, I've never seen you looking more contented and comfortable than you are when you're with Brian – then why shouldn't you grasp it with both hands? You deserve happiness. After all you've been through, this is your chance. Take it!'

'It's not that simple.'

'Brian loves you, you know that.'

'He hasn't said so.'

'He doesn't need to. It's written all over him when he looks at you.'

Gwen didn't answer, but it was plain that the ironing was completely forgotten.

'And you return his love. That's easy to see too.'

'No!'

'And why shouldn't you? You've got a lot of years left ahead of you, and the chance to spend them with a man who really cares about you. I tell you, Gwen, I wouldn't mind being in your situation.'

'Mike still loves you. He spent three hours telling me so the other evening.'

'Then he has a mighty funny way of showing it. Whenever he sees me, all he does is go on and on about what a wonderful time he's having with other women.'

'He's bluffing. There are no other women, none that matter anyway. It's you he wants, Trish.'

Tricia shook her head. 'I don't believe that. I think this is all about power. He didn't want me, but can't bear the thought of anyone else having me either. That's why he's trying to be at the house all the time. How long ago did he start that conservatory, and it's still not finished yet? And now he's talking about starting on the garage roof, so that if he has his way he'll be popping in and out keeping an eye on me for years to come.'

'He just wants you to give your marriage another chance.'

'No way.'

'Trish, are you sure? You've been through so much together over the years.'

'How right you are, and that's why I know I couldn't go back to that again.'

'Then you must tell him once and for all. He believes he can make you change your mind.'

'Oh, I've told him. He chooses not to listen.'

'I think he's lonely.'

'I recognise that feeling. I was lonely within my marriage for years.'

'Poor Mike.'

'I'm sorry, Gwen, but there'll be no happy ending here, not with me. Mike will survive. There'll be some doting lady to console him, you can count on that.'

'And you? Who'll be there for you?'

Tricia smiled broadly. 'Funny you should ask! I might have quite a choice. Just look at this lot.'

Out of her bag she drew a manilla folder full of letters.

'I put an advert in *The Times* personal column.'

'You didn't!'

'Thirty-two replies! And at least thirty-one of them are interesting.'

'What happened to the other one?'

'He sent a photo of himself starkers . . .'

Gwen shrieked with laughter.

'Sent me a poem too. I didn't know you could get words like that to rhyme, the dirty old man!'

'And the others?'

'Well,' said Tricia, pulling out the letters to flick through them, 'I can take my pick – a doctor, an architect, a man who seems to have made a fortune from home with his own e-mail business . . .'

'How old are they?'

'In their fifties mostly.'

'Can you be sure they're single?'

'I only know what they tell me, but most of them are divorced, three or four are widowed and there are even some who've never been married at all.'

'I wonder why?'

'Precisely. I've filtered them out already. My shortlist is down to ten now.'

'You're planning to meet them? Complete strangers?'

'They won't be strangers for long. And we'll talk on the phone first.'

'But they could be sex maniacs.'

'Hmm,' agreed Tricia, grinning broadly.

'You'll have to be careful about how you meet them.'

'Of course, I'm not stupid. But I enjoy male company, and this is one way to meet suitable men that I'd never cross paths with any other way.'

Gwen came over to look through the pile of letters, reading snippets from a few, chuckling over some of the photographs, admiring others. Finally, she sat back with a smile.

'Well, good for you. There are some smashing letters here.'

'Right! Perhaps somewhere in that pile is the love of my life. Perhaps not – but won't it be fun finding out!'

'And talking of finding out, won't you be worried if other people discover how you meet these new friends?'

'Do I care what people think, is that what you mean? Not one bit, Gwen. It's no one's business but my own. I want to find love again, *real* love, not possession and control which was all I ever got from Mike. If putting a small ad in the papers helps me find Mr Wonderful, then I'll give it a go – and to hell with what other people think!'

And as the two friends laughed, Gwen's eye fell on Richard's photo propped in a prominent position on the mantelpiece – and she thought of Brian.

✻   ✻   ✻

'Right, is that it? Sure you don't need a hand with the lasagnes?'

Margaret smiled gratefully at Gillian. 'All under control. They've been in the freezer for the past two weeks. And the gammon's done, so are the apple pies and cheesecakes, which means I'll only have the salads to do in the morning. I can make those up when we get back from the church.'

'Good job we haven't got any little terrors around this weekend.'

'Funny, I quite miss them. They may have me running round in circles when I've got a houseful, but without them it's a bit quiet for me now.'

Gillian came to perch on the kitchen table beside Margaret as she put the finishing touches to the icing on the christening cake. 'No regrets then?'

'No, partner, definitely not!'

'I can't believe how quickly it's all picked up. When did we first start talking about these riding holidays?'

'Just before Elizabeth was born. Less than a year ago.'

'And the work on the house took about three months, didn't it?'

'Those bedrooms badly needed doing though. I had no idea how much potential we had in this house until you suggested opening up the attic space. We'd never have managed last weekend without it. That was our biggest group so far — twenty-two twelve-year-olds!'

Gillian grimaced. 'That school sent the whole class for a weekend of horse-riding. I don't think the poor ponies knew what hit them!'

'It's a lot of work for you though. Those animals need to be groomed and exercised every day even if you haven't got any little darlings here.'

'My girls are pretty good, and there are all the local

lessons too. Yes, it is hard work, but I love it. Even Simon is impressed.'

'He'd only be impressed if it makes money.'

'That's why he's impressed. The books are looking quite healthy, if I say so myself.'

'All I care about is that the bank manager thinks so. In fact, did you realise that he sends his daughter here for lessons now? That new girl, Jane? John Diggens is her dad.'

'Well, I hope he's a gardener in his spare time. He can order his geraniums as well when he comes to pick her up.'

'Just as long as he doesn't expect to collect a pint or two of milk while he's here. That's a thing of the past, I'm delighted to say. I certainly wasn't sorry to see the dairy herd go, I can tell you.'

'What about Roger? He must miss them.'

'Oh, he did for the first few weeks, until he realised how wonderful it was *not* to have to get up at five o'clock on winter mornings.'

'He's changed colour, have you noticed? He's lost that greyness that always used to be in his face.'

'He's happier than I've seen him for ages.'

'Taken years off him!'

Margaret chuckled. 'When I look at him now, I catch a glimpse of the handsome young man I married.'

'How romantic!'

'Oh, he always was!'

'He wouldn't like to give my Simon a few lessons, would he? Travelling up and down to the City every day wears him out. I never see him awake in the week, and he's good for nothing at the weekend.'

'Tell him he'll get more sleep if he comes up with a business idea which he can operate through the internet. An e-tailer, that's what Martin calls Roger now.'

'Is he doing well? Are the plants selling?'

'As fast as Roger can produce them. Now he's got the

packaging and transit better organised, he can deal with much larger orders. One of the big garden centre chains ordered several thousand plants just last week. They're quite interested in several other hybrids he's come up with too.'

'So it's looking good?'

'The future certainly seems a lot more promising than it did this time last year. In fact, if it goes on expanding at this rate, Martin is talking about giving up his job to run it full-time. In fact, the farm holidays and the geranium business don't take nearly as much work as keeping a herd used to, and we're making twice as much money. And it's all thanks to you, Gillian. If you hadn't come up with the idea ...'

'If you hadn't been exactly the person you are – a capable, organised homemaker – none of this would have worked.'

For a moment the two women beamed at each other, before Gillian caught sight of the clock above the Aga.

'Heavens, must rush. Got a lesson at five. See you tomorrow then. Simon will bring the wine over this evening, and we'll both be at the church in good time for the service.'

'Thanks again.'

'And wear that lilac outfit of yours. It suits you!'

'It'll show the splashes if I make a mess putting out the food in the morning.'

'Then use a pinny – but wear the lilac. You have a romantic husband!'

And with a wink and a wave, Gillian was gone.

'If I can't sit in the front, I'm not going!'

'Madge, I get nauseous in the back.' Celia's lips were set in a hard thin line. 'And that seat is mine. I always sit in the front. I have my hankies and map books close at hand in the door pocket. Can you navigate?'

Madge pretended that she hadn't heard the question.

'Might as well go home then. If I try to squeeze into that back seat, you'd need a crane to get me out.'

'The navigator needs to sit beside the driver. It's only common sense.'

Madge picked up her voluminous shopping bag, and leaning heavily on her stick began to walk away.

'Madge, get in the back. You know you don't want to miss this christening!'

'I don't, but I can't. Goodbye, Celia. You can explain to Gwen why I'm not there.'

At that moment Graham's head appeared from inside the boot which he had been filling with various bags and packages.

'Tell you what, I'll sit in the back. If you drive, Celia, and Madge sits beside you, you can carry on bickering all the way, while I doze quietly behind you.'

Celia stiffened, her face red. 'You're missing the point again, Graham. There's a principle at stake here. Madge always demands her own way, and I've had enough. You're my husband. You should stand up for me.'

Graham didn't even bother to glance at her as he climbed into the back. With a look of gloating triumph, Madge made her surprisingly sprightly way into the front passenger seat, leaving Celia only one option. Eventually, with an exaggerated, theatrical sigh, she got behind the wheel, and after several minutes of precise seat, mirror and heat adjustment, she tuned into Radio 4 and pulled away from the house.

Madge gave it all of thirty seconds before she retuned the radio to a golden oldies station. Then pushing back her seat, she smiled, closed her eyes, and within minutes was snoring soundly.

'You look wonderful!'

'Really?' Gwen peered anxiously in the hall mirror. 'This suit isn't too bright? Or the skirt too short? When I bought it years ago, this length was all the fashion.'

Brian turned her to face him, planting an affectionate kiss on her forehead. 'You've got great legs, so show them off! And that colour is delightful on you.'

'I don't want to look like mutton dressed as lamb.'

'I know.'

'Especially not on this occasion.'

'I do understand – and you look lovely, believe me.'

'Why am I so nervous? I've met Roger and Margaret several times now, and I see Kate, Martin and the baby at least once a fortnight.'

'Because there's never been a gathering quite like this one, where all the players are together under one roof. It's only natural you should feel a bit apprehensive.'

'It is?'

'It is.'

Gwen smiled up at him. 'Were you always this sensible and reassuring, or is it just today?'

'Oh, I guess I'm simply a nice chap to have around. You should try it more often.'

'How often?'

'For the rest of your life?'

Gwen's face suddenly became serious.

'Brian, don't. I need more time ...'

'You certainly do. A lifetime, in fact. Come on! We'll be late if we don't get a move on.'

He turned to open the front door, watching while Gwen picked up a brightly wrapped christening present for Elizabeth. As she walked towards the door, she suddenly stopped to smile up towards him.

'I'm glad you're coming today. Have I already told you that?'

'Several times. I'm glad too.'

Stretching out a hand to touch his cheek, she looked into

his eyes with warm affection.

'Thank you.'

His only answer was to brush the softest, most gentle of kisses across her lips. For a moment they held each other's gaze, before he took her hand and led the way out to the car.

'For heaven's sake, Graham, give that camera to me! You've got your finger over the lens!'

Graham took a deep breath, before looking up to glare directly at his wife. 'Three things, Celia. Firstly, don't speak to me like that. Secondly, I practically run a local government finance department. I am quite capable to taking a simple photograph without your help. And thirdly, my dearest, this shot would be sadly lacking without your delightful presence. So stop fussing, and go over to stand beside Madge. Right everyone, smile please!'

For a second Gwen caught Susie's eye, recalling memories of another photo session at another family gathering. Richard had been with them then, twenty-five years of happy marriage behind them, a bright future ahead ...

And then the moment was gone as the assembled crowd grinned broadly while cameras clicked and flashed. Standing in the centre of the group, with Kate on one side of her and Paul on the other, Susie looked down at the sleeping child in her arms. Her god-daughter had no sense of occasion. Elizabeth had bawled through the baptism, been wide awake on the journey back from the church, only to fall sound asleep on Susie's shoulder the moment they reached the farm. Unused to carrying babies, especially a sturdy youngster who was surprisingly heavy, Susie looked round for a seat so that she could cradle Elizabeth more comfortably. Seeing that she was settled, Paul blew her a kiss as he picked up his camera and slid quietly off into the crowd. He hadn't been interested in taking formal group shots, preferring instead to catch intimate, unprepared moments of the afternoon's events. Susie watched him go as she felt Elizabeth cuddle in towards her. Unexpected tears pricked Susie's eyes as she looked down at the baby's fine golden hair, the long blonde lashes, soft skin and perfect tiny fingernails.

Her baby would have been perfect too. She might have had her mother's red hair and pale skin, with Paul's ready smile and dark eyes. What joy she would have brought to them both – if only she'd been allowed to live.

There was a sudden flash. Paul was kneeling in front of her, camera to his eye as she stared at him, unable to speak.

'Next time I take a photo of you like that,' he said softly, reaching out to touch her, 'the child in your arms will be ours.'

Grasping his hand, she nodded dumbly, overwhelmed with love for him.

Over the other side of the garden Madge was comfortably straddling the length of a wooden bench, her back supported by a honeysuckle-clad fence, when Gwen brought over a brimming glass of sherry.

'Here, I've brought another piece of that apple pie for you too.'

'With ice cream?'

'Of course – and cream too,' smiled Gwen, taking the cushioned garden seat opposite. 'You look well, Madge. How are you feeling?'

'Mustn't grumble. My back's creaky, and my legs ache, but I could be worse.'

'I've got another pile of magazines for you. I'll bring them over in the week.'

'Have you left the crosswords for me?'

'I've had no chance to do crosswords lately. Time seems to fly by.'

'When you're enjoying yourself?'

'That's what they say.'

'And are you enjoying yourself, Gwen? It's been a hard time for you. You've had more than your share of shocks and sadness.'

Gwen nodded with a sigh. 'Perhaps family parties are a time for bringing the past close again. Here I am at Elizabeth's christening, with my mind full of memories of our twenty-fifth wedding anniversary celebration. Do you remember what a happy time that was for us all? I could never have imagined then that I'd have been widowed for more than a year by now, with a newly found daughter and grandchild. Here I am, surrounded by a group of people who never even knew Richard, yet I feel I'm part of this circle. I have so much to learn about Kate, all those years to fill in, and it's been difficult to stop myself wanting to be with her every day.'

'Mustn't be too pushy though,' said Madge, digging her spoon into the apple pie. 'I know you're anxious to make up for lost time, but Kate has a life and family of her own.'

'I know. It's taken me a while to realise my involvement can only be on her terms. I've learned to wait until she invites me, to offer help knowing that sometimes it's not needed. Margaret is the mother who matters to her.'

'Besides, you have Susie.'

'Yes.'

'She seems happy enough. What do you think of her Paul?'

Gwen looked across to where Paul sat close to Susie, both looking down at Elizabeth on her knee.

'I think he's good for her. She's quite a handful, but he seems to bring out the best in her.'

'Will it last, do you think?'

'If you mean, will they marry, I'm not sure that matters as much to her generation as it did to mine. But yes, I think they're happy, and he obviously adores her.'

'So you're free then? Both daughters off your hands and getting on with their own lives. What about you getting on with yours?'

'Oh, I'm doing all right.'

'Nice chap, your Brian.'

'He's not *my* Brian.'

'Oh yes he is, if you want him to be.'

'It's too soon, Madge.'

Madge carried on eating for a while, finally laying down her spoon before leaning in towards Gwen.

'Take a tip from me. For nearly all of my eighty years, I've lived alone. It didn't matter so much when I was younger. I even quite liked having my own place where I could simply please myself. But now I'm old and weary, and every bone in my body aches – and loneliness feels like a prison. Sometimes I don't speak to a single soul all day long. No one really cares how I am, or whether I'm coping. You're almost in your fifties now, and the only thing you can be sure of in the years that lie ahead is that you will grow older. Don't go through that alone, Gwen. If you have a choice to share your life with someone whose company you enjoy, grab your chance with all your heart. Otherwise you might find yourself like me: old, crotchety and very lonely.'

Gwen sat back thoughtfully, glancing over to where Brian was walking with Roger out of the kitchen garden towards the geranium greenhouses and enclosures.

'He's asked me to go to Paris with him.'

'When?'

'Next week. It's all come up so quickly. I need more time to consider a suggestion like that.'

'Paris, eh? That would be difficult for you.'

'How could I possibly go with Brian to a city which reminds me so much of Richard?'

'Why Paris? Is there a special reason for him asking you there?'

'A Monet exhibition. He knows how much we'd both enjoy that.'

'So go!'

'It's not that simple, is it?'

'Isn't it?'

'I shouldn't feel like this so soon after Richard's death. It's not right.'

The old lady took a large sip from her sherry glass. 'Richard would want you to find happiness again.'

'Do you think so?'

'His whole life was centred around you and Susie. He'd be pleased to see Susie settled with her Paul. And I believe he'd like you to marry again too.'

'I never mentioned marriage!'

'No, but Brian would, if you'd let him.'

Gwen didn't answer immediately, lost in her own thoughts. Madge gathered another mouthful of apple pie on to her spoon before she spoke again.

'I'll expect a postcard then. Now, I need the loo! Give me your arm, then I can pick up a piece of that cheesecake on the way back.'

Out in the geranium gardens, flanked by gleaming new greenhouses, Brian was clearly impressed. Roger had taken great pride in showing him round the neat rows of new cuttings, the sophisticated watering system, the fields near the farmhouse that until a few months earlier had been pasture land for the dairy herd, now transformed into a thriving nursery garden business. There was an air of success about the place, evident not just in the fields and greenhouses, but in the stable blocks, paddocks, grazing areas and farmhouse. Hall Farm was bristling with enterprise and activity.

'Roger, this is a real credit to you. You've found a niche in the market, and filled it. Congratulations!'

Never a man of words, Roger simply nodded quiet acknowledgement of the compliment.

'But after a lifetime of farming, don't you miss it?'

'I thought I would. I still wake up on the dot of five every morning, and have to stop myself getting out of bed to milk the herd. Old habits die hard. But I've been busy. Of course, I couldn't have done it without Martin. All the sales are down to him. And I've got a good lad who comes in from the village every day to give me a hand. May even have to take on another, if the sales keep going up.'

'And I see you're diversifying. Judging from that last greenhouse, you're planning to offer a wider range of unusual perennials in the future.'

Roger put his hands in his trouser pockets, gazing out across his plants as he answered. 'It's always fascinated me to try and breed new varieties. Tinkering with nature, Margaret calls it. When the horticulturist from the garden centre saw some of my efforts, he just flipped. Said I didn't know what a success story I was sitting on. Of course, having all that press coverage helped a lot.'

'Do you worry about not being able to cope with it all?'

'Nope. I refuse to grow more quickly than is safe and right for my plants. I reckon I need another couple of years to bring production up to capacity. Martin thinks he might have to give up his job and go into full-time business with me then, with the internet orders becoming so busy. That might even mean him and Kate moving back to this area, perhaps even taking over this house in time. Who knows?'

'Roger, that's great!'

A look of satisfaction settled on the older man's face. 'Not bad, is it, for an old stick-in-the-mud like me?'

'Not bad at all,' agreed Brian, as the two walked companionably back towards the house. They arrived minutes later to find the sound of music floating across the deserted kitchen garden. Roger's step quickened as he led the way into the large living room, where Kate was sitting at the piano leading the crowd in a joyful singsong. Elizabeth sat

wide-eyed on Margaret's knee, watching in bemused interest
as the grown-ups around her worked their way through a
few familiar songs from the shows. With Martin's hand on
her shoulder, Kate changed the mood then, slipping into a
couple of favourites from the sixties. Standing towards the
side of the crowd, Gwen stiffened as the familiar melodies
brought back poignant memories of long-ago – school
days with Richard, stolen kisses and first love. Through
eyes clouded with emotion, haunted by past moments and
lost years, she watched Kate as she played with the same
expression of concentration which Gwen had seen so often
on Richard's face as he sat at the piano.

Suddenly, she felt a hand slip into hers. Susie was beside her.
Shoulder to shoulder they stood, mother and daughter, bound
in memory, together in grief, united for whatever lay ahead.

And then, as Kate came to the triumphant end of one song,
she switched to another, a tune which was soft and evocative,
instantly familiar to the older members of the gathered crowd.
Gwen's hand flew to her mouth in shock as she recognised 'Sous
le Ciel de Paris', the tune that had been Richard's favourite,
the piece he had played at their anniversary party just before
he announced that he was taking her back to the city where
they'd spent their honeymoon. And as Susie gripped her hand,
Gwen looked up to find Brian's warm gaze fixed on her from
across the room.

'Did you see that?' hissed Celia, digging Madge in the
ribs. 'That Gwen is nothing but a hussy! Her husband hardly
in his grave, and she's flirting openly with that Brian chap.
It's disgusting!'

She sensed rather than saw movement behind her, as she
became aware of Graham's looming presence. His voice held a
note of threat as he whispered so that only she could hear.

'Celia, do shut up!'

* * *

As the evening sun sank over Roger's nursery garden, guests began to drift off. Gwen, Kate and Susie joined Margaret and Gillian in the kitchen, washing, wiping, covering and putting away. Conversation was relaxed and companionable; but then, thought Gwen, that was all due to Margaret herself who was such comfortable company. She thought back to her shock at their first meeting in the hospital, and wondered that she could ever have been nervous at the thought of meeting this remarkable, down-to-earth woman.

In the months since the night of Elizabeth's birth, the two of them had met several times. Gwen's trepidation at visiting the farm in which Kate had grown up was soon dispelled by Margaret's warm welcome. For hours they pored over photographs and school reports, Margaret telling stories of Kate's mishaps and adventures while Gwen shared memories of Susie's escapades. Two mothers. Two daughters. A tie of love which had drawn them together at last.

'We must go,' announced Kate. 'Elizabeth is exhausted, and so am I.'

Wiping her hands on a clean teatowel, Margaret turned to find herself enveloped in Kate's arms. 'Thanks, Mum,' she breathed, hugging her tightly. 'It's been a fantastic day – and you are a truly wonderful mum, the best ever.'

Gwen busied herself with wiping down the draining board, apparently not noticing the emotion of their embrace. Suddenly she felt a hand on her shoulder, as Kate reached out to draw her into the hug. Together the three of them stood, arms round each other.

'I owe everything that I am to you two. Two mums. Twice the love. Doubly blessed.'

With a kiss for each of them Kate broke away at last, disappearing upstairs to gather up the changing bag and other bits and pieces she'd left there. At that moment,

Elizabeth, who had been watching from her high chair, held out her arms to Margaret. With a smile, her grandmother moved over to scoop her out, wiping her mouth clean as she sat down on a kitchen chair next to Gwen. The two women laughed out loud at Elizabeth chuckled up at them, glad of the attention as she crawled from one lap to another.

It was then that Paul's camera clicked, capturing forever the delighted faces of Margaret and Gwen as they sat side by side, the golden-haired baby grinning happily between them.

Susie sent Madge a copy of that photo. It stood in pride of place next to the television set, so that it could bring a smile to her face even if the programmes were lousy. Tonight wasn't bad: two of her regular soaps, then an hour of Michael Barrymore who had always been her favourite.

Backing carefully into her chair, she arranged the necessities around her. Her plate of toast and Marmite, a chocolate muffin and a cup of tea with three sugars were to one side, balanced on a pile of old newspapers. On a stack of magazines to her left were her pills, a fresh bottle of sherry and the TV guide. Changing the channel on the remote control, she sat back painfully, picking up a piece of toast as she reached down the side of her chair to pull out the postcard with its striking picture of the Eiffel Tower.

Dearest Madge, (it read)
Well, this always was the place for honeymoons – so Brian and I tied the knot yesterday in a quiet private ceremony. No fuss – and no doubts either. It seems the skies of Paris have worked their magic yet again . . .

Madge chuckled as she took another bite of toast. That was all right then. And as the familiar music of *EastEnders* filled the room, she settled comfortably back into her chair with a deep sigh of satisfaction.